THE
PERFECT
PLACE
TO DIE

THE PERFECT PLACE TO DIE

BRYCE MOORE

sourcebooks
fire

Published by Sourcebooks Fire, an imprint of Sourcebooks
P.O. Box 4410, Naperville, Illinois 60567-4410
(630) 961-3900
sourcebooks.com

Library of Congress Cataloging-in-Publication data is on file with the publisher.

Printed and bound in Canada.
MBP 10 9 8 7 6 5 4 3 2 1

For my great-great-grandmother, Zuretta Palmer.

Not all heroes go on adventures.

PART ONE

The Maid

CHAPTER ONE

Think of the list that follows: men and women, young girls and innocent children, blotted out by one monster's hand, and you, my reader, of a tender and delicate nature, will do well to read no further.

———————

I WAS SEVENTEEN—OLD ENOUGH FOR BOYS to come calling, even though none of them had, and nothing Mother said could fool me into thinking there was a reason other than the length of my nose and the size of my chin. "Handsome" is about as good a compliment any boy paid me, and that was only when his parents were listening. But I was a hard worker, and I knew my way around a farmyard and in a workshop. Father didn't have sons, and Ruby wasn't worth a thing when it came time for work to be done.

The boys hadn't come calling for me, but they more than made up for that by lining up for my younger sister. She never had a moment's rest at the dance hall, and she'd have been out nightly if Father had let her. As it was, she still went out twice as often as she should have.

Father would scream at Ruby each morning, and I imagine she thought she had it pretty rough the way he handled her. However, he was careful to keep his blows to places where no one would notice the bruises—and she was careful to keep those bruises from getting noticed. I wasn't as lucky, but I made sure Ruby never had a chance to see what he did to me.

It's amazing what a family will do to make other families think everything is normal and fine.

But one evening Ruby came into the room when I would have sworn she was already on her way into town. I was in the middle of changing for the night, and there was Ruby, barging in through the door, all breathless and hurried as she searched for a missing earring she just had to have for the dance.

"Zuretta," she said. "Have you seen my—"

I tried to turn fast enough, but the way she cut off told me I'd failed. Her eyes widened, and the blood drained out of her face faster than if her throat had been cut. The two of us stared at each other, neither of us speaking, for a full minute—maybe longer.

"That was Father?" she asked me at last.

"It wasn't Mother."

She nodded. Once, then twice. "There's a lot there," she said. "On your back. How long has he been doing this to you?"

"Long enough," is all I said. I could take the blows, and I wanted things to stay the same between Ruby and me.

Ruby had never been the sort of person who let things be,

though. She'd march straight to the store and elbow her way into the front of the line if she thought it was necessary. She didn't wait then, either.

"Come on, Zuretta," she said.

"What?"

"We're going, you and I."

"Where?"

"East. North. West. I don't care. Anywhere but Manti, Utah."

"But Mother—"

"Mother knew what she was getting when she married that man. You and I didn't ask for it."

"But what would we do?"

She rushed over to her dresser and took out a bag and began throwing clothes into it, almost at random. "Anything we want," she said, and then looked up at me as an idea struck her. "Chicago." Her eyes were bright.

"Chicago?" I sat down on my bed.

"The Columbian Exposition. Remember? People have been talking about that for months. We'll go to Chicago. We might even see the Pinkertons!"

"We can't afford tickets," I said, hoping some reasoning would work with her.

But Ruby was already packing again. "I'll take some money out of the jar on Father's shelf when we leave. That'll pay for the tickets, and when we get to the city, we'll get jobs and never come back. Real jobs. Maybe as maids in a fancy hotel. Meet people from around the world. Come on, Zuretta! We'll be free!"

I could see the future with Ruby there, just for a moment. Expensive rooms and swaying train cars. *Free.*

But Mother cried out in the room next to ours, and it all came crashing down. "I can't," I told Ruby. "She needs my help. *Our* help."

Ruby licked her lips, thinking. Then she shook her head. "Not from me, Zuretta. I'm sorry, but no more. We all have our agency. God gave it to us to make our minds up. I'm getting out of here now. Tonight. You can come with me, or you can stay here and get beaten whenever Father pleases. I know the choice I'm making."

And I could see that she did, but I knew my choice as well. I thought it was the right one. The sensible one. I said goodbye to Ruby that night.

I never saw her at home again.

———

She wrote me, of course, and I even got to read some of her letters. The ones Father didn't catch wind of, at any rate. (Until we learned to have them sent to a friend and cut Father out of the process entirely.) The letters were filled with marvelous stories of Chicago and the exposition. She'd seen a real-life Pinkerton Detective, and she'd found work as a maid. Though, she refused to let me know where she was living. Everything went to a box at the post office downtown, and she picked it up there. She worried Father might come looking for her, but I thought the odds of him making the journey from Utah all the way to Chicago were slim.

In some ways, the letters made things harder. Father's temper only got worse, and Mother didn't get any stronger. He blamed me for Ruby running off.

I thought I'd been hiding it all well enough, but the bishop called me into meet with him one Sunday. He had a stack of letters on his desk, at least an inch high.

"Do you want to tell me about your father?" he asked.

I did not, so he sat back in his seat and sighed. "What am I going to do with you, Zuretta?" As if I was something to be handled and passed around. A problem that could be solved if he found the right leverage.

I perched in the seat across from him, my back safely away from anything it might brush up against.

The bishop pointed at that stack of letters. "Your sister," he began, then added, "It's not just me she's writing to."

"I can handle him," I said, which was true enough. "Ruby's off enjoying life in a big city. Mother and I will be fine."

The bishop hemmed and hawed about it, but he let me go at last, with a request I tell him if it got to be too much. I promised I would, because a promise was only words.

It all felt worth it when Ruby wrote me about her secret engagement. She'd fallen in love with the man of her dreams, and they were going to elope to Europe at the end of the summer. She wouldn't give me his name or say what he looked like, nor even describe what he did for his career. She was free, and she was happy, and that was all that mattered.

Until her letters stopped.

They'd been weekly occurrences for so long, arriving without fail each Tuesday. When one went missing, I assumed it must have been because of some trouble in the post. By Thursday, I decided the letter must have been lost. Three Tuesdays later, and I could think of little else.

Perhaps she'd eloped early. Perhaps Chicago was simply too busy for the postal service to function properly. But the lies you tell yourself during the day don't hold up to the thoughts that come at night. Ruby might have been hurt. What if she'd been struck by a cart or fallen off a ladder? She might be all alone in a hospital, unable to write.

Then the dreams came. Ruby trapped and alone. Ruby crying in terror.

I might not have been willing to talk to the bishop and accept his offer of help when it was just for me, but for Ruby I'd do almost anything.

That is how I came to be at the train station two days later, a ticket for Chicago clutched in my hand, and not a single soul to see me off.

Some people solve problems, and others pay to have them

solved. I might have wished the church folk had decided to solve mine, but I was grateful they'd offered the money to help me solve them instead.

No one could solve Father.

The train pulled up, and the train pulled away, taking my suitcase and me with it.

A woman approached me, all smiles and happiness.

"Headed to the World's Fair?" she asked, and I only nodded because I didn't trust myself to speak. But her smile was so warm that I felt a small piece of me thaw. "Me too!"

From there she chattered practically the whole way. Her name was Madeline, and she was tall and slender, with light-green eyes and red hair that drew attention to her from everyone who passed. I don't know how I would have even made it to Chicago without her. She knew which way to go to switch trains and where to sit so as to keep the men from "taking advantage of you."

She showed me where to eat and how to keep the costs down, and we took turns watching each other's bags so we could both sleep and not have to worry about getting them stolen.

"We women have to watch out for each other," Madeline told me. "People in the big cities aren't like you and me. They'd rob from their own mother if they could get away with it, and most of them could. I've been traveling for years, Zuretta. Years. I see things other people don't see, and I'm paid very well for it. I have stories that would drain every drop of blood from your face if you were to even *suspect* they were true. Everything from simple theft straight on up to murder."

Perhaps Madeline recognized she'd gone too far, because she reached out a hand and touched my shoulder. "I know it's a lot for you to take in, and I don't mean to scare you without cause, but there are men in Chicago who make people like us disappear. Who cares if another woman or two goes missing? Not the police, certainly."

"Maybe not," I said. "But the Pinkertons do."

"The Pinkertons?" she asked, curiosity in her voice as well as a bit of something else I couldn't identify.

I nodded. "Detectives. They even have a women's division, if you can believe it. They protected Abraham Lincoln. Before he was assassinated, of course. They've gone after Jesse James, Butch Cassidy, you name it. Allan Pinkerton was Chicago's first police detective, though it's run by his sons now. They have their main office over on Washington Street, or they used to."

It's part of why I'd been so ready to go to Chicago to find Ruby. My sister and I had followed the Pinkertons for years. We'd even dreamed about joining the Female Detective Bureau. Spending our lives under cover, finding out everything people wanted to keep secret, risking it all for a chance at justice.

The Pinkertons solved problems. They made a difference. Ruby wouldn't stay lost long, as soon as I could get the Pinkertons on the case.

"They'll charge," Madeline said after a moment. "Not that I want to spoil your dreams, but I'm sure men like that don't work for free."

I nodded again. "Of course. But I've brought some money with me, and once they hear what's happened, they'll have to help me. They've got a code they live by."

"A code." Madeline couldn't have sounded less impressed, and it made me want to defend my heroes.

"Of course! A system of seven rules they made so that people could trust them and depend upon them. Accept no bribes. Turn down reward money. Never raise fees without the client's pre-knowledge. They're honorable."

"I think I'd try the police first, just the same," Madeline said. "It's their job to find missing people. Better to hold onto your money for when you need it."

She had a point, even if a big part of me still wanted to meet the Pinkertons in person. It was good to have options, after all, and, if the police proved unable to help me find Ruby, it wasn't as if the Pinkertons wouldn't still be there.

―――――――

The country changed on the way to Chicago. It was hard to see if you weren't looking for it, but, once you noticed it, the difference was striking. As if, somewhere in the rickety swaying of the train and the smoke from the engine, you'd gone through a door to another world, like Alice through the looking glass except with a powerful locomotive churning up mountains and over rivers.

Before the trip, I thought I'd gone plenty fast, because I'd ridden a horse at full gallop from Mt. Pleasant to Spring City, just to show James Carver I could. But this made any horse ride feel like crawling.

I tried to picture Chicago in my mind: a city with a million people! I'd heard tales of how tall the buildings were, but that was all they could be. Tales. You couldn't make something ten stories high. It would be like trying to build a house of cards. Someone would sneeze, and the whole thing would come tumbling down.

I fell asleep on that train, and I didn't wake until Madeline was tapping my shoulder and telling me I didn't want to miss the view of the "Windy City." Not that you'd know it from the buildings. All the gas lamps and electrical lights lit the horizon with a fiery haze. The whole night sky dimmed in comparison, as if so much light on earth had made the stars bashful in return.

It was a city where everything could, and probably did, happen, from princesses to paupers.

I'd be there in an hour or less.

I took another look at what I'd brought. A bag with my clothes. A small purse with $14.67 left in it. I'd felt so rich when the bishop had handed me $75. It was more than most men earned in half a year, and I'd spent $60 of it just for the train ticket. But I needed to find Ruby, and having money in my purse wasn't going to get me any closer to it. The train might have been expensive, but once I was in the city, I'd be able to make the remaining money stretch.

Hadn't Ruby talked about getting a job in a hotel? I'd earn my way through this and save up enough to go back to Mother, and never mind the fact that two tickets home would be $120. Ruby and I could ride emigrant status, and that was only $45 each. True, it was only a rough plank for a seat, and we'd be elbow-to-elbow with every other passenger in that car, but it would get us to the same place just as good as the second-class ticket.

All the worrying in the world didn't stop that train from getting to the station, and when it did, Madeline took me by the elbow and ushered me forward. "Can't gawk around too much, Etta," she said. "Do that, and you mark yourself a tourist. That's exactly what they'll be looking for."

She didn't have to tell me who "they" were.

"Besides," she said, "I know a hotel three blocks from here that charges reasonable rates. Not like most places that'll take a dollar or two and only give you a bed full of bugs and a head full of lice in return. Follow me."

Once I was in the city, I saw it wasn't as perfect up close as it seemed from far away. It was like someone had taken Cinderella's castle and added garbage and smells that you didn't notice until you were walking through the front door.

You didn't see all the people from far off, for one thing. If I'd thought I'd be rid of people once I got off the train, I had another thing coming once I was in the city. Everywhere you looked there was someone else.

The lights that looked like fairy dust from afar turned out to be windows with people, and it didn't seem so magical when those people were yelling or throwing things out of them.

Even this late at night, the city hummed with activity. People bustled from place to place. The clatter of horses' hooves on the streets, coupled with the ungodly rattle of iron-sheathed wheels rolling along behind, was nothing compared to the smell—no, the *stench*—of that many people living that close together. We wouldn't have packed our cattle so tightly next to each other, yet here were humans doing it of their own choice.

I had to stop in the middle of the street and take a few deep breaths, because, for a moment, I was a bee trapped in a hive with other bodies scurrying around me in every direction.

Ruby would have loved this. Of that I was sure. I tried to see it through her eyes: not as bodies piled high set to crush one another, but as bustling excitement. Possibilities. Ruby would see them all as people to meet and friends to make.

I'd have to be more like Ruby if I was ever going to find her again.

The hotel Madeline brought me to was four stories tall, and our room was on the top floor, higher than I'd ever slept in my life. You could look out the window and see the city alive below you. I stood there for a few minutes, staring at the crowd down on the street, somehow hoping I might spot Ruby somewhere.

Before I'd made it to Chicago, I'd had a hard time thinking how Ruby might have lost touch with me, but now that I saw all those people, all those dreams and hopes and fears, I didn't wonder. That many people could swallow you up and not even leave a ripple to show you'd existed.

Tomorrow, my search would begin. With Madeline to show me where to go and whom to speak to, things would be easier. Whether they were handled by the police or the Pinkertons, tomorrow, all my problems would begin to be solved.

CHAPTER TWO

The first taking of human life that is attributed to me is in the case of Dr. Robert Leacock, a friend and former schoolmate. I knew that his life was insured for a large sum and after enticing him to Chicago I killed him by giving him an overwhelming dose of laudanum.

T HE ROOM WAS TOO QUIET.

It took me a moment to remember where I was and what had happened yesterday. As I stared at the strange ceiling (yellow where it should have been white), the sun just coming through the curtains for this time of day, it all came back to me. The trip from Utah. Meeting Madeline. It was time to find Ruby.

I sat up. The bed next to mine was empty. No sheets. No pillow. No sign of another person in the room at all.

"Madeline?" I called out, though who knew why? It was just the one room, and I could see every corner of it from my bed.

I got out of bed, dressed only in my simple nightgown, the floor cold against my bare feet. I went to fetch a dress from my suitcase, but my suitcase was gone. A pit yawned open in my stomach as I checked under the bed, hoping it had gotten pushed underneath somehow.

Nothing was there but dust.

My pulse quickened, and my breaths came faster, but I fought the urge to panic. Madeline could have gone down to settle our bill. Or she could be out buying us breakfast, and she'd taken my suitcase with her so she could keep a close eye on it.

But it was all a foolish hope, and I knew it in my heart already. I went through the motions (hurrying downstairs, asking the attendant, looking outside the main door), but it was just as I'd feared.

"Madeline" had run off with my suitcase. My clothes. My shoes. My purse. Every single thing I'd brought with me from Utah was gone. I didn't have a scrap of cloth to my name except my underclothes and the light blue nightgown I had on. She probably would have stolen that too, if she could have done it without waking me.

I walked back up the stairs in a trance, my mind not wanting to fully process the predicament I now found myself in. When I came back into my room, I noticed a slip of paper that had fallen under my bed. I picked it up: Ruby's photograph. Whether it had been left behind by accident or Madeline had taken some pity on me, I couldn't say, though it still did little to mend the hurt and confusion I felt inside. I sat there on the edge of my bed and tried, unsuccessfully, not to cry.

How could I have been so foolish? Had Madeline known she

was going to steal from me the moment she'd met me, or had it taken time for her to decide I was naive enough for her that she'd be able to get away with it? All night I'd slept soundly in that bed. How could I not have woken up?

But I knew how. The trip had exhausted me. Madeline must have known it too.

I'd dreamed of joining the Pinkertons one day. They would laugh me out of the building if I ever suggested it. Women detectives didn't get duped like this.

An hour passed. Two, perhaps. Each time I thought about going outside to find help, I'd clutch my nightgown around myself and decide to think things through a while longer. But I'd only paid for one night at the hotel, and the owner didn't take too kindly to me staying in the room all day.

"But I've been robbed!" I tried to tell him, my face covered in tears and sobs choking my words.

He didn't even blink. "You people ought to know better than to come to our city without a lick of sense. Go tell the police. It's their job to care about such things, not mine, and I'd appreciate it if you didn't spread the word that you were ever here. People are safe in my establishment. Those that aren't fools, at least."

There's only so long you can sit on a bed in an empty room wishing you'd done things differently. No matter how deeply I longed to be anywhere else, there I was standing in front of the doors leading out to the streets of Chicago.

My heart was in my throat. I'd die of shame the moment I stepped outside. The entire city would stop and stare at me in my nightgown, stunned by how foolish I looked and how stupid I'd been. But the hotel owner shoved me out, and even that last moment of hesitation was stolen from me.

No one stopped. A few men passing by eyed me up and down, and I ducked my head, expecting some comments, but nothing came. The city kept on moving. There were some snickers and sneers, but in the end, it didn't seem like they cared any more for my predicament than the hotel owner had.

Come on, Zuretta. I had come to Chicago with one purpose: find Ruby—or, at least, discover what had happened to her. I'd felt so independent when I left my Father's house, my head high, confident I was doing the right thing. But it hadn't taken more than a few hours before I had been cozied up to by a con woman. At that moment I'd have given anything to let someone else make choices for me again.

If I kept at it like this, I'd never amount to anything. Ruby wouldn't stand for it.

So I had to do what Ruby would do. As soon as I had the thought, I felt my chin lift. *Don't let them see you're uncertain,* I could hear Ruby say. *You deserve better than this, so go out and demand it.*

I strode up to the next person I saw on the street, an older, overweight woman in a purple dress and a scowl across her face. "Where is the police station?" I asked, and I was proud my voice didn't tremble. There was no way I'd go to the Pinkertons in my current state. But Madeline had been right about one thing, even if she'd lied about everything else: it was the job of the police to help people.

The woman stopped short, and her eyes widened as she noticed me for the first time. Once she realized she looked like a struck fish, she closed her mouth. "Which one?" she asked after a bit of sputtering.

"The closest one," I said. I supposed Chicago was so big it needed more than one station.

"Two streets south and three to the east. You can't miss it."

As I walked through the streets, I realized why I wasn't as remarkable to others as I was to myself. Chicago was bursting with people. I'd thought it was busy the night before, but that was because I hadn't seen it in full action. There were at least twice the number of people out now as there had been yesterday. Maybe three times. Vendors selling flowers or fruits from carts. Shop owners talking to customers. People milling around, staring into buildings as they passed. More horses than I would have expected as well, pulling far more carts and carriages than I thought possible. (And bringing with them far more manure than any sane person would want to smell.)

In a smaller city or town, my nightgown would have been the most interesting thing on the street, easily. Here in Chicago, there were so many other things to distract from it. My back straightened, and my shoulders relaxed.

Halfway there I noticed a young man, perhaps a year or two older than myself, had started to trail behind me. I didn't notice him at first, but, when I turned to check for traffic when crossing a street, he was there. And, when I turned again to look for the source of a tremendous racket (a milk delivery truck rattling with all its bottles), he was even closer and staring right at me.

I whirled to face forward again, blushing and hating myself for it. Visions flashed through my head: being abducted or assaulted or even just having him call out to me. It was to be expected that I might draw the attention of some less-than-upright men, especially in a city this big. If I could get to the police station, it wasn't as if he would do anything to me there.

Then again, I'd only glimpsed him twice. I chided myself. Just because a young man was looking at me one time didn't mean he was wicked. He might be walking the same direction I was. I could slow down and allow him to pass, but what if he were really trying to catch up to me? Then I'd be playing right into his plans.

Instead, I crossed the street, ducking between the carts and horses to go stand in front of a clothes display on the opposite side. In my head, I counted off the seconds. When twenty had gone by, I'd check once more to—

"Excuse me, Miss?"

A voice spoke from right behind me. I yelped and turned to see the young man standing there. He was a foot taller than me, had dark brown hair, blue eyes, and valiant effort at a mustache, though it did distract a little from his large nose. He wore a gray suit. He smiled at me, and his teeth were very white.

I backed up a few steps until I bumped up against the store window. "Please go away," I said, though it came out as more of a squeak.

He frowned a little in confusion and leaned forward, cupping his hand to his ear. "Excuse me? I didn't quite—"

"Please. Go. Away." That all came out much louder than I'd wanted it to this time. Loud enough that some of the other pedestrians threw glances our way. My blush only deepened.

The man's eyebrows raised. "I'm sorry. I just wanted to—"

I turned and started walking again, hoping he'd take the hint and not press matters. The urge to turn and see if he was following was great, but I managed to fight it off for thirty yards. When I finally did give into it, he was still trailing, with a curious expression on his face.

Fine. As long as he didn't pester me. I'd get to the police, and he'd realize his mistake and wander elsewhere.

By the time I had gone the last three blocks to the station, I'd almost gotten used to being out in public practically undressed. I eyed the brick building for a moment.

If it weren't for the fact that the young man had also paused half a block down from me, I might have wasted even more time on the doorstep. He was studying me, and who knew what thoughts were going through his head?

The inside of the police station was big, filled with an open room with offices and hallways leading off it. The main doors led into a waiting area with a line of people queued to speak to the police. In the front half of the room, officers moved here and there about their business, ignoring the regular citizens.

That job fell to a single man. A middle-aged officer with a bristly mustache and a weak chin sat behind a desk there, talking to the first person in a line about ten people long. He was thin as a rail, dressed in blue, with two rows of gold buttons on either side of his jacket, arranged in pairs all the way down it. He wore a matching flat-topped blue hat with a short brim at the front.

He might have been telling the man in front of him that he "cared deeply for the citizens of Chicago and, most particularly, for those that had fallen on hard times," but from his red face, pressed lips, and clipped words, what he meant to say was "Why are you wasting my time, you simple-minded ingrate?"

Maybe I'd be better off turning around and going back to the streets where I was more anonymous. Give the man time to calm down. Come back when it wasn't so busy.

But this was Chicago. For all I knew, this was as empty as it got in here. There was also the fact that, when I turned to look back at the door, the young man from the street stood three people behind me in line. He had the nerve to smile at me again.

I faced forward and planted my feet, wishing once more that I'd had the common sense to know when a woman was trying to take advantage of my good nature.

So I shuffled forward as each person made his or her way to the front of the line. I received a few disapproving looks, but no one asked me to leave because of my state of undress.

At last it was my turn. As soon as I approached the man, his eyebrows shot up. "Come to turn yourself in, are you?"

I frowned and looked behind me, unsure if he was talking to someone else. "Excuse me?" I asked when it was clear he must mean me.

"Walking about in your unmentionables, right in the middle of the day." He had a smile on his face now, but it wasn't the right sort. It was a smile that came at my expense.

I blushed again. "I—I was robbed last night. A woman—she met me on the train and..."

He was shaking his head as soon as I started to explain, and I trailed off when his expression became more impatient. "This damned fair!" he exclaimed. "That's the cause of it all. It makes perfectly sensible people lose their minds completely. You wouldn't go about town dressed like this in your home now, would you?"

I shook my head.

"Of course you wouldn't. And if a strange woman were to come to you in Pennsylvania or New York or wherever you're from and tell you she knew where you could stay the night, you wouldn't listen to her, would you?"

"I'm from Utah," I said.

"What was that?"

"I said I'm from Utah."

"What does it matter where you're from?" he asked, his voice getting louder. "One of those Mormons, are you?"

"Yes," I snapped, and my voice was sharp and pointed. "I'm a Mormon. And no, I wouldn't be dressed like this in Utah, because I wouldn't have been robbed there. But I came here to find my sister, and I made the simple mistake of trusting someone who clearly wasn't worthy of it. Perhaps I made the mistake of believing the police in Chicago were somewhat competent and compassionate. But if I'm wrong, then I'll bid you good day and go find someone who can actually help me without degrading me."

The words had tumbled out of my mouth, and I couldn't quite believe they'd come from me once I was finished and they were hanging in the air between the officer and me.

After a pause, the officer said, more quietly and with a bit of anger running beneath the words, "What do you mean by that?"

"Strange," I said. "I would have thought it was quite apparent. But if you're too slow to even pick up on that, then it's clear my time is being wasted here, as is yours."

I turned to leave, and if the officer had been smart, he'd have let me be. True, the young man was there, but he looked as stunned as the rest of the people in line. They'd probably never imagined a girl like me could behave that way, but the officer had it coming. Some people can't abide letting a young woman have her say in public. I knew that from Father and from others in Utah, and this officer apparently felt it in his bones as well, because he stopped me.

"I haven't finished with you yet, young lady," the officer said. "You can't leave here until I say you can."

"Really?" I faced him again. My chin raised a few degrees. I had a sense of why Ruby spoke the way she did. There was a thrill that accompanied it. "Why is that?"

"Because of the way you're dressed, for one thing. What sort of an officer would I be to let a woman parade around like that in my city?" His eyes flicked to the people behind me in line.

I understood all at once that he was worried, not about me, but about what the other people in the room thought about him.

"I would have thought a man entrusted with protecting the disadvantaged would take more concern for a girl like me. I come here looking for help and, instead, am told I am to blame."

"Yes," he said, sitting back from the desk and patting his stomach. "Well, it can't be helped if you bumpkins don't know any better."

I nodded and turned to leave again. "No doubt the newspapers will find that noteworthy as well," I said over my shoulder.

The people standing in line didn't seem impatient or upset. They simply looked from me to the officer, clearly waiting to see what he'd say next. The young man was smiling widely, enjoying the show, I guessed.

The officer cleared his throat. "Come back here, young lady. How many times do I have to repeat myself? You stand and listen to me until I say you can go."

I turned once more and faced him, my arms crossed, my head tilted to let my braids hang down. "Yes?"

"You said it was a woman who stole from you? A woman you met on the train?"

"Yes."

He leaned forward and rested his elbows on the desk. "Then she'll be long gone. They always are, and the newspapers won't be interested. You might as well expect them to write about water being wet."

"You mean to tell me this sort of thing happens all the time, and yet you're unable to bring the culprits to justice?" I might have been irritated before, but that was quickly growing to full-blown anger.

"It's not that simple," the man said. "They leave the city before we can spot them."

"Yes," I said. "Well, my father's lawyer will have a thing or two to say about that, no doubt."

The man was silent for a few moments. "Your father's…lawyer?"

"Yes. We have lawyers in Utah. Very smart ones too. What was your name? I'm afraid I haven't caught it yet."

His eyes narrowed. "Now see here, miss. You think you can come here and make big claims because there's no way of proving you're lying. We don't take kindly to that in Chicago. Admit you have no lawyer and maybe I'll see about finding a home for fallen women where you can stay until you have your feet under you."

I turned to the man behind me in line. "What is his name?" I asked loudly enough for the officer to hear.

"Don't answer that!" the officer shouted out, raising a finger. Now some of his fellow officers really did take note of what was going on. A few of them even stopped what they were doing to stare at us. "Hold on," the officer said, trying to calm himself. "Hold everything for a moment. What is it that you expect me to do?"

"I expect you to help me recover my stolen goods, the same as I would expect from any police force in any city. I also expect your help in locating my sister."

"Your sister?" The officer sounded bewildered.

"Ruby Palmer. She disappeared six months ago after running away from home."

The man pushed his chair back from his desk and stood up. He was much shorter than I expected him to be. Thinner too. "Young lady. The entire world is descending on this city right now. We have four violent deaths each day. Each *day*! Half the detectives on the force are running around looking for missing persons, which might be fine, except none of them are actually finding any of them. We're understaffed, underfunded, and that was before this infernal fair started. So forgive me if I don't leap to rush into every hayseed's problem that comes in off the street."

"I don't want to make your life difficult," I began. "But I also expect you to do the job you're being paid to do. I've stood here for the past hour listening to you berate and belittle every person who came looking for aid, regardless of its merits. Now what is your name so that I might properly report this? Or do you have a supervisor I could speak to?"

The man stared at me. He stared at the other people. Then he sighed, and his shoulders slumped. "Would you mind coming to the back desk so that I can discuss this with you in private?"

The moment I lost my audience, I'd lose most of the bargaining power I had with the man. But if I didn't bend now and then, it only increased the odds of him snapping altogether.

"I won't go to a different room," I told him. "Not with a strange man, and certainly not in my current state of dress. But I'll go with you to the corner over there, where we can discuss this between ourselves in a more private fashion."

He nodded and moved to open a piece of the railing separating the waiting area from the work area. I walked through it and followed him a few steps off to where we could speak in relative privacy and not be overheard. The other officers in the room seemed all too eager to let this particular one handle things on his own.

Once it was the two of us, the officer's voice was low, but urgent and more than a little bossy. "Now see here. I don't take kindly to—"

"If you think I came back here so you could chide me in private, you're mistaken," I said. I had no desire to let him bully me again, and Ruby was right there with me. "I can just as easily go back with the others."

"What do you need?"

"I need you to pay me the attention I deserve."

"I'm overworked, and you already told me you let yourself be taken in by a con woman. I'd say I'm sorry about it, but she's the least of our troubles right now. Honestly, she's probably doing us a favor by keeping some of these idiots from coming to the city. I can file a report, but nothing will come of it. We can't get you your money back."

Part of me withered when he said that. Was I to be without clothes for my entire stay in Chicago? But I reminded myself that was a personal problem. Of far more pressing need was Ruby. "The money doesn't matter," I said. "I'm here looking for my sister."

The officer sighed. "I already told you. The whole city is filled with missing people. Many of them don't want to be found."

"Not Ruby," I said.

A voice came from behind me. "Can I help?"

The officer looked over my shoulder, and his faced melted with relief. "Tom Chalmers! Have at her." Without another word, the officer walked around me and strode off, all too ready to be rid of me.

I turned to see the smiling young man from the street.

He nodded at me. "Miss? We haven't been introduced yet. I hope you don't mind my forwardness. It's just you seem like you could use some assistance, and I don't tend to think you're going to get much of it here. Certainly not with Urville over there."

I folded my arms and tried to gather my thoughts. Urville? That was the man's name? No wonder he was so short-tempered. "How would you be able to help me?"

He held out his hand for me to shake. "Thomas Chalmers. You might not recognize the name, but you've probably heard of my uncle. William Pinkerton?"

I squeaked. It couldn't be helped. I tried to keep a straight face and my emotions in check, but that little squeak of surprise slipped out regardless. It was noisy, though; perhaps Thomas hadn't heard me. "What name was that?" I asked after I collected myself. "Plinkertons? Piano mover, is he?"

He laughed, not even put off by my unfamiliarity. "Detective, actually. Runs one of the biggest agencies in the nation. We might be able to help you."

"I suppose you're always chasing after helpless women," I said. "Easy pickings for your group, perhaps?"

"Hardly," he said. "We have more than enough to keep us busy. But I saw you on the street trying so hard to be brave. I couldn't help but want to learn more. When I witnessed your performance with the police here, that sealed it. Anyone who's determined enough to put old Urville off his game is someone I want to know."

I fought to keep from staring down at my blue nightgown. It made sense. The Pinkertons were honorable. They had their code. Of course they'd be the first to come to the aid of someone like me. But the thought of walking into the main office of my heroes was more than I could bear. "I couldn't," I managed to get out. "Not dressed like this."

He nodded. "All right then. It's settled."

"It is?" I hated my voice for sounding so bewildered and uncertain.

"We'll go and take care of your wardrobe, and then you'll come with me to see if my uncle can't straighten some of the rest of your troubles out. Come on! He's in the office all morning today, but he'll leave right before lunch. We'll have to hurry if we're to make it in time."

CHAPTER THREE

Later, like the man-eating tiger of the tropical jungle, whose appetite for blood has once been aroused, I roamed about the world seeking whom I could destroy.

———

T HOMAS WHISKED ME AWAY TO a department store where he paid for three new dresses, new shoes, a handbag, hat, and gloves. They weren't the most expensive items in the store, but they were still far nicer than anything I'd ever worn.

At first, it felt like a fairy tale. A real live Pinkerton detective had swooped in to rescue me in my hour of need. True, he lacked the last name, but that could hardly be held against him. If he'd ripped back a curtain in the department store to reveal Ruby, alive and well, I don't think I would have been terribly shocked. My head was spinning, and I was too excited by the possibilities.

The butterflies started in my stomach as I was trying on a blue dress that was too loose in the waist. I was looking at myself in a full-length mirror. In the new clothes and new environment, it didn't seem like the same person staring back at me.

I turned and left the dressing room to go directly out to Thomas. He was sitting in a chair waiting for my return, and he stood as I entered. Once again, his face was nothing but smiles, but wouldn't that be exactly what it would be if he were trying to get the best of me?

"It looks—"

I held up a hand to hold him off. "It occurs to me," I started, then struggled for a way to phrase it. What if he were genuine? But I decided the best way out was through. "It occurs to me you might not be who you've presented yourself to be."

The smile left his face. For a moment, my stomach sunk. This was it. I was on to him, and his true colors were going to come out.

"Right," he said. "My devious plan to take you to a department store and get you clothing has been ruined. However will I steal all the clothes I'm about to buy for you?"

When he phrased it like that, I almost folded. Wasn't he right? But I pressed on, even if it was uncomfortable to speak it. "There are more things a young man might want out of a young lady in my position, though it shames me to mention them out loud."

Thomas was the one to blush now, and when I saw his face go deep red, the bulk of my suspicions vanished. He sputtered and fumbled at his pocket for a wallet, digging into it and bringing out a card with his name and PINKERTON DETECTIVE AGENCY on it in finely printed letters. It had seen some abuse from living in his wallet, and I didn't get the impression it was something he showed to people on a regular basis.

Still, staring at it gave us a few moments to collect ourselves before we had to make eye contact again, and seeing the Pinkerton name written down sent a thrill down my spine yet again.

"Thank you," I said, handing the card back to him. "You'll understand my need for caution."

At least that suspicion had been laid to rest. Of course, now that it was, I worried that I'd jeopardized my chances of receiving help from the Pinkertons. Wouldn't that be just the way my trip had been going? Welcome the con woman with open arms only to turn away the real help the moment it was offered?

By the time the clothes were all packed neatly away into a suitcase (which Thomas also bought), I felt even worse than I had to begin with. I couldn't bring myself to discuss how I'd doubted him earlier, but I had another area to focus on instead. Though he'd done his best to hide the prices of everything he was buying, I'd kept a close eye on them and tallied them up in my mind. Either clothes were even more expensive than I'd feared in Chicago, or Thomas had picked a high-end store to do our shopping.

"I'm going to pay it back," I told him as we walked out at last. "Every penny."

He waved it off. "Think of it as my good deed for the day."

I stopped in the middle of the sidewalk, forcing several people behind me to move around the sudden obstacle. "No."

Thomas turned to face me, his head cocked to the side. "No?"

"I'm *going* to pay you back."

"That doesn't make any sense whatsoever," he told me. "How much money did you have stolen from you?"

I kept my lips pressed together.

"Fine, then," he said. "Allow me to speculate. It couldn't have been more than…fifty dollars? And that's probably a large part of what your family saved up for the last several years, I'd wager. I'm not going to say it's nothing to me, but it's certainly a whole lot less for me than it is for you."

"I'll get a job here in Chicago," I said. "I'll earn Chicago wages, and I'll pay you back. I don't need your charity." I already was indebted enough to my bishop, after all.

Thomas smiled again and laughed. "Whatever makes you happy. Just please stop standing in the middle of the sidewalk and let me take you to the head office so we can get this all squared away."

With that, I decided I'd made my point and it would be better not to press it harder, so I allowed myself to be led farther into Chicago.

Now that I was no longer half naked and full of uncertainty, I was able to look at the city during the day with fresh eyes. The buildings were truly incredible, though the height of them all did make me feel somewhat like I was standing in the middle of a chain of dominoes. What would happen if one of them were to shift and topple?

I'd seen the ground move from beneath a barn back in Manti. The whole building collapsed, killing two cows inside and trapping a third.

Enough of that. I had to stay focused. In my new shoes, the brick sidewalks were much harder on my feet than the wooden floors and dirt roads I was used to, and I wondered if I wouldn't regret the loss of my shoes to Madeline most of all. Still, wishing them back would do me no good, so I did my best to move past the loss.

One thing I didn't catch glimpse of in our walk was the Columbian Exposition. "Where is it?" I asked Thomas at last after we came to yet another street that afforded us a tremendous view straight down it, but all it revealed were rows upon rows of buildings and people, people, people.

"The office?" he asked, shifting the package of clothes he'd bought me into his other arm. "A few blocks more."

"No. The fair."

That earned me another laugh. No doubt he'd be telling his rich friends about this after he'd safely handed me over to a lower-ranking detective: the poor farmer girl from Utah he'd gotten an hour or two of amusement out of. "The fair is much farther to the south," he said.

When we arrived at the Pinkerton Headquarters, my feet had

each gotten a large blister on the back of the heel. The new shoes Thomas had bought me might have looked fancy and elegant, but they weren't much for walking long distances. I had to fight the urge to take them off and hold them in my hand when we went inside.

"Here we are," Thomas said, oblivious to my pain. "Now to see if my uncle's still in."

Another building. Another sea of brick and people. I trailed after Thomas, letting him do all the work. I might have objected to outright charity when it came to clothing, but I knew when I was out of my league. Best to keep my mouth closed for now until I had a better idea what was going on.

Thomas and I went up the stairs (five flights!) until we were on the top floor of the building, and I could have sworn the air was thinner. As we passed, a few men nodded to him respectfully. I kept looking for signs of the female detective division, but the only ones we came across were sprinkled behind desks, mixed in with the men, all of them clacking away at Type-Writers or filing reports. I didn't imagine detectives had much to do with secretarial work. I'd heard more women were flocking to that career, but I was surprised to see how many were there. It had to have been at least a third.

At last we came to a door with a man seated at a desk outside. "Jack," Thomas said. "Is my uncle in?"

The man glanced up at us and then continued reading whatever document had been occupying his time before we got there. "Make an appointment, Tommy," he said with an air of exasperation. "You know the rules."

"Right," Thomas said and grabbed me by the hand and strode to the door, opening it without knocking.

The secretary shouted and tried to stop us, but he was too slow. Thomas dragged me into the room and closed the door behind us. I was left standing there, my mouth open and my eyes wide, staring at a group of five men who were all glaring back at me. One of them, a heavyset man with a thick mustache and graying hair, called out, "What's the meaning of this?"

Thomas had turned and walked toward them by that time. "Uncle William," he said to the angry man. "So nice to see you."

If anything, my jaw dropped lower. This was *William Pinkerton* himself? The head of the whole agency? I wanted to crawl under the desk and hide there until they all went away.

But Mr. Pinkerton only grunted once he saw Thomas. He then glanced at the other men and waved his hand toward the door. "Lunch," he said. "Come back in an hour, and we'll approach this with fresh eyes."

They filed out of the room without a word, though they inspected me like a caught fish as they passed.

Mr. Pinkerton stuck his head into the room outside his office. "I pay you to keep my schedule in order, Mr. Stewart. If that's beyond your capabilities, perhaps you should look elsewhere for employment. Think on that the next half hour while my nephew wastes my time once more."

He closed the door and faced Thomas and me. "What's this then, Tommy? Another side project?" His face was clouded with anger.

"No, Uncle. It's a simple, straightforward case that I thought would be good for the agency to take care of. Just a woman who fell victim to a thief."

Thomas's uncle walked around me in a circle to give me a close inspection. It made me feel like a horse on the auction block. "A woman? More like a young lady. In brand-new clothes. You wouldn't, perhaps, have paid for them just before coming here, Tommy?"

"I couldn't have brought her to the agency in her nightgown, could I? It was all she had left."

The man grunted. If I could have shrunk down to nothing at that moment, I would have done so gladly. Facing down the police officer had been one thing, but facing William Pinkerton was far beyond me. It was a miracle my knees hadn't given out. Two leather chairs sat before a large desk for Mr. Pinkerton himself, but I hadn't been offered the chance to rest. And I wasn't going to ask for it.

"Her nightgown?" he asked. "Tell me, Tommy. How was it you came across a young lady in her nightgown? Did you run into her on the street, or were you, perhaps, in the vicinity of her hotel room?"

"I saw her on the street, as a matter of fact." Thomas sounded more than a little defensive. He came to stand between me and his

uncle. "Though I didn't actually speak with her until we were in the police station."

Mr. Pinkerton peered at me again from over Thomas's shoulder, his eyebrows raised. "Was she arrested?"

"No," Thomas said. "She went to report the crime, of course."

The man walked around Thomas and stared me in the eye. "Is this true, young lady?"

I managed a slight nod, to which Mr. Pinkerton sighed. "I'm supposed to believe this little mouse of a girl walked through the streets of Chicago in broad daylight, clad only in a nightgown, to go to the police and complain that she'd been robbed? She can't even put two words together here in a private office."

"You're scaring her," Thomas said.

Mr. Pinkerton sighed even louder and walked around to his desk, where he settled into the large seat behind it and began rummaging through the drawers. "Naturally. She's scared. And so, of course, you rushed to her aid, promising help from the greatest detective agency in the country. Tell me, Tommy. Did you show her that fool business card again?"

Thomas took a few steps back, his hand twitching toward his pocket before he caught himself.

His uncle nodded, finding a box of cigars in his desk at last and taking one out. "I thought so. I wish you'd use that card for something other than getting my agency into problems it has no time or resources to solve."

"Come now," Thomas started.

"You deny it?" Mr. Pinkerton inserted the end of the cigar through a device and clicked it closed. The tip of the cigar fell off and dropped to his desk.

Thomas folded his arms and stood straighter. "Our family has time, money, and resources to do some real good in this city. The things I've brought to you have been important. Every. Single. One."

Mr. Pinkerton nodded. "Very well. You can save the world on your own time, Tommy. But don't be shocked and surprised when you interrupt me in the middle of an important meeting, trailing another of your strays, and I don't leap to the rescue. Be grateful I let you keep your office, and you can thank your mother for that. Now take the mouse away and leave me in peace."

Thomas grunted in frustration, but he grabbed my arm and tried to pull me out of the room. I shook him off, not even realizing what I was doing until my arm was slipping out of his grasp. My heart was going to burst through my chest, but I stepped up to Mr. Pinkerton's desk and forced myself to stare him in the eye.

He stared right back, puffing on his cigar. The words froze in my mouth. I was terrified, but a thought jumped into my head: the memory of Ruby disappearing through the window after she'd fought with Father for the last time. This was for her.

"I didn't go to the police to report the robbery," I said.

Mr. Pinkerton said nothing.

I cleared my throat. "That is, I was robbed, but I was going to go to them in any case. My sister disappeared in Chicago. Something happened to her, and I need help finding out what. I'm willing to pay, except my money was all stolen yesterday. But I've followed stories of your agency for years, and I know if anyone can help me, it's the Pinkertons. I read about what you did with the Molly Maguires and then Marm Mandelbaum and Frederick Ker and—"

"See, Uncle?" Thomas started.

Mr. Pinkerton jabbed his cigar at his nephew, cutting him off, but still staring at me. His eyes were hard and unreadable. Was I supposed to say something more?

"I know there are many people missing in Chicago these days. At least, that's what the police said this morning. But I don't think Ruby is just missing. I think she might be…" I trailed off, not wanting to speak the words out loud, as if, by doing that, it made them more real.

The seconds ticked by. Mr. Pinkerton waited for me to finish, but when I didn't, he said, "Bah. A mouse after all."

"Kidnapped," I blurted out. "Or—or worse. Or she's going to be."

"Why?" Mr. Pinkerton asked and took another puff of his cigar.

"My sister and I have always been close. We tell each other everything. When she came here, she still wrote me every week. She found work at a hotel, and she fell in love with a man. But she wouldn't tell me anything about him or about where she worked. I kept asking, but she always ignored the questions, and she refused to provide a return address. She said it was because of Father, but then her letters stopped altogether. Something's happened to her. Something...bad."

Mr. Pinkerton pushed back from his desk and stood up, walking around it to stand next to me. He placed a weighty hand on my shoulder. "My dear girl, where are you from?"

"Manti," I said. "Utah."

He considered the thought for a moment, then continued. "Never been to a place as big as Chicago, I'd hazard?"

I shook my head. Having him this close had stopped the flow of words I'd managed to carve out.

"Your sister neither, of course. I've seen so many people like you the last year. Drawn to the city by the excitement of the fair and the promise of jobs and new lives. What none of you realize is that the city changes you. Opens your eyes to new possibilities. Some people find that, once they know what else is out there, their past doesn't seem that important anymore. They go new places. Cut ties to family members. Even sisters."

"No," I said. "Not Ruby."

He put his other hand on my other shoulder. It felt like I was being pressed into the floor. Perhaps he meant it to be comforting, but it made my stomach churn with discomfort. "Tell me," he said. "What's more likely? That your sister was abducted, or that she ran off with the handsome young man who swept her off her feet?"

I stepped back, away from his hands. He let me go. "I know

which one I'd like to believe," I said. "I'd love it if Ruby were fine. It would hurt, but I would get over that. But she isn't fine. I know it. *Know* it."

"How?" Mr. Pinkerton asked.

What else was I supposed to tell him but the real reason? "Two weeks ago, I had a dream. I was with Ruby, and we were locked inside a room. A safe, perhaps. We were frantic to get out, but we couldn't."

The detective shook his head. "Nothing but—"

"Fancy," I said, finishing his sentence and nodding. "That's what I thought as well. But I had the same dream the next night and the night after. Three nights in a row, exactly the same, and I had it again last night. I can feel it. I know it's true, or it will be. And I hope and pray it hasn't happened yet, even though I fear I'm far too late. But if that's so, I'm going to find her and save her, and I'm going to make sure whoever did it doesn't do it again."

Mr. Pinkerton exchanged glances with Thomas, but I couldn't tell what that meant. "How old are you? Eighteen?"

My first instinct was to lie, but Mother had raised me better than that. "Seventeen," I said. "I'll be eighteen in September."

"Seventeen?" he said, as if that were all the excuse he needed. "You'll have to somehow find your sister or her killer in a city swarming with new people. And, if you do find him, what are you going to do? You can't confront him. What's to stop him from killing you too?"

"I'll turn him into the police," I said.

"With what evidence? Courts don't accept dreams as part of the prosecution, and you keep saying she was abducted. Stolen. In my line of work, I've found it's much more likely she's been murdered. It's too much work, hiding a person—much less risky to stash a body away. Do you think he's got her corpse locked away in his basement, moldering, waiting for you to stumble across it? I'm sorry. I don't mean to shock you, but I think, perhaps, it's for the best. You need to know what you might be facing if you're right."

"But you could help me," I said. She wasn't dead. I wouldn't even consider it.

He thought for a moment, then shook his head. "I can't. The agency has too many other clients who have paid for their cases to be worked on for us to start taking on new ones for free. And, before you even think of it, Tommy, I'm going to say you can't help this young lady, either. If she's wrong, then you're only wasting your time. If she's right—and I want to emphasize strongly how much I doubt that is the case—but, if she's right, and you get yourself in danger, your mother will have my neck."

"But you could be saving lives by catching the man," I said. "If he took my sister, he could take someone else."

"Young woman, you need to get your head out of fantasyland and bring it back to reality. You've followed our cases, and I appreciate that. But not everything you read in the papers is true, and the bits that are only come along every so often. Most detective work is boring. It involves sitting around and waiting and plenty of research. Almost all the cases have nothing to do with murderers, much less anything to do with multiple bodies."

He walked over to his desk and took out a stack of bills. More money than I'd seen in my entire life. He held it out to me. "Go home," he said. "Get on a train and go back where you came from. Your sister is gone. You thought she'd never give up on you, but a boy came along, and she went head over heels."

I didn't reach for the bills.

He waved them in front of me, his expression becoming annoyed. "I wouldn't do this for just anyone. Who knows why I'm doing it now? Probably to save myself the grief I'll hear from my sister if Thomas gets in trouble again. But I won't offer it again, so do the smart thing. Take it and go."

I stood slowly. Deliberately. I stared Mr. Pinkerton right in the eye. "You mistake me, sir. I'm not here for money, and I'm not here to make things difficult. My sister is in trouble at the least and dead at the worst. I'm not going home until I know what happened to her. If waving money at me makes you feel better about your refusal to help, then fine. But I'll be damned if I take it to let you feel less guilt."

Without waiting for him to respond, I turned on my heel and strode out of his office.

CHAPTER FOUR

*My second victim was Dr. Russell, a tenant in the Chicago
building recently renamed "The Castle." During a
controversy concerning the non-payment of rent due me,
I struck him to the floor with a heavy chair, when he, with
one cry for help, ending in a groan of anguish, ceased
to breathe.*

═══════════

THOMAS RACED TO CATCH UP with me, of course. He couldn't
have had time to do more than stammer an excuse to his
uncle, because I was walking quite fast; he caught up within seconds.
When he did, it was all apologies and "I can't believe he would do
that" and "how in the world could he ever?"

I didn't slow my pace. By then I was out on the streets again,
choosing a direction at random and walking as fast as my feet would
take me, hoping to stay ahead of the tears that wanted to leak out
and praying I could hold things together until I was someplace safe.

Wherever that was.

The street was even busier now, the buildings glowing with the golden light of the setting sun. A gaping hole opened inside me. No one looked at me. No one noticed or cared who I was or what I needed. In the middle of all those people, I felt lonelier than ever before.

Thomas caught at my elbow and held tight, forcing me to slow down. I whirled to face him.

"What?"

He sputtered, my expression apparently taking away all ability for rational thought. "Where will you stay?" he asked at last.

"On a park bench, for all I care." The longer I was standing and not doing something, the more unwanted thoughts intruded on me. Why hadn't I just taken Mr. Pinkerton's money and lied to him? I could have spent it on a hotel room, but instead I'd had to make my grand exit. It was the sort of thing Ruby would have done.

I needed to be smarter than Ruby if I didn't want to end up in the same mess she'd found herself.

Thomas stared at me, his eyes wide and his mouth open. Was he fighting back a smile? I wanted to slap his cheek, though I was back to my old self enough that I didn't.

"I know a place," he said at last. "I'm friends with the owner. It's downtown, and he'll let you stay there for at least a week. That will give you some time to get your feet under you. You won't have to take any money from me if you don't want to, though I'd appreciate it if you'd at least let me give you enough to keep you fed for the next while."

I studied him a moment longer. He was earnest, and he meant well, and it would be foolish of me to turn down more help. "I'm not going to give up," I told him.

Now the smile broke out on his face in truth. "I didn't think you would. You're not like other women."

This only spoiled the moment. I turned around to face the street again. "Very well. Take me to this hotel, and we'll see about the rest."

As we walked, I wondered where this new version of me had come from. Only yesterday I'd been on the train, latched onto Madeline as if she were the one thing saving me from drowning. Just this morning I'd been mortified to be on the street in my underclothes. Yet here I was, fumbling my way through Chicago but somehow still going.

Thomas spoke as we walked. "If you're intent on staying, then you need to be more careful. Don't trust any strangers, particularly ones who seem friendlier than most. There are street hustlers aplenty in Chicago with the exposition in town. Some will try to sell you false goods. Some will try to make you think you broke something of theirs. Watch your money and possessions. Pickpockets are very good at what they do. If anything comes up, find the police. Give them my card if you need to. I will iron things out."

He pressed his somewhat crumpled business card into my hand and continued on, spouting volumes of information. Hotels where Ruby might have gone looking for work. Places I could go for help if things got too much. I was so swept up in it all that I didn't notice at first what the building looked like that he ushered me into: the Palmer House.

I almost stumbled into a sprawl on the floor when I saw our destination. Chicago had already shown me more marvels than I thought possible, from the towering buildings to the throngs of people. But none of it had prepared me for this. The main lobby was at least as big as our personal tomato plot back home with sweeping chandeliers made of gold and crystal and pillars so wide around that I could have hugged them and not even had my hands touch. The carpet was soft and plush and so perfect I couldn't bring myself to walk across it. Instead, I skirted the edge of the room, giving myself time to see who else was there.

Little children darted back and forth in the lobby as nannies snapped at them or hissed in hushed tones. A few men in suits read the paper in the middle of the room in enormous upholstered chairs, sipping coffee through thick mustaches.

I turned to Thomas. "Your friend *owns* this hotel?"

He flushed slightly. "His parents do, but it's close to the same thing. Wait here while I arrange for your stay."

The far wall was taken up by a desk that stretched its entire length. Uniformed employees scurried around behind it, sorting mail or keys or packages. A thin man in a dark suit lorded it over the entire operation, watching his minions and somehow issuing orders without making a sound. He was nothing but smiles and nods when Thomas spoke to him, and then we were heading up the stairs to the seventh floor.

By the time we were safely at my room, I was willing to forgive him for having such an uncle.

"You'll be careful, won't you?" he asked me before he left.

I nodded and even gave him a little smile in return. "I'll be careful."

He reached out to shake my hand, and I accepted. He pressed a much smaller wad of bills into my palm, and I did not turn them away. "I'll check in with you," Thomas said. "If you'll let me."

"I would be very grateful if you would."

He didn't suggest once more that I go home, and for that I was even more thankful.

My room greeted me with high ceilings, tall windows, and a bed with sheets as smooth as a kitten's fur.

I went to look out over the city. Seven stories up! My hands gripped the railing tightly as I peered down to the street below. I was as high as a bird, and an image flashed through my head: wind rushing through my hair and dress as I fell to a messy end on the sidewalk below.

But I stood my ground. When I wasn't looking straight down at the tops of the heads of passersby and horses down below, I could see out across the city. Glimpses of Lake Park to my right, and what might have been a piece of the Art Institute, brand new and holding who knew what wonders of culture.

For a moment, I could feel like I was living my dream. The same one I'd shared with Ruby: Life as an independent woman in the center of society. Refined. Poised.

But with that feeling of freedom and the whiff of attaining my dream came a cold dose of reality. Buildings stretched as far as I could see. It would take forever to sift through them in my search for Ruby.

Ruby had been a bright flame in Manti, but what was a small flame to the bonfire of Chicago? Would anyone have noticed her? Would anyone care if she'd even been killed? It could have been something as simple as an accident. A cart in the wrong place at the wrong time. A slip from a balcony like the one where I stood now.

I stepped away from the window and returned to reality.

If I were going to get this done, I had to start doing something on my own. But what? I lay down on the bed and stared at the ceiling, trying to think over my options. Here I was in one of the finest hotels in the city. For a moment I wondered if Ruby had found work at a place like this. Would she have applied here?

What would the Pinkertons do?

I sat up in bed, my eyes wide. Thomas had bought me entrance into the hotel, but what I did with that entrance was up to me. I could lie here enjoying the feel of the sheets against my skin, or I could go around doing some real detective work. Ruby had wanted to be a maid, after all. This hotel had to be crawling with them. I might not know where to go and what to say to begin my search, but there were maids here who would. All I had to do was ask them the right way.

Minutes later, my cheeks dry and my spirits high once again, I was stalking the floors of the hotel, room key in hand. The halls were lined with plush carpet, identical doors dotting the walls like so many soldiers at attention. If anyone questioned where I was and what I was doing, I was going to feign ignorance. Just another lost bumpkin.

The first few floors held nothing for me but a grouchy old man, a simpering girl and her beau, and a pair of twin girls in matching blue dresses. But on the third floor, I came across a maid's cart in the middle of the hall, parked next to an open door.

I paused outside, listening to the faint sounds of a woman cursing under her breath. I hesitated, then checked myself again. If I didn't have the nerve to talk with a maid and ask her a few simple questions, I was never going to get anywhere in this quest.

Clearing my throat, I rapped on the door frame. "Excuse me?"

The cursing stopped. With a swish of fabric against fabric, a woman strode to the door. I guessed she was in her twenties, maybe five years older than me. A giantess in a white and blue dress with a white maid's hat perched precariously on top of her head. Strands of brown hair were escaping her bun, like prisoners from a jail cell. She dropped into a slight curtsy when she saw me, her eyes sinking to the floor after one brief glare that was quickly curbed. "Pardon, ma'am. Didn't mean to disturb."

For a woman as tall and broad as this, her voice was remarkably quiet. I realized only then that I hadn't thought much about what I would do when I actually found someone to ask questions.

"You're a maid here?" is all I managed to come up with.

She closed and opened her eyes, deliberately, as if trying to calm herself down. "Yes, ma'am."

Why hadn't I come up with something more than a yes or no question? "Have you been a maid long?"

"Ten years this spring, it'll be."

"How did you get your job?" I asked.

"Pardon, ma'am?"

I stood up straighter, trying to look more confident than I felt. "Your job," I said. "How does someone become a maid in this city?"

Her jaw was a square line of frustration. "You apply," she said curtly, as if I'd insulted her mother or spat in her oatmeal.

"Am I bothering you?" I asked her, taken aback. It wasn't as if I'd been taking too much of her time.

She gestured at the hotel room behind her. "Last night a group of men from out of town decided to have more fun than usual. They burned the drapes, smeared honey into the carpet, ripped the mattresses into shreds, and I don't even want to think about the things they did to the pillows. But the room needs to be ready by tomorrow to be let out again, and I'll let you guess who the person is who needs to get it ready. So forgive me if I have little patience to answer random questions from a girl so fresh off the train you can still smell the smoke on her."

There were a thousand things I wanted to say to that woman. They flew through my mind one by one in a blur. Yell at her for being mean. Complain about how rude everyone in this city seemed to be. Chide her for speaking that way to a paying customer.

But I knew what it felt like to be stuck cleaning up after other people's messes. So instead, I tucked the key into the neckline of my dress. "If I help you clean up, will you eat dinner with me?"

You would have thought I'd splashed water in the woman's face, for all the spluttering she erupted with. "What?" she managed to get out in the end.

"I'm new to Chicago, and I'm not doing anything right. I need answers, and all I keep coming back to is how clueless I am. But I do know how to clean a room and get stains out of a pillow. So I'll help you get it done, if you'll come to dinner with me afterward and answer my questions. Even the silly ones."

Now it was her turn to stand there like a fish caught for supper. Long enough for me to worry I'd judged her wrong and my ploy might turn back on me. If she decided to make trouble for me, there was no knowing where that might lead.

"I'll take that as a yes," I said, and pushed past her and into the room, where I was caught short by the smell.

"You get used to the smell after a little," the maid said next to me. "Though I don't suppose our customers will go along with that suggestion."

I stared at the feathers and the stains and the burnt spots in the carpet and the whatever-it-was dripping from the ceiling.

The maid grunted. "My name's Phebe, and if you help me clean this room, I'll not only answer your questions, I'll pay for dinner as well."

"Deal." I squared my shoulders, grabbed a rag and bucket, and went to work.

CHAPTER FIVE

Learning that the man had some money, I induced him to go upon a fishing trip with me, and, being successful in allaying his suspicions, I finally ended his life by a sudden blow upon the head with an oar.

―――――――――

IT WAS A GOOD THING I had a pleasant room to come back to once all was said and done. Cleaning with Phebe took the better part of two hours, and my dress was soaked through with sweat and dirty water by the end of it. Phebe had paled when she'd discovered I was a paying customer, but I hadn't let her back off.

"You promised," I said. "And I accepted. I'm holding you to it. I'll have questions, and I'll expect answers to every single one."

She'd settled by insisting on going and buying dinner for both of us, then taking it to my room, where we could eat in private. "It's the least I can do," she'd said, and I'd agreed. At that point, the thought of going out in public with my clothes the way they were was too much for me to bear.

I'd taken time in my room to air my clothes while Phebe made her trip for provisions, and I was feeling much refreshed when she showed up again, now out of her maid's uniform and looking far less threatening.

"If Mr. Jackson finds out I'm here, I'm sure he'd skin me alive."

I'd pulled her into the room. "Best you not lurk out in the halls then."

She'd brought chicken and rice, and it was one of the most heavenly things I'd eaten in my life.

Sitting there with my belly full and a good few hours of work behind me, I felt the closest I'd come to satisfied since I'd left Manti behind me. I sighed and sat back against the wall. The two of us were eating on the floor, neither one of us trusting our greasy fingers to those sheets or the upholstery.

Phebe raised her eyebrows at me. "How you can make a sound of contentment after what we went through is beyond me."

I shook my head. "Hard work is something I can understand. I'm used to it. You struggle through it, and you know when you're done. But for what I'm trying to do now, there's no telling when I'm finished for the day, and no knowing if I'll ever be successful."

"All right," she said, wiping her fingers on a napkin. "Then let's hear what's so terrible, and we'll see if I can't help you the same as you helped me."

For the first time since I'd woken up in Chicago with all my belongings stolen, it felt like I had a chance.

Phebe—gruff, blunt Phebe—was a person I understood. I didn't have to worry that she had something else in mind when she spoke, because she said and did exactly what she thought. She listened as I told her everything from Ruby leaving to the train ride to shopping with Thomas. It felt even more overwhelming when I spoke it out loud and shoved it into the open.

At last I finished, explaining, "That's where I am now. I need to find her. Everyone says she must have run off, but I know my sister. Something happened, but I don't know what, and my only idea is to try and trace where I think she would have gone until I come across her trail. I thought she might have applied to the Palmer to be a maid."

Phebe grunted. "Mr. Jackson doesn't care how much a girl's eyes flutter or how heavily her bosom heaves. He wants workers who will give him the most for the pennies he pays, and that means experience. He'd have turned your Ruby out on her ear, and never mind how much she might have protested."

With Phebe's help, I learned more in an evening than I would have learned in a month on my own. All about the hotels in the area. Which ones were open to new help. Which ones had managers with wandering eyes and hands. Which ones paid the best, and which ones usually had new maids more often than others.

"It's a hard business," she explained. "There are so many new people flooding in to see the exposition. Everybody's putting up a shingle saying 'rooms available,' and everybody's looking for help to clean those rooms. You can't just go anywhere, though. You want to know you'll be safe and that you'll be paid."

A chill ran down my spine as she said that. What would have happened to me if I'd gone somewhere without Phebe's advice? Could that have happened to Ruby? No. She'd sent letters for months. She'd found a place that had been safe, hadn't she?

Phebe snuck down to the maid's area of the hotel and returned with a map of the city, which we spread out on the bed. "There's two ways we can do this," she said, pointing to the map. "Start at the train stations and work our way out, or start by hitting the ones that make the most sense to investigate first. One's ordered, the other's haphazard. It's up to you."

I stared at the map, tattered and stained in places, the ink faint enough to make you squint, and one whole corner missing completely. "How many hotels do you think there are?" I asked, not willing to commit to an approach yet.

She sniffed. "Hard to tell. We don't care about who's hiring right now. We care about who was hiring six months ago. And I haven't the faintest idea how to figure that out." Phebe trailed off in thought. "Best to cover them all. Your sister worked at one of them, so, sooner or later, you'll come across the right one. But we could still do it by location or jump around by my best guesses."

Mother always taught we should go with our feelings. I clenched my eyes closed and prayed silently. I wanted this all over with—Ruby found and the two of us back on our way again.

I opened my eyes and decided. "We'll start from the middle and go from there."

We worked late into the night, marking spots on the map that I should try. As the *x*'s on the map grew, I found it increasingly difficult to keep my spirits up. Chicago was so large! With each hotel, Phebe had something to say about a maid who worked there now or in the past, filling me in on the wages and the working conditions. She knew which hotels catered mostly to immigrants, which were in disrepair with sagging walls or leaking roofs, which were too close to the train tracks, keeping you up even in the middle of the night. Those were typically the ones that offered board in return for a reduced wage.

"Not that you want to stay there," Phebe said. "Sleep's as valuable as room, in my book. Lose too much of it, and your health will slip. If you're sick, you work more slowly. If you're slow, you lose your job."

As the night grew later, she left a couple of times to go check with the new staff that had come on, getting the latest information she could. Each time she left, I wondered anew: What had I done to deserve such an effort? Phebe didn't know Ruby, and she hadn't known me just hours ago. Yet here she was, scouring the building for tips that might help me and giving up her own free time.

"You should go," I told her the third time she returned.

She waved it off without a moment's hesitation. "We were all new at some point, and Lord knows we all have family that make decisions that aren't worth a wooden nickel. I've got a niece who might be in the same muck as your sister, if she doesn't watch out. If that happens, I'd like to think someone would help me the same as I'm helping you."

It was well past midnight by the time we finished. Phebe sat back on the bed and blew out a sigh. "That should give you a start," she said, pointing at the map. It looked like a maze of *x*'s and lines at this point.

"A start?" I asked.

She gave me a wry smile. "You can't be thinking we got all of them. We didn't make it much farther than Englewood, and most of that is already almost a guess. It'll take more time to flesh it out completely. Where are you staying, when you aren't throwing money to the wind to sleep at the Palmer?"

I shrugged. "I'm not actually paying for this. Thomas covered the bill. I imagine I'll have to look for—"

"You're staying with me," she cut in. "And you'll stay for free."

"No," I said. "I can't keep being a charity case."

"Then I'll charge a fair rate," Phebe said. "If that's what it takes to get you to agree. You need friends in this search of yours. If you turn us all away, who's going to be around to help you when it all goes to pieces?"

At that, I accepted. I would have been a fool not to.

CHAPTER SIX

A domestic was the seventh victim. I thought it wise to end the life of the girl. This I did by calling her to my office and suffocating her in the vault of which so much has since been printed.

———

I HAD THE DREAM AGAIN THAT night. Ruby and I were in a room with no windows and only one door. The walls were smooth and bare, and, when my arm brushed against one, I felt the cold, rippled touch of metal.

Was it a safe? It was an awfully big one, if it was.

A man stood outside the door, his face covered in shadow, his body an outline of darkness against the light from outside. Ruby was crying, tears streaming down her cheeks and her forehead creased in confusion, but I couldn't make out what she was saying.

The man said something back, and then he started to slam the door on us both. Ruby lunged forward, trying to stop it, and she managed to get her fingers around the frame just as the door smashed closed. She screamed in pain. The door had bounced off her fingers, leaving them crushed and bloody.

The man said something that might have been a curse, then reached through and shoved Ruby backward. I couldn't move. I could only watch this unfold, even though I wanted to jump into action and help her.

My sister struggled against the man, but he struck her on the head and knocked her out. The door swung closed easily, casting the inside of the room in darkness.

Then, just like that, I was able to move. As soon as there was nothing I could do, the dream let me do whatever I wanted.

I rushed to Ruby's side. "Who did this?" I asked. "Who is he?"

She shook her head at me, and when she looked up, I saw her skin had begun to turn green around her mouth and rot. "You shouldn't have come," she said, but her voice was missing the emotion Ruby always had. She might have been ecstatic or she might have been shattered, but Ruby had never been in between. She was now. Empty.

"I have to save you," I told her.

She reached up to touch the corner of her mouth, her fingers exploring the rot, then tearing off a large chunk of skin and holding it up to me. I flinched back. A quarter of her mouth was now exposed to the air, making her look like a grinning skeleton was trying to emerge from within her.

"Does this look like it can be saved?" she asked, then examined the skin herself. "I'm dead, Zuretta. Dead and gone. And he'll kill again no matter what anyone does. No one is looking for him. No one cares. You won't know who he is until you're as dead as me. Go home. Father only beats you. This one does much worse."

Suddenly she was joined by fifteen or twenty other girls reaching out to clutch at my clothes, my arms, my hair. I flinched back again, but they pressed forward, unrelenting. I was getting crushed. I couldn't breathe. They were everywhere, and the stench hit me all at once. Rotting meat and decay.

I couldn't get out. Couldn't escape.

And then I awoke.

CHAPTER SEVEN

After considerable correspondence this man came to Chicago, and I enticed him into the Castle, where, while I was engaging him in conversation, struck him a most vicious blow upon the head with a piece of gas pipe. So heavy was the blow that it not only caused his death without a groan and hardly a movement; but it crushed his skull to such an extent that his body was almost useless to [me].

I T ALL TOOK SO MUCH time. Time to walk from one building to another. Time to wait for the person who might have hired Ruby. Time to go back when they weren't there the first time or the second or the third. I might have planned to go from one building to another in a nice, neat pattern, but that lasted all of one day before it began to turn into a zigzag route between buildings.

"I won't be able to afford this," I told Phebe at the end of my first Friday on the hunt as I counted the money Thomas had given me. "You're being more than generous with the rent, but food prices are… We didn't have to worry about them back on the farm. Not as much."

Phebe nodded, worry wrinkles on her forehead.

So I got a job working at a hotel. My experience talking to Phebe had more than prepared me for the answers they wanted a new maid to give them to their questions. It was a small affair, a half hour's walk from the center of the city, but it was money, so what did it matter? Phebe assured me hands would wander regardless of how much money was in a man's wallet. The hotel manager, at least, was happily married.

The weeks dragged by. Weeks of walking the streets of Chicago from the morning until the evening. Day after day of me going to work and cleaning floors and washing sheets and ironing uniforms and scrubbing toilets. Night after night trudging from hotel to hotel asking about workers. Thomas checked in from time to time, offering his help. I handed him my list of hotels and had him pore over it to see what Phebe and I had missed. When he returned, he'd increased the size by a third. I was grateful for the help, but it was hard not to feel discouraged, especially when he couldn't do more to pitch in.

"If my uncle catches wind of it, he could start making trouble for both of us," Thomas explained. "The last thing you want in your search is someone working against you."

I supposed he had a point, but it still felt like he was ducking out early. It didn't matter. At this point, I wouldn't have trusted the search for Ruby to anyone but myself.

I met plenty of maids, and I spoke to managers by the dozens. I saw firsthand how many people Chicago churned through each day. All of them going about their business. All of them strangers to each other.

Manti might have been small, and a town its size brings its own set of problems. People knew me there, but they hadn't chosen to know my problems. I'd thought that was bad enough, but Chicago didn't even care to know my name.

Try asking a person in Manti if they'd seen a blond girl six months ago, of Ruby's age and complexion, and they'd scrunch up their eyes and be able to tell you, with reasonable certainty, yes or no. I had Ruby's photograph still, but, even with its help, days and weeks went by, and no one confessed to meeting her.

Each day that passed, the memories grew a little worse. Each week that went by, the nightmares became more vivid. Dead women stalking me in my sleep.

"You need to rest," Phebe told me one evening a little over a month into my search. "The bags under your eyes are starting to get bags of their own."

I collapsed into the chair by the kitchen table, my head falling into my arms of its own accord. My back was agony, my feet throbbing, and my hands raw. "It's not working," I said without looking up. "None of it."

Phebe came over to rub my shoulders. "It's a long process. You knew that when you started. Don't give up, though. Think about how much more you know now than you did before."

I closed my eyes and tried not to give in to despair. It felt like my body wanted to explode. So much I wanted to do and couldn't. Even speaking it out loud was more than I could bear. There was a vision in my head, and it grew clearer with every passing day: an older version of me, my shoulders hunched and my fingers knobby, still working day in and day out at hotels.

My sister had never been found.

"I didn't come here to start a new life," I muttered.

"What was that?"

I sat up and turned to Phebe. Her hair bun had tiny strands escaping left and right, and she reached up to undo it. "This wasn't the plan," I said. "Or it was, but not like this. Ruby and I were supposed to come here together. She asked me to come, the night she left. If I'd only gone with her…"

Phebe began to brush her hair out, and sighed. "You can't blame yourself for everything, Etta. Unless you mean to tell me you're the one who made her disappear?"

"If I'd been here, then she—"

"Might have been hit by a cart. Might have caught the flu and died. Anyone can play the Might Have game, girl, but no one ever wins. So live your life for the future, and quit questioning the past."

My head sank back to the table.

Phebe continued, the room quiet enough for the sound of her brush strokes to be heard, a sign of how late it was. "You might not have come here to start a new life, but, now that you've been out of that tiny village of yours, do you really want to go back?

"You couldn't do it," Phebe said, placing her brush down. "Go back to being beaten by your father? You're not the same person who left home weeks ago. You started a new life the moment you left your house behind you, so embrace it. Come with me to the fair. It'll take your mind off—"

I snapped up. "I can't. Not while Ruby might be…"

"Ruby is what she is. You're doing your best, but you're finding this might be a longer race than you had in mind. Don't kill yourself trying to finish it all at once. You're bringing in money. You're gaining experience as a maid. You've got grit. Don't give up."

One way or another, I kept scrubbing and sweeping and searching. Those x's on the map kept getting crossed off, even as more were added. Central Chicago was eliminated. The bulk of the east and west were crossed off as well, and I was focusing on my way south, closer to the Columbian Exposition. Bronzeville. Bridgeport. Fuller Park. Construction had been fierce down there. It wasn't the first place a person came when they arrived in the city, but almost all came there eventually.

The Continental Hotel was newer than most. Neat brick. Clean lines. A modest lobby. It wouldn't win any awards, though it would have been one of the nicest buildings in my hometown.

It was late in the evening, and I'd been up early to work the morning shift. My eyes were drooping, but I wanted to get at least three more hotels off my list before I headed home. The farther away my search brought me from downtown, the longer it took me to travel to do the searching. It cost money to take the trolley down here, but it was almost an eight-mile walk.

I had to make each trip count.

There was a trick to getting the hotel manager to listen to me. Go up to him with the same frantic voice and cry for help that I'd tried the first few days, and they all became suspicious. Pose as the maid of a wealthy woman from out of state sent to fetch a wayward daughter, jingling a purse full of coins for a reward, and the response was much more receptive.

It was ironic: If I told the truth, everyone thought I was lying. If I lied the right way, then people would actually speak to me. Though I'd taken to strapping a knife to my right thigh, high up enough so that no one would spot it by accident. That's how life was in Chicago. A girl had to be prepared for the worst, and my years working on the farm had given me more than enough muscle and experience to let me know how to use it. Heaven knew Father had given me practice with taking a beating.

The manager of the Continental had bad breath and a slight stoop to his shoulders that made him look like he'd been caught in a continual shrug. His black hair was slicked back with grease, and his suit was frayed around the edges. "How am I to know you're in earnest?" he asked me, eyeing my clothes, though his gaze kept getting drawn back to the purse.

"A common question," I said, keeping my tone lofty and disengaged. "One that always indicates you know nothing of interest. Thank you for your time."

I turned to leave, and he reached out to grab my shoulder. I froze and stared at the offending hand until it was removed from my person.

"Beg pardon," the manager said, smiling widely to reveal crooked teeth only made worse by the yellow gaslight. He laughed nervously, sending a second wave of bad breath wafting toward me. "What if I were to lead you to a place where you might have more success?"

I frowned at him. "Excuse me?"

"I haven't seen the girl, but I know of a hotel that swallows girls like that for lunch. One after the other. All of them pretty. All of them gone. It might be your lady's daughter fell into the same pit."

"What do you mean?"

His smile grew wider still, though I hadn't thought that possible. "What's in it for me?"

"Nothing until your information proves of real worth."

The smile fled his face in an instant, though at least that made it harder to smell his breath. Onions, I thought. And molding meat.

"Never mind, then." He turned to leave.

"Giving up that easily?"

"I'm a busy man," he said, despite the empty lobby and no sign of a guest even having checked in. I'd been in enough hotels by this point to recognize one that was about to go under. "I ain't got time for women who can't see a good tip when it's right there hanging on the low branch in front of them."

It was impossible to keep the sarcasm from my voice. "I'm sorry. I didn't realize you'd be so upset when a woman didn't immediately thank you for living."

"I didn't—"

"You say you have information. If that information proves accurate and helps my search, I'll return and pay you a dollar and consider it money well spent. But I won't pay a cent for someone's fever dreams."

He sucked at his teeth, staring at the wooden registration desk and picking at one of the wood grains.

"I thought not," I said and left the lobby.

Seconds later, padding feet rushed up behind me, catching me outside the main door. "A dollar?"

I turned. "You have my word."

"Then give me ten cents up front," the man said. "You don't trust me. Why should I trust you?"

"Because all it costs you is to speak. You've already told me about this mysterious hotel, and now I'll be asking around about it. If it's as well-known as you've said, then I'm sure I'll find someone ready and willing to tell me more, now that I know what to ask.

Someone who will do it for free. So do you want a chance at a dollar or a certain nothing at all?"

"The Castle, they call it," he said all at once. "Almost as big as one, from what I've heard. Over in Englewood. Used to be a drugstore, but they built it up and up, and now it still is, on the main floor. Part of it, anyway. But it's got two more of them floors now, and that's where the guests stay."

"Where is it?"

"Five blocks east of here. You can't miss it. Got some of them little bumpy-outy things with the windows."

"Women have gone missing from the place, and no one cares?"

His eyes dropped to the ground, and he gave a half shrug. "There was some private detectives down there, is all. One searching for one girl, and another for another. Nobody thinks nothing really suspicious, is what they tell me, but a man has to wonder, don't he?"

"So it's not quite as sinister as you claimed."

He glared at me. "This city chews up strangers. Women mostly. I see it, even if no one else does."

"Yes," I said. "And you'd love to do some of the chewing, no doubt. Very well. You've given me the information. I'll return to pay you for your troubles should they prove worth my while. Thank you." I left, ignoring his protests.

It was the best nugget of information I'd panned out so far. Still, I didn't feel optimistic when I returned to Phebe's apartment, and she only gave me more reasons to make me skeptical.

"Whatever you do," she told me that evening as we got ready to turn out the light, "don't go barging in asking questions the way you've been."

"I thought you said you doubted the man's word."

"And I do, but it wouldn't hurt you to be careful. Either the man's lying, and you'll quickly see the truth of it, or there's something to be concerned about. You've come out of your shell a great deal from Manti, but perhaps the new you could learn a thing or two from the old version. You can always unbottle caution afterward, but it's impossible to cram it back in when it's already loosed."

It was sound advice, and I did my best to follow it three days later when I found time to go to Englewood. I'd expected to have to dig around to find this Castle the clerk had mentioned, but all it took was a few questions to pedestrians, and I was pointed right to the building. Its actual name was the World's Fair Hotel. When I saw it, I understood where the nickname came from.

The building didn't sit right when you looked at it, as if it shifted around in the corner of your eye. It was dark, for one thing, and made of brick, and the windows didn't line up the way they should. Most buildings would have them spaced evenly across the front, but the Castle had little bump-outs from the wall, with an almost-round tower on the corner itself. It was three floors with no real roof to speak of, so those bump-outs made it seem like something meant for guards and regular patrols.

Though I might have called it "jail" instead.

Would my sister honestly come to work at a place like this? I doubted anyone would want to, though if there were a man involved, that might explain much.

Part of me wanted to rush right in, ask my questions, and never return. But Phebe's advice persuaded me to take my time and observe, asking around to some of the pedestrians to see what they knew of the building before I jumped in with both feet.

I heard stories about its construction and one or two complaints that it had taken longer to build than it should have. The building was managed by a Mr. Holmes, a former doctor who lived on the third floor with his wife. To hear the people tell it, he was a bundle of excitement, always undertaking new endeavors, though somewhat limited by a mysterious senior partner who provided the bulk of the money.

The hotel's strange layout was due to the rocky path it had taken into existence: numerous companies had worked on the building over the years, and one man told me not all of them had been paid. Again, the blame came to the feet of Mr. Holmes's partner or superior. Holmes himself was well liked by everyone I spoke to, although he had an assistant, Pitezel, who many liked far less. He was the muscle behind the management, I gathered.

I had wanted to find my first real lead, but the more people I spoke with, the more it seemed this was another false trail. The sun was well on its way to noon, and I'd spent almost two hours uncovering nothing more than complaints of bad tipping and some circumspect business dealings.

It was time for me to head to work, and I debated leaving early to allow myself some extra travel time. The trip had left me feeling more tired than usual, and the thought of ten hours of cleaning seemed particularly bleak.

Still, I had yet to do my bare minimum: check with the manager to see if he remembered Ruby applying for a job. I knew already Pitezel and Holmes were away from the hotel on business, and I had no desire to waste one more minute on the Castle than I had to. Instead, I took out my dog-eared picture of Ruby and approached a woman leaving the hotel. She'd been pointed out to me as the druggist who ran the pharmacy on the main floor. If my sister had been around, perhaps she would have seen her.

"Excuse me, ma'am," I called out.

She stopped and sized me up. She was an older woman with a mouth that pinched together and a nose a few sizes too small. Her gray hair was in a tight bun, and her blouse and dress were neatly pressed. "Yes?" she snapped.

I held out the photograph. "I was wondering if you'd—"

She didn't even glance at it. "The detectives are hiring women now, are they?"

My hand dipped. "Excuse me?"

"You're after one of those girls, are you not? The Cigrand girl or the Conner daughter? Don't waste my time with more questions. I'm busy enough as it is."

My heart was in my throat. I fought off a stutter and tried

to keep myself from flushing. In vain! "No. I, that is, I'm here for someone else. If you'll take a moment to look at this picture? I believe she was here as a maid, or a house servant?"

The woman sighed and shook her head, but she snatched the picture from my hand and held it out at arm's length, moving it forward and backward as she tried to focus on it. Her eyebrows shot up in apparent irritation, and she shoved the picture back at me.

"Just what we need. Another one disappeared and run off to who knows where. As if two weren't enough."

"I don't understand," I said.

"Ruby hasn't been here for months, girl. She was nice enough while she was around, but she fled like all the others. That's all I know, and I don't have time to waste frittering it away with the likes of you."

She turned and stalked away in a huff, leaving me staring after her with my mouth open.

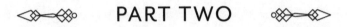

PART TWO

The Detective

CHAPTER EIGHT

Mrs. Cook and her niece had access to all the rooms by means of a master key and one evening while I was busily engaged preparing my last victim for shipment, the door suddenly opened and they stood before me. It was a time for quick action, rather than for words of explanation upon my part, and before they had recovered from the horror of the sight, they were within the fatal vault.

━━━━━━━

I STARED AT MYSELF IN THE mirror one more time, inspecting every detail to make sure it was as perfect as possible. My hair (now dyed a dark brown) was neatly tucked into a tight bun. My dress was freshly washed and pressed. Nothing in my teeth. My face seemed strange with the coat of makeup that Phebe had taught me to use. Far prettier than I was used to. She'd turned out to be an expert at making even the plainest of faces into something much more interesting to look at, though I did wonder what the paints would do when I was up to my elbows in cleaning and laundry.

I'd the farmer's tan I'd arrived in Chicago with. Looking at that person in the mirror, I wasn't sure how many people back in Manti would recognize me. They shouldn't. I was no longer Zuretta.

Just Etta now.

My hand trembled as I reached up to flick off a speck of lint from my red collar.

I felt more nervous now than I had when I was parading through the streets of Chicago dressed only in my nightgown.

Back then, I wasn't worried for my life. Back then, I wasn't about to apply for a job at the same house where girls my age had gone missing. My hands had every reason to tremble.

I took a deep breath and held it, focusing on the last memory I had of Ruby: a smile and a hug in the middle of the night as she slipped out our window. She'd been so alive then. So excited.

This was for her.

I opened my eyes and held out my hand. The trembling had stopped.

With a quick nod to myself in the mirror, I felt at my right thigh to make sure my knife was safely in its spot. I turned, grabbed my handbag, and headed to the door. My room was a far cry from what my home in Manti, Utah, had looked like, even a stark difference compared to the apartment Phebe and I had shared. A threadbare rug, dingy, white walls that needed paint, and a creaky bed as the one piece of furniture. I had to use my luggage as my bedside table. But it was closer to the Castle, and I couldn't very well walk

14 miles each day just so I could see a friendly face when I came home each evening from work.

If I got this job, I'd be able to afford this new room for more than a few weeks. Assuming I didn't disappear as well.

Phebe had suggested in jest that it would be easier to ask questions if I were a maid in the hotel myself. The next day I discovered there was an opening. I'd told Phebe it was God at work. She'd said it was more likely the devil.

Enough thinking about the past. My mind had to be on the present if I hoped to be successful today. I turned the knob and went into the hall. The stairway was rickety, but when I emerged into the city of Chicago, it was to a day full of sunshine and warmth. We were well into Spring, and everyone was buzzing with excitement. The Columbian Exposition had finally roared to full life, and even more tourists were swarming to see it, hard as that was to believe.

The streets were full of carts and horses and people rushing here and there on their morning errands. The moment you stepped outside, you were hit with a wall of noise: clattering hooves, the rumble of iron-shod wheels across cobblestone, the continuous murmur of voices. And there were the smells, too, of course. All those horses made plenty of manure. Smoke drifted in from factories, and many of those people in the streets were far from what my mother would call clean. All of that had seemed so overwhelming when I first arrived. Now it was just another day in Chicago.

The walk cleared my head as I focused on the task at hand.

Cross the street. Head south. Three blocks down. My feet handled the trip in much better fashion than they had when I first arrived, unused to walking on hard roads in new shoes. The shoes were far from new now, and I had hundreds of miles of experience with the city.

The Castle's bulk loomed into view, massive and squat, but I didn't hesitate. I just marched straight up to the pharmacy on the main floor. This could all go wrong within the first few seconds. I'd talked to Mrs. Patterson last week, asking about Ruby. True, it had been a quick conversation, but, if I stood out in her mind or she connected me in any way to my sister, then my hopes of investigating here would be gone.

I'd waited a few extra days in an effort to give her more time to forget me, not to mention the hair dye and makeup. This was my one chance, and it was worth anything and everything I could pay.

A bell by the door chimed as I entered, and Mrs. Patterson looked up from her bottles and smiled at me. She worked double duty at the Castle, supervising the pharmacy and the maids, and always with a sour mood, from what I gathered. I saw no trace of recognition or suspicion. Yet.

"Can I help you?" the old woman asked. She had the same tight gray bun and shrewd eyes, and she wore a plain brown dress with a white collar and white belt. Her employees all claimed she had a suspicious nature, though she hid it well from customers. If she suspected me, would she be able to hide her thoughts?

"I'm here to apply for the posting," I said. "Housemaid?"

Mrs. Patterson lost her smile and grunted, then jerked her head behind her at an open door. "You'll want Pitezel for that, and I'll appreciate you using the servants' entrance from now on." Did her eyes linger on my face longer than they should have, and did she hesitate as I left the room?

I'd known which door I should have used, of course. But I'd wanted to be noticed and remembered now, if possible. The Castle had a reputation for being a place experienced maids avoided. Too many young women had come into the Castle and left before anyone knew their faces, let alone their names. I wanted people to notice me now. I didn't know what was happening to the women, but I didn't want to become another one of them.

So I'd be meeting with Pitezel. He wouldn't have been my first choice, but it hadn't been outside the realm of possibility.

I fought to stay focused as I walked deeper into the building, though my mind kept wanting to think of all that might have gone on here. Ruby must have walked these very halls, not more than a year before. What had happened to her?

The halls were narrow and lined with wood, the floorboards scuffed with use. I passed through a barber shop and a luggage store as well as the offices for a lawyer and an accountant. The Castle could have been any number of store fronts I'd seen in the city since I arrived here.

Mr. Pitezel was back in a storage room. He was a tall, wiry man with sunken cheeks, thinning blond hair, and a thin mustache. He had been a carpenter before Mr. Holmes hired him as his chief assistant at the Castle. He was married and had five children, and that was the extent of common knowledge about him.

He was staring at shelves, making little marks in a notepad and muttering when I arrived. He might not have been a carpenter anymore, but he still had a clawed hammer in a loop on his pants. I stood waiting for him to finish, but the seconds ticked by, and he gave no sign that he had noticed my arrival.

Finally, after a full minute, I cleared my throat. "Mr. Pitezel."

"It speaks," he said, not taking his eyes off the shelves. The tick marks kept being added.

"I'm here to apply for a job?"

Once again, there was no response.

"I was told to talk with you?" I added after another thirty seconds.

He sighed and turned from the shelves at last. "I'm a busy man, and you're interrupting me in the middle of inventory."

The Ruby in me didn't like that tone. Not even a little. "Perhaps you would be less busy if you had a full contingent of maids," I said, trying (and failing) to keep the impatience from my voice.

"Impertinent help is never needed," he told me, and I cursed myself for letting my newfound temper get the better of me.

"I'm sorry," I said. "I didn't—"

"You may go."

I froze in the room, unsure how to proceed. Had I failed that

quickly? Should I try to force the issue, thus sticking out even more in the man's memory and jeopardizing future investigations? Did he want me to stand up for myself or apologize profusely? How could I—

"Excuse me," a voice came from behind me. A man's hand circled my waist and pushed me lightly to the side. "Sorry. Tight squeeze, I'm afraid. Forgive the forwardness."

I moved easily, shocked by the familiar gesture from a stranger, but at the same time, relieved someone else had arrived. The man stepped around me into view.

Shorter than Mr. Pitezel, with a thick mustache and warm brown eyes, he smiled at me, cocked his head at Mr. Pitezel, winked, and somehow it was all fine.

"Dr. Henry Howard Holmes, my dear. At your service." He gave me a slight bow—the most such cramped quarters would allow. "Did I hear you were inquiring for a job at our fine establishment?"

"Y-yes," I said, off balance. "I was…"

He had already turned to Mr. Pitezel, playfully punching the man in the arm. "Benjamin! You know how swamped we are at work." He turned his smile back on me at full force. "But we can't take just anyone, I'm afraid. The Castle is one of the top hotels in Englewood now, and we require our service to match our reputation. What experience do you have?"

"I've been cleaning rooms at the Auditorium Annex for the past year, and I have a letter with me recommending my services."

Never mind the letter was signed by Phebe and penned by me. If they started looking too carefully into my past, I might as well turn around and head out the door now.

Mr. Holmes's eyebrows shot up. "The Annex, eh? I've heard good things of them. They're newer than we are, aren't they? Prime real estate too. Why did you leave?"

"I wanted something farther away from the noise of downtown, and it's less expensive for me to rent a room in Englewood. Plus, the exposition is open now, and I wanted to be able to visit it as often as I pleased. Chances like this don't come around every day, and I heard the Castle was hiring, but if you don't have any positions..."

He patted my shoulder. "You're a godsend. Isn't she, Benjamin?"

His employee only grunted.

"What's your name, miss?" Mr. Holmes asked me.

"Etta," I said. "Etta Smith." I'd said the lie often enough to try to make it roll off my tongue, but I still felt like it tripped at the end when I actually spoke it.

"Fantastic!" Mr. Holmes said, his smile beaming beneath that thick mustache and showing no sign of suspicion. He turned to Pitezel. "Benjamin, can I trouble you to go through the paperwork with Miss Smith? Minnie and Anna have been hounding me to head with them over to the exposition, and I can't say no." He placed his left hand lightly on my right shoulder and cradled my elbow in his right hand, his body closer than I was expecting. Not in a way that made me uncomfortable, but, rather, as an uncle might care for his niece. His expression was earnest and open. "Thank you so much for coming forward. This is the hand of Providence!"

His hands lingered a second more, and then he removed them, clapped twice, and left the room with a last "Providence!" as he disappeared through the doorway.

Pitezel's eyes stayed cold. At last he nodded and jerked his head to the side, indicating I was to follow him.

"You can start today, I assume?" Mr. Pitezel asked over his shoulder as we walked.

I nearly stumbled in surprise. When I had left my apartment this morning, I had worn my nicest dress and taken care to be as presentable as possible. I knew from experience what work as a maid required, but I hadn't dreamed that I'd be starting off right away. Perhaps there were simply a few chores to be taken care of that had slipped through the cracks in the absence of sufficient help. "I'm ready to start whenever I'm needed," I said.

The man grunted and kept walking. "A bathroom on the main floor hasn't been cleaned for a few days, and Mr. Reynolds, the building's owner, has been asking us to make sure it sees attention swiftly. Some of the tenants have complained, but the other cleaning staff have been overworked as it is. Your first task will be to take care of that."

A bathroom? I couldn't help but blanching. The thought of tackling a chore like that dressed as I was... "Could I have time to go home and change first?" I asked.

Mr. Pitezel stopped in the middle of the hallway and turned to face me, his arms folded. "When Mr. Holmes hired you, he said it was an act of Providence. That's because we have things that need cleaning. Now. Not in an hour or three or whenever you feel like returning. If you're a professional, you'll put the needs of the Castle before your desire to keep your fingernails from getting dirty. Do you want the job or not?"

"I'm here to work," I assured him.

"Good. Down the hall on the right is the barber's. Hans. That's where the bucket, mop, and rags are. He'll show you. The bathroom is farther down the hall, on the left. Check in with Mrs. Patterson after you're finished, to make sure there isn't anything else before you leave. I'll expect you back here first thing in the morning."

He walked off without waiting for a response.

The downstairs toilet in the Castle had been broken for at least a few days. There was a sign posted outside the door: BROKEN. Yet, judging from the interior, the sign had been almost completely ignored.

The smell washed over me like a storm front the moment I opened the door. It made the room I had cleaned with Phebe months ago seem like a spotless kitchen by comparison. It was a simple affair: perhaps four feet square with only a toilet, a sink, and a small mirror. Perhaps it'd had a trash bin at some time. There was no evidence of it in its current state, though there was a mound of crumpled pages from a Sears & Roebuck catalogue piled in the corner where a bin might have belonged.

It took the better part of an hour to clean that small space, and at the end of that time, I smelled as bad as the bathroom had to begin with, even after scrubbing my hands and arms repeatedly. My nicest clothes would require multiple washings to recover, and they would never quite be the same. Some stains don't come out.

Still, I felt proud of my work. Clearly Mr. Pitezel had hoped the task would be enough to send me scurrying for the door, but I would have cleaned ten of those rooms if it meant I had a chance of discovering more about my sister's fate.

All that was left to do was to find clean linens and toilet paper. There were no cupboards or closets in the immediate vicinity of the bathroom, and all the efforts I made to search through the surroundings were met with glares and suspicion, not to mention a few pinched noses.

When the fifth place I checked (in the closet next to the jeweler's counter) was unsuccessful (and the clerk there, a fop named Gustavo, yelled at me in Italian), I came up with a new approach. Surely the second floor would have clean linens in abundance. I could go upstairs and search in relative quiet, with no one to complain about the way I smelled.

I was on the fifth step when someone yelled behind me. "What do you think you're doing?"

Mrs. Patterson had appeared in the hallway. I curtsied to her. "Looking for clean linens for the far bathroom, ma'am."

Her face was hard, her lips a thin line.

"I was hired an hour ago," I added, the silence making me shift my feet.

"I'm aware of the new situation," Mrs. Patterson snapped, "even if I may not approve of their selection process. But who gave you permission to go to the second floor?"

The blood rose to my face, and I stammered out, "No one. I—"

"I suppose your ignorance is somewhat excusable," the woman continued, speaking over me. "But we run things according to strict rules here at the Castle. Mr. Reynolds insists on it. You're a first-floor maid. That means you stay on the first floor. Always. I take care of the second floor, and Beth is tasked with the third. All work is handled on a floor-by-floor basis. That way, Mr. Reynolds knows exactly where to place the blame when anything runs amiss."

This was one of the most backward ways of running a hotel I could envision. "And cleaning supplies?" I asked, keeping my question brief to avoid being interrupted again.

"Are kept on each floor separately. If you use too much, we will dock your pay accordingly."

Perhaps the reason maids didn't last long at the Castle was due more to the draconian measures of Mr. Reynolds and Mrs. Patterson. This might be a dead end. I had a hard time picturing Ruby lasting long here. But I was committed now, and if I found she'd moved on before she'd disappeared, at least I might discover where she'd headed next. (And I'd cheerfully quit this job in an instant.)

But all I did was nod and say, "Yes ma'am. I'm sorry. I wasn't familiar with the rules, and I wanted the bathroom to be cleaned as quickly as possible."

She sniffed at me in dismissal. "See that it doesn't happen again. In the meantime, if you're quite done wandering the halls at your leisure, I'd appreciate it if you could take care of the rest of your duties on the first floor."

"The rest of my duties?"

Mrs. Patterson's eyes widened. "Good heavens, girl. You make it sound as if it's a revelation that you should be asked to work at a place once you've secured a position. The first floor has been without a maid for well over a week, and it's not as if Beth and I have had the time to properly cover those chores. I'll need the hallway swept and mopped, the light fixtures dusted, and the garbage cans emptied and rinsed. The rest can wait until tomorrow, I suppose, but all of that absolutely must be done before the end of the day."

There were many things I'd have liked to say to Mrs. Patterson, all of which would have gotten me fired immediately. Some of which might have gotten me arrested. But I bit my tongue. "Yes, ma'am," I said. "Though if you wouldn't mind pointing me in the direction of the toilet paper and clean linens?"

She sighed. "Must you be led by the halter to everything?"

My first day didn't improve from there.

CHAPTER NINE

The fourteenth case is that of Miss Anna Betts, and was caused by my purposely substituting a poisonous drug in a prescription that had been sent to my drug store to be compounded.

———————————

WHAT SEEMED DANGEROUS AT FIRST proved to be very much like any other maid job at the countless hotels I'd visited in the city. There were no pentagrams drawn on the floors in blood. No screams of agony in the middle of the night. No shadowy figures lurking around the hotel late into the evening.

If you discounted the beastly way the management at the hotel treated me, it was like any other hotel I'd seen in the city.

Mr. Holmes was energetic and outgoing. Charming to all, though perhaps weaker than some would wish he could be. When pressed on any issue, he would inevitably defer to his employer, the elusive owner of the Castle.

That man, Mr. Reynolds, came and went with a swirl of a cloak and not even a tip of his hat to show he'd noticed you were there. A tall man with a thin mustache and severe clothes. After three times of him passing me in the hall without so much as a twitch, I called out after him. "A pleasant morning to you, Mr. Reynolds."

He turned and stared at me, silent. Shadows covered his face in the dimly lit hallway, and my stomach twisted uncomfortably.

"My name is Etta, sir. The new first-floor maid. I wanted to thank you for—"

He walked off without another word, leaving me standing in the hall with my broom, feeling like another piece of the furniture. Five minutes later, Mrs. Patterson showed up and told me just what would happen if I were to ever disturb Mr. Reynolds again.

I didn't chance it. Besides, he was hardly ever around, though his impact was everywhere. He imposed such harsh measures on Mr. Holmes that it was a wonder anything could be done at times.

Mr. Holmes had a way about him that made people want to like him. You couldn't stay mad at him for long, and you'd wish he'd somehow be able to rid himself of Mr. Reynolds, even though it seemed impossible. The man was horrid with his money, from what I could tell, and he paid all of us like misers, including Mr. Holmes. But, somehow, we all stayed.

Mr. Pitezel was as gruff and mean as my first impression had indicated. He had a quick temper, though it softened whenever his wife and any of his five children were present. For them, he somehow had a smile and affection to spare. They were darling, the children at least. The mother tended to bark and treat maids poorly. I wondered how it was a group of children like that could come from a man such as him. Not that I should have, remembering Father and how he treated Mother and me.

I already had firm opinions on Mrs. Patterson, and they didn't change. But just because I disliked a person didn't mean they were the next Ripper.

Minnie, Mr. Holmes's fiancée, had come to the Castle with her sister Anna only a few months ago, so they, at least, were above reproach. They were a lovely pair of girls, little older than I, and though I did not have much cause to speak or interact with them, they seemed from afar to be nothing more than carefree creatures, and I envied Minnie's engagement to Mr. Holmes. It was pleasant to think of other people going about their lives in the world and comforting to see happiness still take hold.

For there was none in my heart. Only dark thoughts and narrowed eyes.

What if the culprit were someone who didn't live or work in the Castle at all? A neighbor, or a delivery man? One of the countless customers always in and out of the building, or a guest who came on business at regular intervals?

At times I would pass the staircases and wonder if clues to Ruby's disappearance waited elsewhere in the building. But I was not yet desperate enough to risk such a gamble. The building was no ally to stealth. Floorboards creaked and groaned with every step you took down the main floor's halls, and while it was easy enough to tell if someone was coming, that also meant anyone might follow your own path through the building based on sound alone.

Were there incidents that seemed odd or unexplained on the main floor? Most certainly. Once, as I was walking down the main corridor, an enormous series of *thunk*s and *thump*s came from the room next to me. I thought someone must have fallen over or knocked down a bookcase. But when I went to check, the room was empty and in order. Had the noise come from upstairs, or within the walls?

Another morning, I could have sworn I heard a woman crying softly, a high-pitched wail that drifted in and out of hearing. But no matter what room I went into, the sound grew no louder. In the end I dismissed it as being an upstairs guest, but I still wondered. The Castle had a tendency to creak and groan when the wind gusted outside, as if the entire building were possessed or in pain.

Those experiences reminded me of my own nightmares, with the legions of rotting corpses surrounding me in the vault, and Ruby at their head. But I was not living in a story by Edgar Allan Poe. No one was being bricked into rooms alive or tied down to tables to be sliced open by pendulum-swinging blades.

I knew there was a difference between fact and fiction, and I had to keep my feet firm on the ground. This investigation would turn up something, but when it did, it would undoubtedly be something mundane. A love affair gone awry. A jealous suitor.

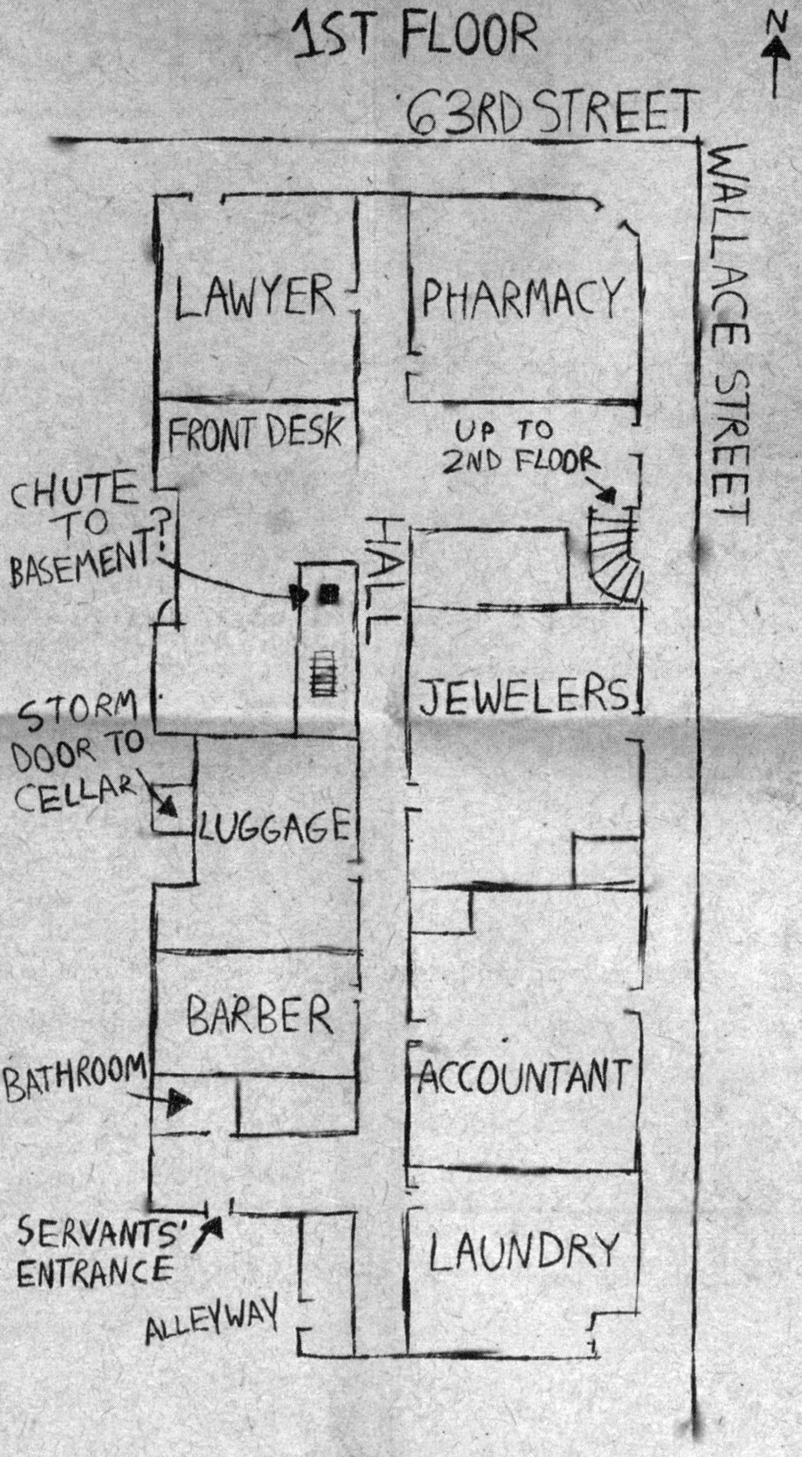
1ST FLOOR
N
63RD STREET
WALLACE STREET
LAWYER
PHARMACY
FRONT DESK
UP TO 2ND FLOOR
CHUTE TO BASEMENT?
HALL
JEWELERS
STORM DOOR TO CELLAR
LUGGAGE
BARBER
BATHROOM
ACCOUNTANT
SERVANTS' ENTRANCE
LAUNDRY
ALLEYWAY

People disappeared often enough in this country without needing some sort of bloodthirsty maniac to be at the roots.

Besides, there were other ways I could find out about Ruby. Her fiancé, for one thing. I had thought, at first, he worked at the same place as my sister, but none of the men seemed suitable candidates. They were either otherwise engaged (literally), or people I didn't think Ruby would look twice at. Hans, the German barber on the first floor, was far too brooding and quiet, and Gustavo (who worked the jewelry store) always smelled of perfume and silks. And he oiled his hair. Even the thought of running my hands through those tangles made me want to reach for a towel. Neither of them could have made my sister swoon.

Whoever it was, I saw no evidence of him, and that hope grew fainter with the end of each day. It was now more than four months since Ruby had disappeared. It shouldn't surprise me that the man in her life had moved on.

Unless, perhaps, he'd been the one to cause her disappearance.

The weeks passed by, and I began to question my strategy. I'd written to Thomas, back when I'd come up with my plan. He'd suggested I was chasing after my tail, but he'd also outlined a plan that had made sense:

If women really are disappearing at the Castle, you need to find out where they're going and why. A string of disappearances

doesn't happen on its own. Look for the person
who's standing out, but don't draw his (or
her!) attention. You want to go undercover?
Fine. That means patience. If you secure
your job, then do it, but expect to be there
for a while. Undercover work doesn't turn up
answers overnight. True, people might drop
hints or clues in casual conversation, but
look for chances to find things that always
tell the truth: paperwork. Nine times out
of ten, if something terrible is being done,
there will be some paperwork that proves it.
A business like the Castle? I'd look at their
files.

I looked for chances to follow his advice, though papers were
few and far between on the first floor. There might have been
something higher up, but I couldn't go there without rousing
suspicions. My searches had all been in vain until one day in the
pharmacy. Mrs. Patterson had been called away to help with a
matter on the far side of the Castle, and she'd ordered me to watch
the store until she came back.

As soon as she was out of earshot, I began rifling through the
drawers. I'd never had a chance to have free rein in the room before.
There were plenty of pills and bottles, bags, and tape supplies. I

came across filing cabinets filled with notes on patients, but I knew, after glancing at the first one, that finding anything worthwhile in there would take hours, if anything even existed.

I returned to the register, dejected. Each time I thought I had an opportunity or a lead, I came up empty-handed. But my eyes caught a corner of red peeking out from beneath the till. My breath caught as I drew it out: a small notebook with well-worn pages. I glanced behind me, certain I would see Mrs. Patterson rushing back into the pharmacy.

No one was around.

I practically tore the book in half in my haste to open it and see what it contained: page after page of tiny, neat handwriting. All of it in code.

9.18.89—R. H75 L44

9.19.89—PC. H68 L50

9.20.89—S H80 L58

It didn't take much thought to see it for what it was, however. The dates were a dead giveaway. I'd worked on a farm enough to know people who kept careful track of the weather, though who knew what use Mrs. Patterson would have for such a journal in the city? An old habit, perhaps? She had more than ten years of daily logs in that notebook!

I flipped deeper in, praying it wasn't all just more of the same.

After a long section of blank pages (waiting in line to be turned into weather journaling), there were basic records on how the pharmacy had been doing. Monthly profits or losses. She was making some money, but she was far from a rich woman, if this was all she had. After that, however, she listed another section in code:

RP—3F: S2.92 E9.92

NS—1F: S4.92 E7.92

BG—1F: S7.92 E12.92

JG—2F: S10.92 E4.93

Like upon line of that, just like the weather reports. The second numbers might have been years. This was 1893, after all. What did the first set mean? It wasn't until I glanced at the last entry that it clicked into place:

ES—1F: S4.93

With no second set of numbers. ES. *Etta Smith*. 1F. *First floor.* S4.93. *Started April 1993.*

This was a list of all the maids who had worked in the Castle!

Footsteps were coming down the hall. It was all I could do not to rip the sheet out of the book. I glanced over the list as fast as I could, trying to estimate how many names were there. They began in 1889, and there had to be at least twenty names on there—maybe more. I snapped the book shut and shoved it back underneath the register just as Mrs. Patterson returned.

She glanced at me, her eyes sharp. "What have you been doing?"

"Just wiping down the register," I said, thankful for the rag I'd been holding in my hand.

"Don't touch what you're not told to," she said, but the remark didn't have much bite behind it. She seemed distracted by something else.

I went back later to see if I could check the book again, but it disappeared from its storage place. Still, those names were enough to keep me going. More than twenty maids in the space of four years? True, some of that might be dismissed by Mr. Pitezel and Mrs. Patterson behaving so beastly, but maids across the city put up with far worse in return for steady wages.

If even half of them had disappeared under mysterious circumstances, that made for a slew of questions.

That discovery was enough to get me through the next few days, but discouragement set in soon after. What had I found, really? Evidence that maids didn't like the Castle, but that they were being abducted? Nothing in there would convince anyone who didn't want to be convinced. Phebe told me to stick with it and not give up hope, but to come so close to my goal and be frustrated made me want to get reckless. There I was, walking about my day with a razor-sharp knife strapped to my thigh, and for what? Each morning I wondered anew what I thought I was doing.

If I were on the second or third floors, surely there would be more I would be able to discover.

Mr. Pitezel's actions, for example, became ever more suspicious. He would disappear on mysterious errands during the day, and when I asked after his whereabouts, no one could give me a straight answer on three separate occasions.

One evening I was staying late polishing a silver serving set that Mr. Reynolds insisted be cleaned until it gleamed as new. And, of course, it had to happen right then, and not an evening later.

In the middle of my grumbling, I heard something crash to the floor, followed by a series of loud thumps descending the stairs.

I rushed out to find Mr. Pitezel glaring at a large trunk that must have slipped out of his grip as he was descending from the second floor.

"Well?" he snapped at me, his face red and his lips in a terse frown. His hand dropped to the clawed hammer that was perpetually hung from his pants, almost as if he meant to threaten me with it. "Don't you have anything better to do than to come out and stare at me like a cow?"

I blushed and returned to my silver, though I did wonder what might have been in such a heavy trunk. A task from a guest? Certainly possible. But what guest would ask for a trunk to be brought down so late at night?

Hadn't I noticed his children dressed in expensive clothes? Far finer materials than anyone working at the Castle should be able to afford. Heaven knew Mr. Reynolds didn't pay enough to cover that, and the man never came out of his living quarters to even check on how things were at the hotel.

Was Pitezel lining his pockets by stealing from guests? Or selling women into some sort of servitude? I'd heard of worse. And what did Mr. Reynolds really do? Perhaps he went about in disguise during the day, like a king or a prince in a Dickens novel. I could picture him doing any manner of devious deeds. A man who treats you like luggage in public will you treat you even worse in private.

None of these occurrences would convince Thomas or the rest of the Pinkertons to take interest. Could I go to Mr. Pitezel and confront him directly? Or, perhaps, it would be better for me to approach Mr. Holmes and win him to my cause or lie in wait until I found some real information about Mr. Reynolds. The man had to eat sometime, did he not? If I could follow him in the city, I might get more of a sense of where he came from and what he did after hours.

But each time the feeling came to me, reason won over in the end. It was too risky, and serving women were expected to interact solely with Mrs. Patterson. Approaching any one of the men was forbidden, for reasons I did not fully understand. In any case, I didn't know my allies from my enemies, and so I continued on in silence.

Waiting and watching.

CHAPTER TEN

This attachment was particularly obnoxious to me, both because Miss Cigrand had become almost indispensable in my office work, and because she had become my mistress as well as stenographer. I endeavored upon several occasions to take the life of the young man and failing in this I finally resolved that I would kill her instead.

T HE FIFTH OF MAY STARTED much like any other day. I'd shown up to work and been set to the laundry by Mrs. Patterson. A family had stayed in the hotel the night before, and their baby took ill during the night, soiling three sets of sheets and five towels in the process.

So the morning had passed with me up to my elbows in water and suds, scrubbing and working at the washboard until my fingers were raw and my shoulders ached.

As I was taking the third set of sheets out back to hang in the sun to dry, two men approached. The first was at least six feet tall and had to weigh more than three hundred pounds, much of it fat. A short mustache sat on his upper lip, a small patch of hair that barely extended past his nostrils on either side. He waddled as he walked, his toes turned outward, and the bulk of his weight around his middle. He was joined by a small man as thin as the other was fat. The large one was in blue, and the short one in brown, and together they seemed as mismatched a pair as you could hope to discover.

"Good day, Miss," the thin one said, removing his hat to reveal a head of thick blond hair. "May we have a moment of your time?"

I glanced at the load of sheets in my arms and wondered if there had ever been a man to ask a more foolish question. The fat one rushed forward, plucking the sheets from my hands. They seemed to magically shrink as they made their way from me to him, the overbearing load turning into little more than an armful. "Allow me," he said. "You were going to hang these up, were you not?"

"You'll get your fine suit damp," I told him, for I hadn't wrung the sheets out as much as I ought to have.

He only laughed and gave me a charming smile for someone so large. "Far worse has been done to it before, I assure you."

I shrugged and nodded. "If you're willing to help me, I'm willing to give you some of my time. The trade seems fair."

The short man slapped his friend on the arm. "The trade seems fair. Did you hear that? If only all such transactions could be as straightforward."

I led them around to the clotheslines, and the fat man surprised me by how quickly and nimbly his fingers danced through the chore, finding pins and setting the sheets in place with a practiced hand.

His short friend did the talking.

"My name is Mr. Stanley, and the fine gentleman hanging your sheets is Mr. Oliver. We represent two detective agencies."

My heart leapt into my throat. "The Pinkertons?" I blurted out. Was it possible someone else had hired them where I could not afford to?

Mr. Stanley gave a little laugh, then shook his head. "Nothing so grand as that. Out of state. You would not recognize the name, I'm afraid. But we are employed nonetheless."

"By different agencies, as a matter of fact." Mr. Oliver was already done pinning the laundry to the line, though he made a few small adjustments to the job, straightening folds that didn't need the extra work, then stepping back to inspect his work.

"That's true," Mr. Stanley added. "We met here, where our paths crossed. I've been contracted by the Cigrand family to locate their wayward daughter."

"And I by the Conners," Mr. Oliver said, turning to face me again. "Have you heard of either of them, by chance?"

I shook my head, at a loss for the feeling that had settled into my gut like food gone sour.

"A sad tale," Mr. Oliver continued. "Ned and Julia Conner were a young couple who moved here from Davenport in Iowa, along with their twelve-year-old daughter, Pearl. Ned was hired on at the Castle to work the jewelry counter. Julia found employment in the same building as a bookkeeper. They lived on the second floor in some of the family rooms, and life seemed happy, for a while."

Mr. Stanley took over. "Until Ned began to suspect his wife of being untrue. It happened within months, really. Ned absconded in the night, abandoning Julia and Pearl to go back to Iowa with his sister, Gertrude. Julia and Pearl disappeared as well. Vanished. The family is distraught, and they hired my colleague's agency to track the latest movements of Ned, Gertie, and the rest. I, on the other hand, was hired to find Miss Cigrand. A similar story, in some respects. Emeline Cigrand moved to Chicago with her fiancé. She hired on at the Castle as a secretary, and the two of them disappeared in the middle of the night, leaving no word of where they were going. Her parents hired me."

Mr. Oliver clapped his hands and wiggled his fingers as he spread his arms. "Which brings us to the present day. I meet my colleague at this establishment, and the two of us discover we are both on similar hunts, with similar results. No one has seen anything or heard anything."

"Do you think someone at the Castle did something to them, then?" I asked, my heart a lump in my throat.

Mr. Stanley laughed. "What? Do you mean do we think there's a Jack the Ripper housed within its walls? Nothing nearly so dramatic. We've both interviewed the staff repeatedly, and there's been no signs of anything sinister at work."

Mr. Oliver nodded sagely. "Evil will out, you know. Murderers simply aren't capable of the careful planning and attention to detail necessary to hide their crimes from any competent investigator."

"It's true," Mr. Stanley said. "They simply don't know enough of modern science and techniques. We're always one step ahead of them. You have no need to fear that."

Would they say the same if they knew my own sister had disappeared here under the same circumstances? I did not trust either of them enough to confide in them, however. I had worked too hard and too long to get into my current position to risk ruining it by placing my fate in the hands of two strangers.

"You needed me for something," I said. "I assume it wasn't simply to be an audience to the tale of two tragedies."

"Quite right," Mr. Oliver said. He hitched his pants up around his voluminous waistline. "Quite right, indeed."

Mr. Stanley looked to either side of us and lowered his voice. "We have come to put a new theory to the test. One which, perhaps, connects this all and does so in a surprisingly straightforward fashion."

"Only too true," Mr. Oliver said. "For, if there is one thing we have noted in our years of investigating, it's that all sorts of crimes share one connection. Money."

"Money?" I asked, frowning.

"Money," Mr. Stanley confirmed. "Men do things for basic motivations, and the most basic of these is greed. People want what they cannot or do not have. When you think of that, isn't the connection obvious? Mr. Conner worked in the jewelry department. Miss Cigrand as a secretary, who, no doubt, had the occasion to examine the books and order records of the Castle. Both lived in the same building, working with valuables."

He finished with a flourish, as if he'd already proven his point. I shook my head, wondering what I was missing. "I'm afraid I don't—"

"Treasure!" Mr. Oliver almost shouted. He raised his eyebrows, apparently taken aback by his own volume, then lowered his voice and repeated the word.

"What if Mr. Conner set aside jewels, one at a time?" Mr. Stanley asked. "Not so many as to be noticed, but enough to add up."

Mr. Oliver spoke. "But, then, his wife discovered his plot, and they had a falling out, with both of them so distraught over their lost love that they abandoned the jewels completely."

"That's where Miss Cigrand comes in," Mr. Stanley said. "She finds record of the embezzlement, takes the jewels, and absconds to Europe!"

Mr. Oliver nodded eagerly, even as the small hopes I had begun to gather were dashed on the rocks below. These men were puffed-up fools.

"We simply need an inside source to corroborate."

"What are the two of you doing back here?" A new voice spoke from behind me. Minnie had walked around the corner, and her eyes were as full of fury. While she tried now to be assertive and commanding, like the fiancée of a man as important as Mr. Holmes ought to be, her shoulders slumped in contrast to her words. A sign of weakness and hesitation that inevitably came whenever she tried to assert herself. The Mississippi accent she carried didn't help, blunted only somewhat by her time at school in Boston.

Mr. Oliver and Mr. Stanley removed their hats and bowed in tandem. "Miss Williams!" Mr. Oliver exclaimed. "Mr. Stanley and I looked for you first, but you weren't to be found."

"Neither high nor low," Mr. Stanley added.

"Then no wonder the two of you struggle to find the ones you've been tasked to follow," Minnie said, clutching at her red skirt in irritation. "My sister and I have been in the pharmacy the past hour, which sits directly by the main entrance."

From behind her, her sister Anna appeared.

Mr. Oliver turned to Mr. Stanley. "Did you not check the pharmacy, my dear sir?"

"Twice," Mr. Stanley said. "Or was it the jewelry counter? I'm afraid I'm not sure. I might have gone to the jewelry counter the second time, thinking I'd already gone to the pharmacy the first. That explains the second trip, I suppose, which I did wonder at."

Mr. Oliver returned his smile to Minnie and Anna. "A

misunderstanding, I'm afraid. Though it did provide us the opportunity to speak with this charming new maid you've hired."

The sisters glanced at me, twin expressions of caution on their
faces.

"They were helping me with the sheets," I explained. "From
the...accident the Stone family had in the evening."

A flush blossomed in Minnie's cheeks. She always did struggle
with frank and open discussion, even in passing. "I'll thank the two
of you to finish your meetings swiftly, and then leave us in peace once
more. There has still been neither hide nor hair of either woman or
family seen here, and you've had my word on several occasions that
I would inform you the moment that situation changed."

"Of course, Madame," Mr. Oliver said. "But, with a new
maid, we couldn't in good conscience ignore the opportunity. Our
employers have trusted us to leave no cranny unexplored. You can,
surely, understand their driving desire to find their lost loved ones."

"I was almost through speaking to them," I piped up, anxious
to have one more chance with the detectives. "Five more minutes,
in honor of the families' loss?"

"Five minutes," Minnie said after a pause. She and Anna
returned to the depths of the Castle, leaving me with Mr. Oliver
and Mr. Stanley. If I could only trust them! Fools or not, I was
desperate for something to change. For help, wherever I could get
it. The words bubbled out of me, almost on their own.

"Women are disappearing from this house," I whispered, my

nerves quickening my tongue. "Many of them. Not just your assignments. Maids. Young ladies. They come here, and they disappear. I believe someone might be abducting them."

The words hung in the air in front of me. The two men stared at me with twin expressions: eyebrows raised, mouths open, hats still in their hands.

Mr. Oliver broke first. The smile returned, and he chuckled. "I think someone's been reading too many detective stories."

"Have you been inside the Castle?" I hurried to ask. "They don't let maids up to the second or third floors. There are strange sounds in odd places. I haven't—"

"Next you'll be telling us the place is haunted," Mr. Stanley said, "and that we should be on guard against ghouls and demons."

"No, my dear," Mr. Oliver said, patting my shoulder. "You can't put any stock in the stories printed these days. Nothing but pure sensationalism. A case like Jack the Ripper's only comes along once a century, perhaps, and this is America. We don't kill women in this country—slice them open and scatter their insides about. We do, on the other hand, embezzle large amounts of money and jewels. If you happen to—"

I turned and fled, leaving the two of them standing there. It was all I could do not to run outright. Yet again, I'd trusted someone enough to ask them for help, and yet again I'd been disappointed. Let them look for treasure on their own time and not waste mine.

Minnie and Anna were waiting for me, the two of them huddled together in the entryway, whispering. They broke apart when I approached. "What were they really after?" Minnie asked me.

I glanced behind me, almost wondering if the two detectives might have trailed along in my wake, but the hall was empty. "As you supposed," I said. "They were after more information on two women and their associates. They seem to believe they disappeared over stolen jewels?"

Anna scoffed and said, "Complete nonsense." She walked past me to go outside without another word.

Minnie grimaced. "Forgive her. She's overly protective at times, even when there is no real cause. Those two detectives are a nuisance, but only because they choose to loaf around collecting wages for no real work when they might be better served going elsewhere and investigating something worthwhile."

I blinked a couple of times, trying to follow that sentence. "You don't believe them?"

"I don't understand how it can be so difficult to hold onto hired help these days, though I suppose the exposition draws so many of them here. Then, once they've seen it, they move onward. I haven't seen Beth since yesterday, and I'm sick with worry. The wedding is coming up, and I don't have time to run a hotel and keep it clean. Mrs. Patterson is stretched too thin as it is."

"Is Beth ill?" I asked, forcing my voice to remain as calm.

Minnie shook her head. "She always sends messages when she's under the weather, and we heard nothing this time. I can't understand what makes so many women abandon these jobs. We pay worse than some, yes. But better than many, wouldn't you say?"

"How many maids have you lost?" I asked.

"Well, Beth for one. Before her was Zinnia, and before that was Mary. Mrs. Patterson rattled off a long list of maids she'd blazed through before Anna and I arrived. Ethel was here for a month, I believe, and, from what I was told, Ruby lasted something like...three?"

I licked my lips. "Ruby? What a peculiar name. Where did she go?"

"She was gone before I came here. If I knew why any of them left, then I might stand a chance of convincing them to stay. One day they're here, and the next they're not."

"Does it pay any more than the first floor? The third?" Because people trust other people who have clear-cut motivations, and nothing cuts clearer than more money.

Minnie cocked her head to the side. "Well, yes. Might you be interested?"

I didn't have to hide my eagerness. "Very much so, though I would hate to take a job from a woman who's fallen on misfortune."

"We need workers who can do their job. She might show up again with a reasonable explanation, but, if she doesn't, the work still needs doing. Usually Henry insists on knowing the maids longer before he allows them upstairs, and Mr. Pitezel likes to interview them as well. We've had maids with sticky fingers, and nothing ruins the reputation of a hotel faster than theft."

Kidnappings might do the trick, but I kept that opinion to

myself. Instead, I said, "I don't mean to reach above myself too quickly, but if it's help you need, I'd be happy to provide it. I have a little brother who'd like to see the exposition before it closes, and I've been trying to save enough money to cover his train fare."

I surprised myself with that lie. Particularly with how well constructed it came out, and it drew on the family connections I knew Minnie held dear. Though heaven help me if she were ever to ask to meet my brother.

"That's a shame," Minnie said. "Where are you from? Your name was…Edith?"

"Etta," I said, smiling and giving her a half curtsy, all the while wondering if I wasn't simpering too much. If she began to tell how desperately I wanted this, she might get suspicious. "I'm from Colorado."

"Well, Beth might not have gone anywhere. For all I know, she broke her leg. But, if she doesn't show soon, I'll speak to Henry. What's the use in being engaged to the man if I can't persuade him now and then, right? I'd love to avoid another search for a maid."

I blushed and nodded, relieved.

Two days later, I was promoted.

CHAPTER ELEVEN

A little later I killed her by administering ferrocyanide of potassium.

———————

MRS. PATTERSON INTRODUCED ME TO the new responsibilities as soon as I arrived in the morning. Her expression told me what she thought of the promotion, and I wondered once again if it weren't possible for a short, squat, elderly woman to be the cause of all the disappearances. I would have given the consideration more credence, except for the fact I knew full well how easily Ruby would have evaded anything this woman might have sought to inflict upon her.

My sister never would have been one to let a woman like Mrs. Patterson get the upper hand.

As I approached the stairway to the second and third floors, my stomach tumbled over itself, and my knees felt weak.

Nonsense. As if I'd suddenly be dragged into a corner and stuffed into a box the moment I walked up a few steps. I'd been here for weeks and seen many visitors ascend and descend those stairs. So why did a weight settle over my shoulders as I went up, and why did the hallway darken?

Dark wood lined the corridors, all freshly constructed. I'd assumed the upper floors would be the mirror of any of the countless hotels I'd toured during my stay in Chicago. Straight halls and doors to either side. The architectural bar for a hotel was not a high one, and those who wished to save money would not go out of their way to experiment. Yet when I arrived at the second-floor landing, I saw nothing more than a closed door to my left and a short hallway that turned sharply to my right, revealing only two closed doors along its stretch.

"Well?" Mrs. Patterson asked.

I'd stopped in the middle of the steps, and the older lady eyed me now with no small amount of annoyance.

"My apologies," I said.

"I believe you mean, 'My apologies, Mrs. Patterson.' You might have been able to get away with frivolity when you were downstairs, but you're an upstairs girl, now, and that means responsibility, manners, and respect. There are plenty more where you came from, and don't forget that for an instant.

"I've turned more than one girl out in the middle of the night, and more than a few have slunk out with their tail between their legs. Too cowardly to admit they couldn't cut it, and it doesn't take a private detective from the East to tell you that. So, if you're quite done gawking at a place you have no right or reason to think about, follow me and quit dawdling."

I nodded, keeping my eyes on the floor and hoping the Ruby in me was able to bite her tongue. "Yes, Mrs. Patterson. My apologies, Mrs. Patterson."

She sniffed and continued up the staircase.

I had hoped to glimpse some of what this forbidden floor hid, but such a glimpse would not be possible from the stair landing, even had I been alone. Leaving the mysteries of the second floor behind, I followed Mrs. Patterson, a few of the floorboards creaking as I went.

At the top, the staircase opened into the expected straight hallway with doors to either side. Light came through the windows behind me, but the hallway itself had few gas lamps. It would be darker than a guest would like at night. The hallways were also narrow as a rabbit warren.

Perhaps the mysterious owner had demanded they use as much space for rooms as they could. It had been built for the exposition, after all, and it wasn't as if the tourists flooding the city would be here for more than a few days. It made sense to pack as many in as they could, and never mind the complaints that might follow.

Mrs. Patterson led me down the hall, which turned at an odd angle. Most buildings had corridors that branched off perpendicularly, with straight intersections. This one lurched from side to side, sometimes turning forty-five degrees, and sometimes ninety, and sometimes somewhere in the middle.

I quickly lost track of where I was in the house, with no windows to orient myself to the outside. It made me miss Manti's open spaces and inviting mountains. We passed closed doors on either side, tunneling ever deeper into the upstairs.

A staircase appeared heading down on the left, smaller and more appropriate for maids, as one might expect in a hotel. It didn't match up with any staircase on the first floor that I was aware of. "Shouldn't I be using this back access?" I asked.

Mrs. Patterson didn't turn around. "You will use the staircase we came up, and only that staircase. You are not to go down or up any other staircases in the building. If you can't follow simple rules, we will happily find a girl who can."

At last we came to a final left turn, and I discovered windows once again. Judging from the scene I caught through the curtains, we were back to the same side of the building we'd started on, having made a U-turn in the middle of all that mess.

We were in an open room with windows on one side and doors on the other three. But the doors didn't line up like they should. The one on the right was practically in the hallway, leaving a huge space of flat wall that felt unbalanced. The one on the left had the opposite problem: it had been stuck almost next to the windows themselves. It gave the room an unsettling feeling, as if it had been drawn by a five-year-old or a madman, and it made the hair on my neck tingle.

"You will stay here from now on," Mrs. Patterson said, turning to the wall opposite the window and opening the door.

I stumbled midstep. "Excuse me?"

She turned to glare at my impertinence. "If you will be cleaning the family quarters and the rest of the third floor, Mr. Reynolds requires you to live on the premises. You didn't presume the increase in salary wouldn't come with additional responsibilities, did you?"

"No," I said, scrambling to think. "I haven't told my current landlord, and—"

"We will be providing room for free," Mrs. Patterson said, clipping each word. "I should think this would come as a pleasant surprise to a woman in your position."

She was right, and never mind the fact I suspected someone in this house of kidnapping or worse. Any other girl in my situation would be ecstatic to save such a great deal of money, but I couldn't forget the fact these quarters would have been Beth's just days ago. What had happened to her, and would I share the same fate? I curtsied. "I'm sorry Mrs. Patterson. It only came as such a shock. But I'm grateful. Really, I am."

Mrs. Patterson tsked and shook her head, then turned to the task at hand: showing me my room.

It was a cramped space crowded with two other doors, one to my right and one across from me. There was a small bed and a nightstand and a dresser, but no windows. With the doors closed, it would feel like a prison cell. I couldn't quite touch both walls when standing in the middle, but only because I was shorter than some.

"Where do those go?" I asked, pointing to the other doors.

"They lead to guest rooms and are to remain locked unless we let your quarters to a guest. Leave whatever you want here, but it's time I show you around the floor to give you an idea of your cleaning assignments."

If I'd thought things had been strict on the main floor, that was because I hadn't been introduced to Mrs. Patterson's approach to the upstairs. There were more than twenty-five rooms on the third level. Some big and square, others tucked into corners and odd-shaped. Some doors were locked and against the rules to enter. Others had specific keys I would have to request to obtain access.

There was Minnie's room, Mr. Holmes's room, and Mr. Pitezel's quarters. While the latter also lacked windows or outside access, the former two were light and spacious and almost felt normal. I kept getting turned around, forgetting where I'd come from and how to get to where I was going.

We came to the office, and I stopped short. There, across the room, was the door to an enormous safe. The door hung wide, thick and monstrous, revealing a shadowy green interior big enough to be a room.

Straight from my nightmares about Ruby.

If I were to inspect it, would I see claw marks where my sister had tried to escape? Could it truly be one and the same? Perhaps it was the sheer size of it that made it seem so similar. .

Mrs. Patterson barely gave it a glance. "You don't need to clean in there. Mr. Holmes had it specially installed at the request of Mr. Reynolds. These used to be his offices."

"He doesn't work at the hotel anymore?" I asked, surprised.

"Where he works is none of your business," Mrs. Patterson snapped, though there might have been a hint of a blush around her cheeks as well. Had I hit on a sore spot or something she wished to avoid?

All in all, it was a dizzying introduction to what was to be my home for the next long while. The house held its mysteries; a normal building didn't need to leave its rooms in such a jumbled disarray.

"Why is everything so mixed up?" I asked at last. I couldn't help it.

Mrs. Patterson stared me down, considering whether it was worth her time to answer me or not, no doubt. "We had to hire and fire several construction crews and architects over the years. Shoddy workmanship, sloth, and inexperience, I'm afraid to say. Mr. Pitezel had to enforce it as well. It's a case of too many cooks, but the soup was already made by that time, and it would have cost too much to make it anew. That's the last you need worry about it."

How incompetent would an architect need to be to not understand how to finish a basic floor plan? But I let the matter drop and kept my eyes open for other details that might explain what was going on.

Mr. Holmes came upstairs while Mrs. Patterson was showing me where the towels and clean linens were stored. His face lit up as soon as he saw me.

"Etta!" he exclaimed, striding toward me and reaching out to shake my hand vigorously. It made me feel respected and safe.

If the truth were to come out about this hotel, it would ruin Mr. Holmes. But wasn't he at least somewhat to blame? He ought to take greater care of what went on during his watch.

Assuming he wasn't the one causing it all.

"Has she shown you your room?" he asked me, clapping me on my shoulder. "Everything to your satisfaction?"

"Yes," I said, and wished I weren't blushing.

"Excellent!" he said. "Come to me if you have any concerns. I'm off for a meeting with Mr. Reynolds. He's come from his apartment downtown, but I'll be back this evening, and I trust I'll hear nothing but great things about you. We're so lucky you found us!" He hurried off as quickly as he'd approached, always moving, always doing.

As I continued my training, I wondered again at Ruby. She'd fallen in love with someone here. Who would it have been? Never Pitezel, and Mr. Reynolds was never to be seen. But Mr. Holmes? Handsome, a doctor, charming, and well-mannered Mr. Holmes? I could see Ruby falling for him quite easily.

Except he was now engaged to Minnie. Then again, hadn't one of the detectives claimed he'd been engaged before that as well? I would need to unfold the course of events that had led to those arrangements, though Ruby might have fallen for someone else. A hotel guest, or someone who lived nearby. She'd been so secretive about it in her letters.

My money was on Mr. Reynolds. He reminded me of Father

in more ways than one, and I could picture Ruby wanting to break through with a man like that. Force him to notice her. If she saw a challenge—someone who ignored her where everyone else couldn't leave her alone—she would always rise to it.

If I could come right out and ask around about her, perhaps I could solve this mystery in less than a day. But if I asked the wrong person, I might join my sister's fate. There was no telling who the wrong person might be, and as soon as I asked questions, there was also no telling whose ears those questions might eventually fall on.

So I kept my head down and paid close attention to Mrs. Patterson, despite how irritable I found the woman. I needed to stay here for as long as it took. Until people began to trust me, and conversations could turn naturally to the past, as they always did among acquaintances. Or until I uncovered something in that third-floor office, perhaps.

The answers I sought would come to me, if I could only be patient.

CHAPTER TWELVE

I confined him within the secret room and slowly starved him to death. Of this room and its secret gas supply and muffled windows and doors, sufficient has already been printed. Finally, needing its use for another purpose and because his pleadings had become almost unbearable, I ended his life. The partial excavation in the walls of this room found by the police was caused by Latimer's endeavoring to escape by tearing away the solid break and mortar with his unaided fingers.

THE THIRD FLOOR MIGHT HAVE been a rabbit's warren, but after a week of cleaning its rooms, seeing to the trash, dusting its furniture, mopping, sweeping, and sweating in every room on the level, it became just another place.

Though some things didn't add up. My fourth day up there, I'd been tasked with tidying the main hallway. I set myself to the job, the broom scratching softly against hardwood floors as I worried at the state of my investigation.

My ears caught a faint cry, a wail at the edge of hearing. I paused, listening in silence, unsure of the sound. It had been so soft. The wind outside?

The sound didn't repeat, so I resumed my sweeping, chiding myself for letting distractions interrupt me. I worked farther down the hall, circling another staircase that descended to the floor below, but then I stopped and stared at it, thinking through my position in the house once more.

This staircase led down where the first floor had no staircase leading up. This one must have only led from the second floor to the third.

It was in between the time for arrivals and the time for check ins, and that gaping hole to the lower floor seemed more than a little inviting and intimidating.

Would a real detective shy away from some actual investigating just because they were frightened of an old woman like Mrs. Patterson? I propped the broom next to a side table and put a hand on the banister, gazing at the staircase.

What did I expect to find? I'd had nightmares since I moved into the Castle: Bodies strung up from the ceilings in the guest rooms. Blood and carnage draping the halls. But that clearly was only my imagination running wild. No guest had ever complained, after all. But I wouldn't know what was there until I explored.

I reached my foot out to take the first step, then froze. What if Mrs. Patterson came back upstairs? She was known to do surprise checks on the staff. "Making sure we were all in our place," she put it.

Better to be sure.

I darted back down the turning hallway to the main set of stairs, treading down them as lightly as I could. Hannah, my replacement on the main floor, was scrubbing the floor at the side entrance, and she didn't look up as I went by.

Mrs. Patterson was arguing with a customer, her voice carrying clear down the hall. "No, that's not what we charge for aspirin, and we never have. We run a respectable business here, and if..."

I sped back up the stairs, holding firm to my newfound resolve. I'd go down the staircase and peek around to the count of fifty. Just enough to get a taste for what was there. What could be so sinister that Mr. Reynolds (or Mrs. Patterson?) would forbid anyone else from seeing it?

Then I was back on the third floor, staring down at that new staircase once again. Why did I have butterflies? It was a building, nothing more, and this was for Ruby.

After the first step, the others came more easily. As I descended, I was filled with confidence. Pride that I had gone through with it. I was no shrinking violet, standing to the side as—

"Etta?"

I shrieked and whirled, stumbling in mid-stride on the step and tumbling backward. Only a tight grip on the railing kept me from careening down the staircase.

Mr. Holmes stood at the head of the stairs, gazing down at me in confusion. "What are you doing?"

"I thought I heard a guest calling for help," I blurted out, the first thing that came to my mind.

He paused, listening. "I don't hear anything now. Hello!" he called out. "Anyone in need of assistance?"

Nothing but silence. My pulse pounded in my ears. I had been caught. What would happen?

I stammered, "I—I must have been mistaken." It rang so hollow.

Mr. Holmes took the first few steps toward me, then reached out his hand. I walked up to him, and he escorted me back to the third floor. He kept my hand in his and took my shoulder in his other, gazing into my eyes. "I know how tempting it can be. Forbidden fruit. But you must follow Mr. Reynolds's rules to the letter. I like you, Etta. We can't afford to lose you right now, but I know what would happen if Mr. Reynolds were to find out."

"Find out what, exactly?" I asked, wishing he of all people would push back against the tyrant. "Why does he insist on these silly rules? The third floor, the second floor. It makes no sense."

"It's some European approach to the business," Mr. Holmes explained. "I can't pretend to understand it, but Mr. Reynolds read it in a book somewhere, and, once he got it into his head, it had to be done. The man reads too many books. I don't think he'd ever really run a hotel before. He wanted to do it for the exposition. Thought money was to be made. But he kept reading books throughout the construction, and it made him change his mind a hundred times. Each change meant a tweak to the building plans. The result is a mess, but we're making money, or, at least, enough I suppose…"

For a moment I debated going to him with my questions. I wanted an ally. Someone on the inside who might help me with my search. Would it be too hard to tell him about Ruby outright and see what he knew?

But I remembered what had happened with Madeline when I'd first arrived in the city. Did I really know Mr. Holmes well enough?

The moment passed, and I said nothing.

"You have to stay to the third floor," he ended up concluding. "I don't want you to be let go."

I nodded but didn't want to let the matter of Mr. Reynolds drop entirely. "Where is he each day?" I asked. "How does he enter his offices without me ever catching sight of him?"

"He prefers late nights and early mornings," Mr. Holmes said, his tone beginning to grow curt. "And he's been known to fire people who ask too many questions. Believe me, the less you have to do with him, the better."

He patted my shoulder and went back down the hall.

I considered going back down the staircase right then, but, instead, I retrieved my broom and resumed my duties for the day. Though I also contemplated on the fact that, for a building with floorboards as noisy as the Castle had, Mr. Holmes had eerily been able to come up on me unawares. Some measure of this suspicion dimmed as I paid attention to the rest of the third floor. It wasn't nearly as loud and creaky as the first, though who knew why.

I didn't give up my investigations. Rather, I focused them on what I had access to. Just because the third floor wasn't the treasure trove of information I'd hoped it would be didn't mean it was a lost cause. For one thing, it's where Mr. Reynolds's office resided. Could I finally get some real information on the reclusive master of the Castle?

A few times, I came close. The offices were in the middle of the floor, overlooking the street. I'd been in to clean them, of course. Nothing too remarkable about them, other than the safe. A desk of cherry and a fine leather chair, papers stacked around the room in neat piles. I inspected a few of them long enough to verify their contents. He had signed contracts in his name and opened mail addressed to him at this building.

I wrote down the names of the companies that had worked on the Castle, but when I went to talk to them, they wanted nothing to do with me. A woman inquiring after a four-year-old construction project? All of them wanted to know why, first off, and I didn't have a good enough reason to provide them.

The filing cabinets in the office held old catalogues, brochures about the Columbian Exposition, transit maps for the city, and little else. He did have an entire drawer devoted to medical supply companies, but that might have been connected to the pharmacy somehow. Maybe he was looking to get another business to move into the Castle? Mr. Reynolds didn't appear to be a person who wanted much to do with details. Either that, or he was incredibly orderly. Cleaning his rooms only meant dusting and polishing. I never even saw a crumb to sweep.

I'd see Mr. Holmes go into a meeting with him, sometimes with Mrs. Patterson or Mr. Pitezel trailing along in their wake. They all had serious expressions on their faces, and Mrs. Patterson would fidget with her hair incessantly as she waited in the hall before they were allowed in. But Mr. Reynolds never came to the door to let them in, and no matter how many excuses I came up with to loiter around the area, I never caught more than a glimpse of him when the door opened or closed.

There had to be another way into that office. A secret passage or a hidden staircase, though I scrubbed every inch of that floor on my hands and knees, knocking periodically on the wood to see if I could hear a hollow space beneath. All I came up with was blisters. I tried the walls, pressing in places on the molding or searching for areas that might have hidden an entrance. Some of the walls in the Castle were horsehair and plaster, but others were nothing more than painted wood. Mr. Reynolds's office had one such wall, replete with knotholes of various sizes. I thought one of them might be used to pull a section of the wall outward, but they were all boarded up on the other side of the wall through some trick of carpentry I didn't understand.

I stomped my foot in frustration, angry with myself for finding nothing but at a loss for more ideas. The Castle felt like a jigsaw puzzle with half the pieces missing. Surely it couldn't be so hard to find at least a few of the hidden clues. As I stood there thinking, my neck began to itch with that feeling you get sometimes. As if someone was watching me. The Castle itself? I turned, studying the wooden wall with all those knotholes. It would be a simple matter to hide a peephole amid all those opportunities. I pictured Mr. Reynolds lurking in the walls of the Castle, moving from floor to floor unseen, yet watching what was going on around him.

For a moment, I thought I saw the wood behind one of those knots *shift*. I hurried over to it, scraping at the backing, trying to move it or twist it to the side. It stayed firm, and I eventually had to resume my duties. I took care to study the other painted wood walls in the Castle, however. Just because it sounded like something out of a Gothic horror didn't mean it was impossible or even unlikely.

Perhaps I could detect any secret rooms or passages by measuring the dimensions of the rooms I had access to. Nothing so grand as using yardsticks for precise measurement—I didn't want to risk having my investigations scrutinized. But I could measure with my feet, placing my right heel against a wall and then touching my left heel to my right toes, followed by my right heel to my left toes. In this manner, I could tell how many "feet" were between any two distances.

Over time, I transferred my measurements onto a piece of paper, starting with the entire dimensions of the building (checked

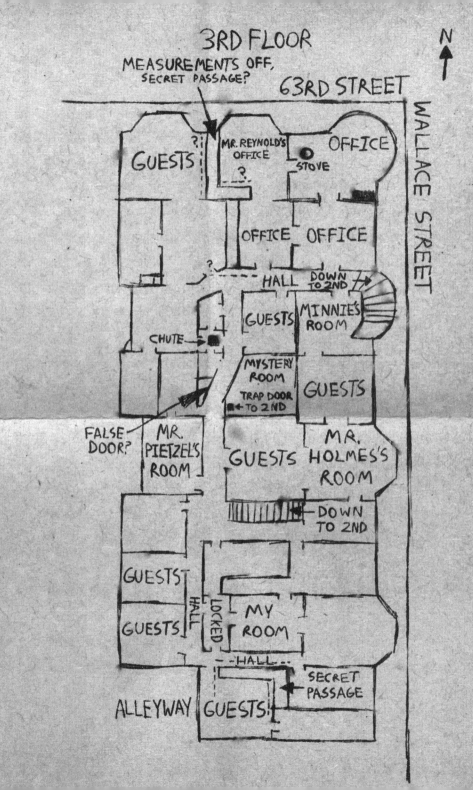

from outside) and filling in the rooms and hallways that touched the outer walls first. There were some areas that stayed stubbornly blank: a space in the middle of the back of the building where my map said there should have been a room, a spot to the north of the rear hallway that might have concealed a hidden passage. The second door in my own room was permanently locked. (Mrs. Patterson said it was "under renovation," even though no workers ever came near it.) In another area where the hallway turned diagonally, a door stood that made me doubt my method. According to repeated measurements, there could have been no room behind it. A flaw in my approach, or a false door?

Of course, the doors being left permanently locked didn't stop me from trying the knobs from time to time, hoping I'd catch one open by luck.

Mr. Holmes and Mr. Pitezel came upon me in the middle of one such jiggle of the mysterious extra door. I gasped in surprise when they came around the bend in the hall, my hand leaping off the knob as if burned.

"What are you doing?" Mr. Pitezel's eyes narrowed, his tone dark.

It took a moment for me to find my voice. "I got turned around, is all."

Mr. Holmes laughed it off. "You certainly did. Should we show her, Benjamin?"

His companion only glowered, but Mr. Holmes reached into

his pocket and took out a key ring, sifting through it for a moment before finding the right one. He unlocked the door and opened it, revealing a flat brick wall. The door was a facade, after all.

Mr. Holmes laughed louder and pointed to the bricks. "Do you see that? That's what comes when your carpenters don't speak to your masons. Lesson learned, though I'd appreciate it if you didn't tell the guests about our blunder."

Easy for him to dismiss, but all those little "mistakes" added up to a building that confused you in unexpected ways. I wasn't the only one to become lost or turned around. Guests would come up to me asking for directions multiple times. Some of them laughed off the experience, chalking it up to their unfamiliarity with big cities. Chicago was attracting people from across the globe, and I would hear a score of different languages on the street and in the rooms. But many of the other hotels had people come and stay for a week or two, unwilling to leave so soon after having made such a long journey to get here.

No one stayed that long in the Castle.

Some of them would say they were planning to be there for a longer visit, but no one would last longer than three or four days. I heard some complain about the layout, and some reference the smells. One man was particularly upset about a gas leak he swore had started in his room in the night, though I could find no trace of the smell when I went to air out the room later that day.

Many of the guests simply left early. I'd go in to clean their rooms to find them empty. One morning I found an entire suitcase left behind in the family's haste to leave. Mr. Pitezel said he would take care of it, and he ushered me out of the room. Maybe that was where he found the expensive clothes his family would wear at times.

Seeing Phebe to catch her up on my search became more difficult, now that I was living at the Castle, but it was all the more important. If anything were to happen to me, it would be up to Phebe to come to the rescue. Thomas's residence was much farther away, but he was involved in our plans as well. Word would get to her first, and she'd call in the cavalry if it came to that.

Phebe and I would meet for breakfast or dinner every three days at a restaurant a few blocks from the Castle. Each time I'd make the walk, I'd see the buildings of the exposition towering in the distance. The Manufacturers and Liberal Arts building was said to be so big it could hold the entire standing army of Russia. Buffalo Bill Cody was down there, across the street from the main fair. And, of course, there was the Wheel that Mr. Ferris had constructed, though soaring two-hundred-fifty feet into the air on the rim of a giant iron disc sounded like a good way to get a broken neck.

At night the new electric lights lit the entire complex, setting the sky ablaze. No wonder they called the place the White City. I would have loved to see it, even for an afternoon, and Phebe encouraged me to do so.

"It's such a grand time," she said one day, two weeks after I'd moved into the Castle. She was having eggs and bacon for breakfast. "What with all the money you're saving by not renting an apartment, you can certainly spare the funds. It would do you good to get away from all that doom and gloom."

I poked idly at my hash browns. They'd let them burn on the bottom, and I missed the way Mother would spice them with cinnamon. "What if Ruby knew I were here in Chicago and wasting time with the exposition when I could be helping her?"

"It seems to me Ruby did what she wanted to do. How many times did she leave you behind to get beaten by your father while she was out dancing?"

"It wasn't like that," I said.

"It was exactly like that," Phebe stated.

I shook my head. "I have to find her. She's in trouble. I had a nightmare last night. Mrs. Patterson had her locked in the pharmacy in a secret room under the floorboards. Ruby was there, tied up the whole time as I walked back and forth above her, none the wiser."

Phebe stopped eating for a moment, pushing the food around on her plate instead. She glanced up at me once, then twice. "You know," she began, then continued picking at her eggs.

"What?" I asked, exasperated.

She put her utensils down, placed her hands on the table, and stared me in the eye. "You've been in this city for months now. Do you really believe Ruby is waiting for you after all this time, trapped and captive? She disappeared more than half a year ago."

A flush crept up my face, and I broke her gaze, focusing on my hash browns instead. Forcing them into my mouth. *Chew. Swallow.* Shying away from the thought that my sister might be dead. The longer I stayed at the Castle, the more it felt like a place no one simply walked away from.

It held onto you. It wanted to possess you, like some sort of iron maiden from medieval days, clutching you tight in its metal claws, stabbing you with a hundred spikes and draining you of life.

"I know my sister might be dead. Murdered." I said at last, breaking the silence. I tried to keep my voice level, but it still trembled when I spoke that final word out loud at last. "All the more reason to find her killers and not get sidetracked by bright lights and loud music."

"Well," Phebe said, forcing brightness into her voice, "If you're not comfortable going, don't. But what of your investigation? Have you discovered anything new? Is it really that Pitezel?"

"I'm not sure," I said, relieved she was willing to let the other conversation topic slide. "He has the temper and lack of character it would take to kidnap women, or worse. Just the other day I saw him whip a horse bloody when it was too slow getting out of the way of the main entrance. The delivery man was furious, but Pitezel glared at him and swore he'd do the same or worse to the man if the horse wasn't moved immediately. A big man, this fellow was too. Twice the size of Pitezel, but I didn't blame him for turning white and scurrying off. Pitezel has an expression that could chop wood, and with that clawed hammer of his always to hand, it's a miracle he hasn't brained anyone yet."

"So it's him," Phebe said. "Go to the police, or at least to your boy Thomas at the Pinkertons. They'll investigate him."

I shook my head. "I need to have proof. Don't you remember what Thomas wrote last time?"

"No, but I have a sinking feeling you're going to remind me."

I reached into my handbag and leafed through the letters I kept there. They weren't safe to leave at the Castle, where anyone might come across them. Finding the right one, I unfolded it and read.

Not everything has a sinister explanation. You keep mentioning things that are nothing more than circumstantial. If something were really happening in that building, there would be real proof. We can't go to my uncle with claims. They won't convince him. We need hard evidence. At the very least, eyewitness accounts.

I set the letter aside and stared at Phebe. "He's getting more and more like that each time, questioning everything. I think he's beginning to write me off as just another delusional girl. What would happen if I were to call the Pinkertons and persuade them to investigate Pitezel, and he turned out not to be the culprit? I'm going to have trouble enough convincing those detectives to show up in the first place. The second I bring them out on a false charge, I'll never see them again."

"So your plan is to wait until you've been murdered too, and have me ask for help then?"

When said like that, the truth of the matter seemed bleak. "I don't think it will come to that," I said. "I'm piecing things together over time. I need proof. Something tangible and obvious that anyone can understand. Give me another month, and I think I'll have it."

Phebe sawed off another bite of bacon and popped it into her mouth. You'd think the food had been cooked by one of the fine French chefs in the exposition and not by a man in a grease-stained apron. My eggs tasted like sawdust, or perhaps that was just my appetite.

"So," Phebe said, after she had finished her bite. "What are these mysteries you're discovering? If I'm to bring the Pinkertons in like the cavalry to the rescue, I'll need to know whatever I can to convince them."

"The entire house is a riddle. My biggest suspicion, apart from Mr. Pitezel, rests on this elusive Mr. Reynolds. He's funded a hotel, a druggist, doctor's office, glass bender's workshop, barbershop, and a restaurant, all in the same building. Quite the mixture of store-fronts, but the smells don't add up."

She paused with her fork halfway to her mouth. "The smells?"

"The doctor's office is on the east end of the building, but I smell things that should be in a surgeon's workshop on the other end, by the glass bender. Other times I smell lye on the breezes, coming from the basement."

"So go to the basement and find out," Phebe said. "Pretend you're…throwing something away."

"But there *is* no basement. No doors lead to it. No stairs descend there. I don't even see any windows from the outside, though I see a storm door that must lead down there."

"Nonsense," Phebe said, rolling her eyes. "People don't make mysterious basements."

"You don't understand," I continued. "The walls don't make sense either. They're scattered back and forth on the first and third floors with no real relation to each other. It's as if a five-year-old constructed the place."

"So Mr. Reynolds has no business being near a building plan. That's hardly evidence to bring the Pinkertons running."

I pushed my plate away from me, giving up on food entirely as I counted off the other peculiarities I had noticed. "There are staircases that lead between one floor but not to the other. Doors that open to blank walls. I hear screams sometimes, coming from within rooms that don't exist."

"If it's as sinister as all that, then surely the guests must realize something. You might be barred from the second floor, but what do the people say who *do* go there?"

"I've asked a few, but I'm the hired help. Most have no interest in speaking to me, and many stay only a few nights. To them, the Castle is a novelty. The crooked hallways a curiosity and nothing more."

The tightness around her eyes and the set of her shoulders showed Phebe was far from convinced. How could I expect anyone else to believe me?

I continued, forcing confidence into my voice. "The Castle has secrets, and I'm convinced they're waiting for me, either on the second floor or in the basement."

Phebe's eyes widened as she realized my intent. When she spoke, each word came out slowly, as if she were worried speaking it might influence me. "In other words, places you've been forbidden to go."

I nodded.

"And you've decided to go there anyway."

I nodded again. "Mrs. Patterson and Mr. Pitezel already suspect I'm there for ulterior motives. They constantly check up on what I'm doing. I'm going to go to the second floor. Tonight."

"Tonight?" Phebe's eyes were wide and white.

"If I don't return to visit you here tomorrow morning, I want you to go to the Pinkertons. Tell them about the second floor and the basement. If I'm not here, it will mean I've been taken, or my body has." Speaking it aloud—giving voice to my suspicions and fears—made the words sound hollow in my ears. As if these were risks someone else was pondering. As if it wouldn't be my lifeless eyes staring out at nothing that the Pinkertons would find if my plans went wrong.

"Are you sure?" Phebe asked, her voice dropping to a whisper. "Absolutely?"

I gave her a single nod. "The longer I wait, the harder it will be to convince myself. I need to do it. For Ruby."

CHAPTER THIRTEEN

It will be remembered that the remains of a large kiln made of firebrick were found in a basement. It had been built under Mr. Warner's supervision for the purpose of exhibiting his patents. It was so arranged that in less than a minute after turning on a jet of crude oil, atomized with steam, the entire kiln would be filled with a colorless flame, so intensely hot that iron would be melted therein.

T HE WORKDAY DRAGGED ON, EACH chore seemingly endless. My mind kept running over my plan as I washed sheets and swept corridors and tidied rooms. Somehow I found a moment to sneak outside and check the storm door leading down to what must be the basement. It might have come straight from Manti: a metal door slanted against the brick wall to cover the top of a staircase.

It was locked, as always. Opening it would require me to obtain a key from Mrs. Patterson, Mr. Pitezel, or Mr. Holmes. The longer I stayed outside gawking at it, the more suspicious anyone else might become.

I'd wait until it was well past midnight and explore the second floor, instead. The Castle was at its quietest then. I'd bring a candle with me and shield it with my hands, wandering the halls like Tom Sawyer and Becky Thatcher through the caverns.

If anyone came upon me and asked my purpose, I would say I heard someone calling for help and rushed to their aid. And, if they claimed to hear no such thing, I'd attribute it to the wind. True, Mr. Holmes might grow suspicious if I used the same excuse with him twice, but perhaps I could use that to my advantage. Use it as a reason to bring up the disappearances and see what he thought of them.

Still, the knot in my stomach grew as the hour hand inched its way across the large clock hanging on the third-floor landing. Perhaps there were other routes to explore. It might be safer to call for Thomas at least. I'd been avoiding him, mainly because I didn't want to risk him finding out what I was doing. What if he stayed a night in the Castle and could confirm my suspicions? After all, when I last talked to his uncle, I'd only had theories. Now I'd done the important legwork. I'd found where my sister had disappeared. That was enough to be proud of, was it not?

But the memory of their dismissal last time was still bright in my mind. The feeling of shame as they ignored my pleas for help hurt almost as much as the memories of my father's abuse. It was one and the same. Inflicted on me by men who thought they could and should control me and my future.

It was the memory of father's beatings that made me stay in the Castle and complete my preparations. I had endured them. I could face whatever horrors waited for me here. If anyone thought they would prey upon an unsuspecting flower, they would soon learn the errors of their ways.

But it wouldn't be enough to simply walk down those steps and through the halls of the second floor. What did I expect to do? Go from door to door, knocking at each one to inquire if they had seen any missing women or dead bodies? This was a functioning hotel, after all, and even if most of the usual maids were barred from the second floor, the guests were not.

With that in mind, I set aside a piece of paper and the stub of a pencil. Perhaps if I could sketch out the second floor as I'd done the third, I'd come across some information I might be able to use to prove my suspicions were real.

Midnight came and went. I lay in my bed listening to the creaks and groans of the house around me and trying not to think of what might come.

My heart pounded in my ears as one o'clock approached. I got out of my bed and crept to the door, pausing.

Was that the sound of my heart, or was it the noise of someone beating on a wall somewhere beneath me? A single image flashed through my head: a man bricked into a sealed room with no exit, slowly suffocating as the air ran out.

I listened again. Silence.

Tricks of the mind, and nothing more.

The door opened without a squeak. I lit my candle and crept out.

I had worked in the Castle long enough and late at night enough to know the noisier spots of the third floor, and so I moved from side to side, spot to spot, traveling a path I'd memorized during the quieter hours of the day. I'd use the main staircase so I could be certain of my starting point. At night, in the dark, I had no desire to try to begin my search on tentative footing.

No matter how much I might have wanted to hunch and scurry from shadow to shadow, I forced myself to walk with a straight back, my head high. If someone were to see me, they needed to see a woman confident in what she was doing. I'd heard a cry for help, and I'd gone to investigate.

That didn't stop me from eyeing the doors to either side of me as I wended down that crooked hallway. One of them might open any moment. What if the killer or kidnapper knew I was suspicious and waited for me even now? What if this is what Ruby's last night on earth had been like?

I kept walking.

At last the staircase opened at the end of the hall, dark as pitch, like a bear trap waiting for a fool to place her foot in its middle.

I didn't miss a beat, placing a hand on the banister and descending to who knew what madness.

Sixteen steps, and I was there. It took me a moment to remember my paper and pencil, hastily shoved into my skirt's waistband.

Was my hand shaking as I reached for them and smoothed the paper flat on my skirt?

No more than it ought to.

Taking a deep breath, I headed down the hall and began to map out a sketch of the floor.

It isn't the easiest thing, holding a burning candle in one hand and tracing a crude representation of a floor plan in the other. I estimated distances by counting my paces, paying attention to the placement of doors and windows to guess the number of rooms, though I knew from elsewhere in the Castle that was sometimes a foolish endeavor.

This floor was even more curious than the one above it. That one had hallways, even if they lurched from side to side. As soon as I reached the first bend of the hall on the second floor, it led me to an open room with five doorways. A bookcase stood on one side, along with a writing desk and a few padded chairs. A sitting room of some sort.

That room had an open door, which led to another room and on to another, so that the "hallway" was nothing more than a series of connected chambers. At each one, I would pace off the dimensions, set my candle down, and scribble on my map.

Only in the third room did I notice perhaps the strangest thing so far: the floors didn't squeak at all. I could explore freely, as quietly as if I were walking outside on hard ground. Someone must have been taking special and continuous care to keep it like that, especially when the rest of the building was so noisy.

In a way, that should have been comforting; it made it less likely someone would hear me walking. But I couldn't help also considering that, even as the floor's silence aided me, it also helped whoever might be trailing along behind me. I couldn't know if I were being observed, or if someone were, even now, approaching me, hands outstretched, ready to grab my neck and snap it or crush it until all breath ceased.

I whirled to face behind me, certain someone had snuck up while I was counting or drawing. The room was empty, though that didn't calm my pounding heart. My neck tingled like I was being watched from the darkness. My candlelight pooled around my feet in a pitifully small circle. Plenty of the walls on the second floor were of the painted wood variety; any one of those knot holes might conceal an eyeball, or anyone might be around a corner or ducked into a shadow.

Waiting.

Perhaps it was the circumstances under which I was conducting my exploration (the flickering candlelight, the constant fear of being discovered, the lateness of the hour), but I became lost multiple times during that search. The rooms blended together in size and decoration and even the placement of furniture, and I retraced my steps often to regain my bearings.

Each time, I worried what would happen if I needed to escape. If someone were to attack me, should I call out for help? Of course not, because, with my nerves the way they were, I might well perceive anyone I met as a threat. In panic to get away from someone who turned out to be nothing more than a guest of the hotel, I might alert the real culprit to my presence.

Though I wouldn't know if they were friend or foe until it was too late, and, by then, I might not be able to cry out at all.

Besides, I had my excuse prepared. That would be enough.

It didn't help that, when the series of connected chambers opened up once more into a hallway, that hallway branched and twisted even more than the third floor, with some of its twistings leading to dead ends. I was caught in the Labyrinth from Greek lore, and somewhere in here, the Minotaur lurked, waiting for my head.

While I was standing in the middle of one such passage, trying to decipher how it was I had doubled back on myself, I caught a snippet of a voice. Faint and distant. Muffled.

Crying for help.

I paused, looking up from my map and straining my ears to see if the sound would repeat itself, but nothing came to me. My imagination, bringing my excuse to life.

Studying the map, I realized I must have come through a different set of chambers than the ones I had first found myself in. They had looped me around, and if I went to my right, I would be back on my way to the main staircase.

I thought.

To test the theory, I headed to the right, paying attention to the furniture and the doors. Sure enough, I found myself back in the first room I'd come to, with the bookcase and the padded chairs, which meant that the hallway on my right would take me—

"Help! Please, someone!"

This time there was no doubt in my mind that I had heard the voice, nor could I mistake the tone of desperation. It sounded far off, but it was a woman's soprano, and it was followed by choked sobs and...pounding? The noise of fists beating against a wall?

I rushed over to stand next to the bookcase, placing my ear against the plaster. The sound was no greater, so I switched to the opposite wall. Now the thuds were clear. So sharp I could have sworn they shook my cheek as I pressed it against the cool surface.

"Can't breathe." Followed by chokes and gasps of panic.

Abandoning all plans of stealth, I tried the door on my right, directly next to the wall where I had heard the plea. It was unlocked, but it led to an empty closet.

I headed farther down to the right, but the rooms refused to loop back to where I'd heard the voice. So I rushed to my left, trying to find the door that would lead me to the captive. But there the hallway again curved off in the wrong direction.

I could still hear the screams in my head, though they must have been more from my mind than my ears. Was I going mad? This felt too much like the nightmares of being trapped in the safe, scrabbling at the walls, surrounded by dead women.

I had to get to that person. Had to let her out. Not just to save her life, but to find out who had done it. To take her to the Pinkertons and end this charade once and for all.

All capacity for deep thought had left my mind. I ignored the map I'd spent at least an hour crafting, instead rushing foolishly through the corridors, thinking only of finding that victim.

Three things happened at once. The first was that I realized I was completely turned around and lost. The second, which compounded the first, was I whirled too quickly for my candle, and it blew out, leaving a faint puff of smoke trailing in the air.

The third, and most definitely most important fact, was that I glimpsed a body in that instant when I whirled and the candle went out. A man standing at the far end of the hall, facing away from me.

I was lost in the dark. And I was definitely not alone.

I froze, willing myself to stop breathing, even though it was impossible. My heart was pounding too quickly, and I couldn't just stand there holding my breath. I would pass out, only to find myself trapped in a room of my own when I awakened, no doubt. If I ever were to awaken.

Because, while the man might have been nothing more than a hotel guest alarmed by the noise of a woman's footsteps madly dashing by his room in the middle of the night, what had he been doing, standing in that corridor, still as a stone, facing away from the sound of the noise?

And without a candle of his own to light the way?

He might not have seen me in that instant before darkness fell, but he must have seen the light of the candle. He knew I was there.

I backed up until my shoulders touched a wall, my feet making no noise whatsoever, though that was hardly any comfort, for it simply reminded me that he would make no noise, either. If it were the kidnapper or the murderer, then he knew this floor far better than I could. It would be like me walking through my house back in Manti at night, where I knew the placement of each chair and table whereas a stranger would bump into all of them with every step.

Someone spoke in the darkness. A harsh whisper that carried easily through the air but didn't betray anything of the speaker's actual voice. No accent that might give me a clue. No peculiar manner of speech that might give him away. It was as if the whisperer were deliberately removing any trace of that from his voice. "I know you're there," he said. "I know you've been looking for me."

It gave me a general idea where he was, at least: still in front of me. Only then did I remember the knife I always kept strapped to my thigh. I raised my skirt, reached down and unsheathed it, though it did little to calm my nerves. I had no training with it, after all, and I'd never considered I might be fighting blind. I edged to my right, sidling along the wall and hoping I would come to a doorframe soon. Anywhere other than here would be a safer place for me.

"You must be Ruby's sister," the whisper said. "I could see that in your face the moment I first saw you."

Could that be Pitezel? Yes it could. But it could also be Mr. Holmes, could it not, or the mysterious Mr. Reynolds? What about Hans the barber, or Gustavo? Just because I was not overly familiar with the person didn't mean they were exempt from suspicion.

I kept edging sideways until I hit a second wall. I was in a corner, trapped.

"Do you know what I did to your sister?" The whisper was closer to me. Not ten feet away, and straight in front. He must be standing in the middle of the hall, blocking any exit I might take. I fumbled forward with my right hand, feeling the wall for anything that might give me a different escape. Not two feet away, I felt the opening of a doorframe.

"I could show you," the voice whispered. "She didn't go quietly, I'm afraid. Your sister was a screamer. But screaming won't help you in the Castle."

At last I found the doorknob. It squealed slightly as I turned it, but as I pushed inward, it stayed fast. Locked.

The whisper laughed. "Not locked. That one doesn't go anywhere, though I applaud you for trying to get away."

So he knew exactly where I was and what I was doing. What was the point in hiding?

"Scream, and I'll kill you right now," he whispered, anticipating my thoughts. "I have a knife, and more than enough experience to know where to put it, darkness or no. There is a room right next to us. I could whirl your body in there before anyone else arrived. No one would be the wiser. Half this floor is empty this evening. Don't test me."

"What do you want?" I asked, the words stumbling out of my mouth. My hand began to cramp around the knife's handle. I was gripping it too tightly.

"I've never been chased before," came the reply. "It's invigorating. What would you do if you found me? I think I might continue to allow you your search. But I didn't want you to think you were unobserved. I can stop you whenever I want. Reach out and slice you like I'm gutting a fish."

At this, something whipped through the air to my left. It tugged on my blouse, and a blossom of pain spread out on my arm. Had he cut me, or was that my imagination? Panic took over. There was no way to know if the voice meant what he said, or if he were stringing me along until he felt like cutting my throat.

I would not become another corpse. Not without a struggle.

Putting my head down, I barreled forward, one hand held out to ward me against any walls I might run into in my blindness, the other slashing back and forth through the air with my blade.

The man gasped as he heard my steps thundering forward. I ran into him, flailing my arms and legs, trying to connect with anything vulnerable. I knew my blows had strength behind them, for I had years of work on the farm. My finger got caught in his suspender button on his trousers, and I thrashed to get loose, ripping it off in the process. The knife, on the other hand, did no good whatsoever.

The man blocked my first blow, making my wrist go numb. I only managed to hold onto the knife through luck.

Whether I managed to strike him in earnest or he simply let me go, somehow I was beyond his body, and I hurried onward, crashing into a wall and careening to my left, where I tripped over something and slammed into the floor. The voice's claim that half the floor was empty must have been true. No lights came on. No one called out to ask what the commotion was.

I could have sworn I heard footsteps behind me, slow and methodical, approaching me even now. I scrambled back to my feet and continued forward, limping now but still desperate to get to anything that might be considered safety.

"Help!" I called out, as if the whisper had held my voice in check until now, when I realized I was beyond him and might have hope of escaping. But my cry was swallowed by the darkness, and for a moment I was back in the safe in my dream, captured and clawing to get out, with no one to hear my cries.

Until a lamp appeared in front of me, and Mr. Holmes was there in his bedclothes, his hair askew, and his face white with fear.

"Etta?" he said, holding the lantern high to get a better look at me.

I must have been an absolute fright, and I couldn't come up with anything to say in response other than a blubber and whine. My whole body shook as the fear washed over me.

"Your arm," Mr. Holmes said. "You're hurt."

I glanced at where the pain had come. My entire sleeve was dripping red with blood.

He put his arms around me, and I flinched back, too confused to know whom I could trust. I studied his earnest eyes and unkempt appearance, wondering if it could be an act.

Through my panic, a single thought exploded, all at once. I had to make up my mind, now. Could Mr. Holmes be the whisperer? He was in his bedclothes, and the man I'd struggled with had been fully dressed. Just how suspicious was I supposed to become? If I could not trust Mr. Holmes, who came to my aid in the middle of the night, then I could trust no one in this infernal house, and I would best be served putting it all behind me and never returning.

I knew what had happened to Ruby now, after all. Murdered. She wouldn't want me to stay around waiting for the same thing to happen to me. I had nothing to prove anymore. True, I didn't know who had committed the crime, but I had his admission of guilt.

I could rejoin Phebe. My life lay before me. I could see the world.

Every sensible thought in my brain demanded I ignore Mr. Holmes's offer of help, rush down the stairs and out into the night and never return to the Castle.

But the Ruby in me demanded something quite different. Never mind if her counterpart in real life would have wished me head to safety. My Ruby wanted revenge. Wanted that voice to feel the same terror I'd endured. The same wrenching panic my sister would have experienced. And he never would if I ran.

I considered the possibility that more women would fall victim to the Castle, but it was an afterthought. A justification I latched onto to give me further cause to stay the course.

Just as quickly as the thought had exploded, it settled on a plan.

I reached up and accepted Mr. Holmes's outstretched offer of help. If he were the whisperer, he could kill me now, and that was a risk I had to take. Because the whisperer wanted to play a game, and I was willing to bet my life that it was one I would win.

Mr. Holmes led me upstairs to his office overlooking the street below. I sat in his desk chair, shuddering. My mind might have made the decision to stay, but that had not done much to calm my body's troubled nerves.

He took out scissors and a bandage, expertly snipping away the sliced fabric of my blouse sleeve and inspecting the cut. "This was done by a knife," he observed, caution in his voice. But he said nothing more as he cleaned the wound and bandaged it. The peroxide stung when he applied it, but I didn't make a noise.

The wound dressed, he threw a blanket across my shoulders, then sat in another chair and stared at me, giving my nerves time to calm themselves. There was a clock in his office, and I watched it go from 1:52 to 2:12 before he spoke.

"Can you tell me what happened?"

By this time I was breathing somewhat normally, even if the memory of that voice in the dark was still fresh in my mind. I touched my bandaged arm. In the pitch-black, there was no way that man could have known where my body was. He'd lashed out with the blade, and he might just as easily have stabbed me through my heart if he'd gone a foot to the left.

Could that voice be Mr. Holmes? My heart didn't want to believe that. His eyes were too full of concern. His face so open and earnest. That mustache of his gave him a serious look, no matter the subject, and now it made him look like Wild Bill Hickok, ready to rush in and save me from any danger.

"You told me not to go to the second floor," I said, weighing my words carefully. "But I heard someone call for help. It was the middle of the night, and I didn't want to wake anyone. But I got turned around down there, and my light went out. I stumbled against something sharp. I'm not sure what it was, but I was so frightened..."

I trailed off, hoping I could rely on the tendency of men to think little of women when grit was called for. They inevitably did it when I wished they would not, would it be too much to ask that, just this once, he would do the same?

Mr. Holmes sighed. "Truly? No one attacked you?"

I spread my hands helplessly. "It was an accident. I swear. I panicked."

"This is why we have rules in the hotel. The second floor can be a bewildering place. Next time, come find me before you head down on your own. You might have broken your neck."

He continued to chastise me, and I received it all, grateful I didn't have to come up with any more of an explanation. Whoever was hunting the girls in the Castle, I had drawn his attention. I was chagrined I had put up so little of a threat. My fearsome knife might as well have been a feather, for all the good it had done. But I at least had some experience with it now. That had to count for something.

I had something of his, as well: the suspender button from the back of his pants. It even had a shred of fabric still attached. True, he might patch it, and he might simply discard the pants, but he might overlook at, as well. It wasn't a large rip, but I knew to look for it. Perhaps I'd notice someone in the Castle with a mended rip in the same place and a button to match.

I might not have had much evidence yet. Nothing that would convince the Pinkertons or Thomas to come do a real investigation, but I was scaring someone. Somehow as I left Mr. Holmes's room and walked back to my own, I lost the fear that had settled into my gut. Instead, I wanted to leap into the air. I was making progress. Real progress.

And I wasn't going to back down until I came away the victor.

CHAPTER FOURTEEN

It was into this kiln that I induced Mr. Warner to go with me, under the pretense of wishing certain minute explanations of the process, and then stepping outside, as he believed, to get some tools, I closed the door and turned on both the oil and steam to their full extent. In a short time not even the bones of my victim remained.

R UBY WAS WAITING FOR ME in my dreams two nights later, sitting next to my bed on a chair, a lone candle in the room casting a flickering light over the scene.

Her blond hair had lost much of its vibrancy, and it had begun to fall off in pieces from her scalp, leaving her head with a patchy look, like a rag doll whose yarn was fraying. Her skin was decaying much faster now as well, turning green and black across her entire body to the point that, if I hadn't seen her in my dreams earlier, I never would have recognized her.

Though her dress—that I would have known. The same red

dress she'd worn to countless parties and dances. The same fine fabric she'd taken such care of, brushed and pressed and pampered. The one she'd panicked over when she'd spilled vinegar on it.

It hung loosely, the red soiled and wrinkled, the material ripped and tattered so you could see through it in places to more exposed bone and peeling skin beneath.

She didn't seem to mind.

"I told you to stop coming, Zuretta," she told me after a moment. She had yet to look at me, her lanky hair shielding her face as it hung down. Her voice was soft, but recognizable. It sounded resigned.

"What choice did I have?" I asked, sitting up in bed. The room was just as it had looked when I'd fallen asleep. There were my slippers by the bed. There was my dress laid out on the dresser, waiting to be worn. "I had to find you."

Her shoulders slumped. "I warned you against it, but I suppose it makes sense. You never were good at doing what you were told."

She jerked her head up to stare me full in the face, revealing two holes where her eyes should have been. Her lips were dry and withered, flaking apart to reveal swathes of teeth and a swollen black tongue. Her nose flapped to the side, like a door left ajar, revealing more of her skull beneath.

I flinched back, and as I did, hands reached out to grab me and pull me in close to the wall. Other women and girls, each of them rotting to nothing but still strong as iron, their hands loose skin around sharp bones. No matter how hard I struggled, their grip only tightened. The stench hit me like a wave: rancid meat and decay so sweet I gagged.

Ruby stood, gazing at me with a blank expression.

"You'll join us," Ruby said. "And your beautiful skin will peel and crack. It won't be long before you smell the same and lose all hope of salvation. You'll wish you'd listened to me. Pray for it. But it will Be. Too. Late."

I fought harder, to no avail. "What can I do?" I called out. "How can I stop this?"

The hands dug into me, pulling me flat against the wall so I couldn't move even to breathe. Ruby crawled up on the bed to face me, stopping less than a few inches from me, the smell overpowering. "You didn't listen then, so listen to me now. Avenge us. All of us. For everything he ever did."

She lunged forward, mouth gaping wide to swallow me whole.

＝＝＝＝＝

A floorboard squeaked outside my bedroom door.

My heart was still pounding, my breath frantic, and my body covered in sweat from the nightmare I'd endured, so it took a second and then a third squeak for the sound to come to my full attention.

That alone wasn't alarming. I had been a light sleeper of late, never knowing when another of my nightmares might return.

Guests were constantly moving about in the night, often with little rhyme or reason.

A squeak was nothing compared to the clarity of that terror in my sleep.

Except the sound didn't repeat itself again from farther down the hall. All three had been close by, and in a building as noisy as the Castle, that meant something.

Another squeak sounded, still right outside my bedroom door.

Someone was standing there.

I fumbled for a candle, my hands shaking hard enough that the first match went out before I could get the wick lit. I sat there, waiting, knowing whoever it was could now see light from beneath my door.

My breath's pace didn't slow, and I focused on staying still, straining for any sound. Any sign they might be leaving.

My doorknob turned. Slowly. Almost silently. But not silently enough for me to miss the slight hiss of metal on metal.

I had locked it, the same as I always did. I was safe, wasn't I?

Or had this been the last sound Ruby heard as her end approached?

Was I to call out? Stay quiet and wait for them to go away? Who would come to my aid, and would they arrive in time? I knew this hotel was dangerous, and I shouldn't have been surprised when that danger finally began to manifest itself.

The doorknob turned the other way. The attempt foiled.

Until a key rattled in the lock.

My heart leapt into my throat, and I lunged for my knife, hidden in a small slice I'd made in my mattress. My mind tried to find a reasonable explanation. The hotel was confusing. It could be a guest who was simply turned around. He was being cautious to avoid an embarrassing encounter in the middle of the knight.

But the key was turning, and I didn't know who was out there, and I didn't know what they'd do if they gained access.

"Who's there?" I called out, my voice loud in my ears. There was no shake to it, I didn't think. No sign of the fear lancing through my gut. My knife's handle was cool and reassuringly solid.

The key removed itself from my lock, and a voice muttered something…and was answered by another voice in the hall!

"This is my room," I said, because they knew I was now awake, so why not give them the opportunity to go elsewhere, if elsewhere was where they wished to be.

Footsteps left down the hall, and I followed their noise in my mind, tracing their path as they turned the corner and headed back into the depths of the third floor.

But only a single pair of footsteps.

There was still someone outside my door.

"Is there something you need?" I asked. "Are you lost?"

The seconds ticked by. Did they think I assumed they'd gone? My palm was sweating on the knife's handle, making it slick and uncertain in my grip. At last a voice answered, low and gruff. "It's me, ma'am. Mr. Pitezel. We've had complaints of a roof leak from above, and I need to see to the ceiling."

The thought of that brute coming into my room at this hour was enough to make my skin crawl. "There's been no leak here," I told him. "I'd thank you to give me some notice before skulking about my doorway at so late an hour."

"It could damage the building, Etta. It can't wait until the morning. Now let me in, and we'll both be back to sleep all the sooner."

No doubt. But would I ever wake up? "I've told you once: there's no water in here. No drips and no signs of damage. Your leak must be elsewhere, if it exists. You may inspect my room in the morning when I'm about my business, and you can take any damages caused out of my paycheck if you must. But I will have my sleep now and hear you say goodnight and depart."

He punched the door hard enough to rattle its hinges, but he also turned and stomped away down the hall, back in the same direction of his accomplice, leaving me in peace once again.

But it was hours before I could sleep, and when I did, my dreams were filled with rotting women and a smiling Pitezel, dancing with one after another.

PART THREE

The Prey

CHAPTER FIFTEEN

Finally, by alternately starving him and nauseating him with the gas, he was made to sign the securities, all of which were converted into money.

I WOKE THE NEXT MORNING WITH newfound determination. It's amazing what a potential attack on your life will do for your personal motivation. Whoever was at the root of this mystery, they were getting much bolder. They knew I was hunting them, and they were escalating their efforts against me.

Did it have to be Pitezel, though? There could be no disputing he was outside my room during the night, but I'd heard two sets of footsteps. Perhaps the infamous Mr. Reynolds, revealing his true nature at last? Or one of Pitezel's hired laborers? I could not believe Pitezel really had just come to inspect my room.

But one thing was now clear to me: it no longer mattered what Mrs. Patterson or anyone else thought of my actions. If my life was in danger, then I had to abandon caution and find out what I could. Just a few key pieces of evidence would be enough for me to go to Thomas or the Pinkertons, and I was confident that once the Castle was properly inspected, all its mysteries would come to light. The maggots and vermin could try to wriggle back into the shadows, but it would be too late.

A large part of me wanted to abandon my chores and run to Thomas today. Only the memory of all those men, staring at me in disappointment, held me in check. I wanted something tangible I could use to prove my story, or I worried I'd be dismissed as being "overly emotional."

So that morning, after I finished with my sweeping and dusting and mopping, I headed for Pitezel's personal quarters. He was out on an errand given him by Mr. Reynolds and wouldn't return for an hour at least, so I had free rein of the third floor. I wouldn't get anywhere in my search if I didn't start pushing boundaries.

He had a habit of leaving his door unlocked, likely because he assumed the staff was too terrified to risk his wrath if he found them in his room. I knocked lightly at the door, confident he wasn't in, but still intent on keeping up appearances. After a moment, I entered.

The room was sixteen feet square, with a bed, a wardrobe, a dresser, a desk, and a nightstand. All of it was in good repair and tidy, the walls a neat white and cobweb free. I hurried over to the desk and pulled out the drawers. They were sparsely populated with blank pieces of paper, writing instruments, and a checkbook that revealed nothing more than a series of expenses for doctor visits, though Pitezel had a strange way of noting the tallies, summing the debts together instead of subtracting them from an initial amount.

The dresser revealed clothes folded and put away in an almost military fashion. His nightstand held a single picture, drawn by one of his children: a family of smiling stick figures, with a sun shining down above.

I rifled through his wardrobe, searching for the torn pants, but found nothing but well-pressed clothes and shined shoes.

I kept glancing at the door, my ears straining for the sound of footsteps. I checked behind the furniture and underneath it. The headboard of the bed and the mattress. I inspected the desk drawers for false bottoms and the wardrobe for a false back, knocking at the wood and running my fingers over the smooth surface, hoping to find some latch or button that might reveal a hidden chamber.

Who knew what it might hold: Newspaper clippings about missing women, locks of hair, bloody knives? I found nothing.

Then I heard footsteps coming down the hall, the floorboards squeaking. I dashed to put the room back in order, glancing over it to make sure I hadn't forgotten anything. Was it Pitezel? Had I delayed too long? One of the drawers was still open partway, and I rushed to close it. Any moment the door might open—

But the footsteps continued past the room and down the hall.

Enough. My search had been fruitless. I should have gone back to my normal routine, but something about having already taken one risk left me wanting to take more.

I darted out of his quarters and strode to the main staircase and took it to the second floor.

Did my heart beat a quick staccato in my chest? What of it? I ignored the warning and barreled forward.

I used my crude sketch from last night—bloodstained from my wound—as a base to plot out the exact layout of the floor. The halls twisted this way and that, just as I had surmised when I came here in the dark. Two different doors opened to a blank wall, though I was certain Pitezel would simply blame that on faulty construction.

At first I thought my nerves were affecting my calculations, but as I grew more accustomed to my task, I was certain some things didn't add up. The main hallway was two feet thinner toward the far end of the Castle, wasn't it? In another spot, the hall ended much too soon, leaving a space at least ten feet long and the width of the hallway unaccounted for. A few of the rooms were smaller on the inside than they were on the out.

At last I took out a fresh sheet of paper and began to count off steps again, doing my best to re-create the floor plan as accurately as possible. I was beginning my first measurement when a couple came down the hall, laughing at something the man had said. I curtsied to them and ducked my eyes, at the same time wondering how anyone could feel so lighthearted and oblivious. The entire building made me nauseous, yet here the two lovers were without a care in the world.

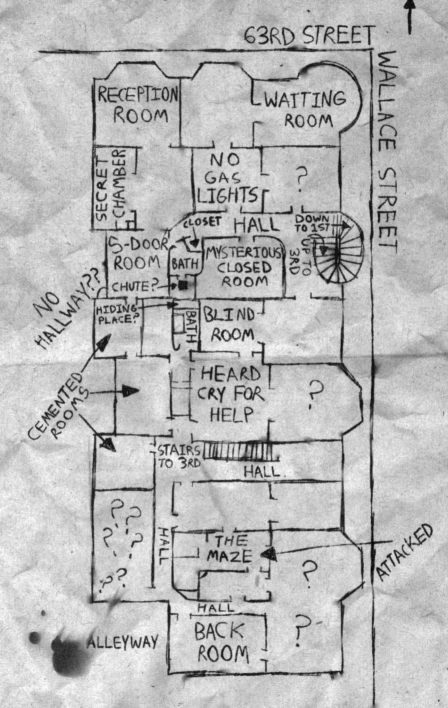

Once they were safely out of sight, I resumed my measurements.

There were hidden chambers on that floor. Many of them. One room was completely bricked in—I measured the outside walls on every side around it, and I knew it must exist, but I could find no entrance, concealed or otherwise.

Yet another room had no gaslights, though it had a gas connection. The spout was concealed up in a corner for some unknown reason. My stomach twisted uncomfortably, and I hurried out of the room.

I turned my focus to smaller details, inspecting the locks to the rooms, discovering latches that could fasten from the outside. With each revelation, I became more elated and disturbed. Elated, because this was the proof I'd so desperately needed. Disturbed, because of what it all implied. Someone had been methodically constructing this building to do all manner of evils on its guests and inhabitants.

And they had yet to be caught.

Every corner I turned uncovered another mystery. Hardly any gas lights in the hall. A ladder hidden within a closet. A chute that led to the depths of the building. Did it connect to the elusive basement?

I was leaning in to see if I could tell how far down it went when I heard the shuffle of a footfall behind me. I shrieked and whirled to see a guest standing there, staring at me.

"How do I get to the main floor?" he asked. "I'm afraid I've gotten turned around."

I fumbled out a response, which I was reasonably certain was accurate, though, at that moment, I wasn't sure if I could have given directions to get to the room right next to us. He accepted them, however, and went on his way.

But when I'd heard the footfall and discovered it was just a guest, I'd been convinced someone was about to shove me down that chute, where my body would careen back and forth, my face slamming into the walls, my neck snapping as I hit the bottom. It was a packaged thought, all tied up and ready for me to understand with a quick burst of insight.

I'd taken enough risks for one day. Didn't I have enough evidence now? Surely it was sufficient to bring Thomas over to my side, and once I could convince him to come in person, pairing my story of Ruby with the facts I'd found in the Castle would be enough to bring the rest of the Pinkertons.

The events at this hotel had gone unnoticed, but they were a sweater with a single strand dangling from it, one I'd dutifully unwound and exposed, where it was now waiting to be pulled. If that strand could be pulled the right way, the rest of it would all unravel.

I stuffed my map into my dress and hurried to safer territory. No one saw me. No alarms were raised.

In a day or two, when I had a good chance to take leave without making anyone suspicious, I would pay Thomas another visit.

CHAPTER SIXTEEN

The Williams sisters come next.

———————

T HE NEXT MORNING DAWNED WITH the usual countless chores around the hotel to get done. Several of the rooms on the third floor needed airing, the bathrooms had to be mopped, and Mrs. Patterson had decided to remind me what I was really paid for by handing me extra tasks, since I had been unable to explain to her what exactly I'd done with myself the day before.

I found myself eyeing every man's pants I came across, constantly searching for the torn button—the evidence that would finish this investigation immediately. True, I suspected Pitezel the most, but I had to remember it could be anyone, and he could have accomplices. A neighbor. Guest. Laborer. I began to pay more attention to suspender buttons than I did to faces and expressions, and it became a habit: always keeping a lookout for the torn pants.

At 10 a.m., Mr. Reynolds stormed through the hallways,

shutting himself into his office without saying a word. An hour later, Mr. Holmes stopped in to ask me if I'd seen Minnie or Anna leave.

I shook my head, my arms up to their elbows in suds as I worked at scrubbing stains out of the bed sheets. "Their doors were closed when I was about my business this morning," I told him. "I never saw them opened. Perhaps they're still sleeping?"

He wandered off without another word, his expression clouded with worry.

I thought no more of the matter for many hours. Minnie and Anna could be flighty at times. Just because they had overslept was no reason to begin to fret. In the Castle, it took much more than that to be noteworthy, and my focus was elsewhere.

Yet their door remained closed past lunch, and Mr. Holmes kept pacing the halls. Finally he came to me, asking if I wouldn't enter their chambers to see if they were ill.

I did as asked. The rooms were empty. Beds either already made or unused. Mr. Holmes's uneasiness began to settle into my stomach as well.

All their clothes were gone. The closets were cleared. Trunks disappeared. It was as if they'd packed their suitcases in the middle of the night and absconded from the Castle.

Mr. Holmes's eyes widened when I showed him, and he began to run his fingers through his hair.

"This is how it was with Ruby," he said, staring at me in panic.

I stumbled forward in surprise. My knees ceased to function, and I almost collapsed to the floor. I clutched the wall to steady myself, blinked, and asked, "Who?"

He sighed and waved off the question, turning to walk back down the hall, but I rushed to catch up with him. I grabbed his shoulder and turned him to face me. "Who were you talking about?"

"I was engaged before I met Minnie. To a lovely girl named Ruby. But she disappeared one day from the Castle, and I never heard from her again. Sometimes I think I'm cursed. I'm sorry... I shouldn't have brought it up."

He was my sister's infamous suitor? It was as if the information didn't want to settle into my brain. She just disappeared one day? Had he tried to find her? What had he done to go to her aid? Watching how he behaved now that Minnie had vanished gave me little hope that anything had been done for Ruby.

But it could be different now. I was here, and I could give Minnie and Anna the chance my sister hadn't had.

"We must check the premises," I told Mr. Holmes, my voice low and urgent.

Before we had even begun, however, Mr. Pitezel came up from the first floor, an envelope held out in his hand. I froze the minute the man entered our presence, my mind running through the things he might have done to those poor women. What if they were asphyxiated in one of the guest rooms? What if they had their throats cut?

Mr. Holmes snatched the letter and tore it open, reading it

over frantically. His shoulders slumped, and his hand dropped to his side, the letter falling out onto the floor.

I picked it up before Pitezel could get there.

Dear Henry,

Anna and I have had the most distressing news. Our brother wrote to us of some trouble at home. Trouble too terrible for me to want to write down into words. I cannot tell you the pain it causes me, but I believe I must end our engagement immediately. You do not deserve a woman tainted with scandal, as I now will be.

Perhaps I shall be able to clear my family's name, though that seems impossible to me now. If I do, I will return to you, and, perhaps, fate will smile on me, and you shall still be unmarried.

Thank you so much for all you have done for us, and please do try to think of me with a forgiving, tender heart.

Yours always,
Minnie

I studied that letter as closely as I'd ever read a document in my life, checking the small details: the curve of the *l*'s, the way the letters flowed, the placement of the commas. It seemed to be done in Minnie's hand, and if the writing seemed hesitant or forced at times—words that stopped in the middle, the pen lifting before continuing, slightly disconnected—didn't the subject matter justify it?

Pitezel tried to take the letter from me, but I shoved it into my waistband, giving him a glare as I did so. He scowled back, his face so dark and foreboding, I took a step back in fright. But I was with Henry, and there was nothing Pitezel could do to harm me.

I returned his stare. "Don't you have other chores that need doing?" I asked him, my voice cold and clipped.

Mr. Holmes seemed to come out of the pit his mind had fallen into, and he blinked and stared at Pitezel. "Yes, please, Benjamin. Go ahead. I'll be fine."

The man slunk off like a fox leaving the chicken house. I hurried to Mr. Holmes as soon as Pitezel was out of the room.

"He took them," I whispered, the words coming out as a hiss. Minnie and Anna might even now be locked somewhere in this building, and I'd do whatever I could to save them. These last events had brought everything together. Pitezel was the man, and he had to be stopped. "They might still be alive."

Mr. Holmes stared at me blankly. "What are you talking about? No one took anyone. That's written in her hand. What could have caused her such shame?"

Could he really be so dense? I took a breath and spoke slowly and rationally. "Women have been disappearing at the Castle. I've noticed it ever since I arrived. I think someone is taking them. Maybe even murdering them. You yourself said Ruby disappeared the same way. Which is the more logical explanation? That two more fell into the same trap that consumed others, or that they suddenly discovered some mysterious shred of information that caused them to throw their entire lives into disarray?"

"There's a third option," Mr. Holmes said. "I could be cursed. Perhaps it's something in my bearing. Women are repulsed by me, but unable to—"

I slapped him across the face, startling us both with my action. For an instant, rage shot through Mr. Holmes's expression. His eyes narrowed and his face hardened, and then it was gone, even though I wished it would stay. He *needed* to be upset by this. "I deserved that," he said.

Just when you wanted men to behave like men, they turned around and became timid mice. "Don't you understand?" I asked. "They could still be alive! We could go to the police, but I fear we don't have the time."

"I've searched the entire premises," he responded morosely.

"Have you been to the basement?" Now was the perfect chance for me to broach that topic.

"There is no basement."

I blinked in surprise. "Then where do the storm doors on the street lead to?" I asked.

Mr. Holmes cocked his head to the side and froze. "I've never seen an entrance to the basement inside the building," he said at last. "There were no basements in the building plans I signed off on. I would think I would have noticed one being constructed."

"Surely you weren't present for the entire construction process. Is it not possible Mr. Reynolds arranged for it? We need to go see him. Talk to him now! I'm sure if you were to—"

"He's too busy," Mr. Holmes said. "He doesn't like it when he's interrupted during the day."

It was all I could do not to slap him again. "Too busy? This is your fiancée's life we're speaking of. I'm sure he'd understand. You meet with him often enough, and I saw him this morning. He's in his office right now. Come on!"

Mr. Holmes moaned and hung his head, tearing at his hair.

"What did I say?" I asked.

When he looked up at me, his eyes were rimmed red. "Tell me you do not think Benjamin is at the root of this. Swear it!"

It was such a quick change of subject, I had to take a moment to make sense of the question. I backed up a few steps and shook my head. "He's been the most suspicious character in all of this from the beginning. Why?"

"Oh, if my trust were to have been the cause of it all," Mr.

Holmes began, then checked himself, took a breath, and started over. "I...I'm afraid there's something you must know."

I waited for him to continue.

"Mr. Reynolds doesn't exist. He never has."

The words hung in the air between us, not making sense. "Excuse me?"

"He's a fiction Mr. Pitezel suggested I create to explain away any troubles that might come up during business practices. People are readier to be on your side when they believe you're simply following orders. So why not attribute any contentious decisions to a man that didn't exist?"

Now it was my turn to stare. "Doesn't exist?"

Mr. Holmes shook his head.

"But I've seen him! The man scowled at me not more than an hour and a half ago."

"You've met a person we *call* Mr. Reynolds. A man I pay to play a part here at the hotel. You could go to the man you think is Mr. Reynolds, but as soon as you asked him any real questions, you'd know straight away."

"But what about his incessant rules?" I asked. "The stipulations about who can go to which floors, and—"

"All made up by Benjamin. He thought it would reduce theft."

"*Reduce theft?*" I could barely contain myself. "How much of your operations have you turned over to the man? Did you never think to question him even for a moment?"

"I valued his advice..." Mr. Holmes trailed off for a moment, then squared his chin. "The time for that is in the past, however."

"No," I insisted. "You can't simply gloss over something like that. A fabricated manager? Did Minnie know?"

"Of course she did," Mr. Holmes said. "I only keep it from the staff to make things simpler. I'll rue the decision forever if it's made it so that Minnie was taken from me. If you think there's even a chance she might be trapped somewhere in this house, where do we begin?"

"The basement," I said, clearing my head and trying to focus. "If Pitezel has hidden it even from you, then it must be central to his operations." I grabbed him by the arm, and we rushed downstairs and outside.

The sun was beginning to set, and the streets were on fire with golden light. A few of the maids gasped in surprise as we sped past them. Mr. Holmes had caught some of my sense of urgency, for I stopped having to drag him, and he ran forward on his own.

We came to the metal door, and Mr. Holmes crouched beside it, taking out his key ring and working his way through the options, one at a time. The lock was a hefty bolt, but eventually he found the correct key. The lock snapped open, and he flung it to the side. He heaved the door up and swung it wide, another piece of smooth sidewalk. No stairs. No basement entrance.

The storm door led, quite literally, to nowhere.

I got down on my knees and pounded against the sidewalk.

It had to be fake. Had to have a catch or a release or a switch. It didn't make any sense! Why would they have put the iron door on the street in the first place? But the concrete was solid, and all I succeeded in doing was scraping my hands as I pounded against it.

"Come up from there," Mr. Holmes said, even more dejected.

"It's a trick," I said.

"The Castle was built by too many different crews." Mr. Holmes walked down the stairs and placed a hand on my shoulder. "I know you want there to be an explanation. Something that unlocks a sinister plot against Minnie and Anna and Ruby. But all that's there is incompetence, I'm afraid. My own and others. You said to take the simplest explanation, and that's it. Not murderous intent. My inability to manage building crews."

I stared at the mortar in disbelief. Could it be true? "But Ruby..." I began.

"People change," Mr. Holmes said. "It happens. They don't always tell us why. Perhaps she ran away from me for some slight I gave her. Or she might have fallen in love with another man, and she didn't want to admit it. I might never know why Minnie left with Anna, but blaming it on a mysterious conspiracy will do me no good."

I allowed myself to be led away. He put the lock back in place, and we went back inside the Castle. My mind refused to cooperate. I wanted to come up with something that made sense of it all. As soon as the front door, I turned to Mr. Holmes.

"We're going to drop this," he said.

"But I—"

"No. Now is not the time for false hope or mad fantasies from Poe. I wish to be left alone."

I stared at him, wracking my brain for some excuse to keep pushing. But I'd already overextended myself. Perhaps put myself in danger. So, at last, I nodded. "You're right," I said, hoping my voice sounded meek. "I've been letting myself get carried away."

Mr. Holmes walked to the main staircase and paused. "It's been a trying day for us all. You surely have better things to do than stay here and watch me brood. I suggest you return to your regular duties. The sooner we can put this behind us, the better."

And that was that.

CHAPTER SEVENTEEN

Having secured all the money and property Miss Williams
had it was time that she were killed. I ended her life with
poison and buried her body in the basement of the house.

───────

"P OLICE OR THE PINKERTONS," PHEBE told me that night after
I had informed her of all the recent developments over a late
dinner. "If you wait any longer, you're as likely to end up on the
business end of Pitezel as you are putting the man in handcuffs.
Likelier, I'd say."

I nodded. "I wanted to go earlier in the day, but Mrs. Patterson
was always looming over me, and Pitezel seemed far too interested
in my whereabouts. You don't think the Pinkertons will simply
brush it off? It's not as if I have solid evidence. Even finding time
to come here to speak with you is becoming almost impossible."

"Didn't you say that Thomas fellow was sweet on you?"

I blushed and wished I hadn't. "He helped me in a time of
need, yes."

Phebe shrugged, diving into her buttered roll with jam. Nothing could separate that woman from an appetite. "Men have their issues, I'll grant you that. They have to be handled in particular ways to get what we need out of them, but it's not all that complex in the end. You'd be surprised what a man will do for a shy smile and a few flutters of the eyelashes."

"It shouldn't be that way," I snapped.

"What?"

"Men don't need to do that to other men to get what they want," I said. "They simply go up to the people they want to do business with and talk to them."

Phebe laughed so loudly several heads in the cafe turned to stare at us, and I shielded my eyes from them. "Men don't just speak their way through problems. Oh, some do—I'll grant you that, the same way some women are able to as well. But many men don't. They bully. They lie. They wheedle. They'll even beat each other senseless when they don't get what they want. We all use what we can, how we can. You've got a pretty face when you aren't slinking around and trying to blend into the wallpaper. It would be a waste not to use it."

I forced my hand down and sat straighter. Did she really think I had a pretty face? "What if he says no?" I asked.

"Then you're no worse off than you are now. It'll take two hours of your time. Is that so much to sacrifice? Because if Thomas listens, then he very well might be able to solve all your problems."

"I wanted—"

"To solve them on your own," Phebe said, jabbing a fork in my direction. "I understand. But that's what you'll be doing by going to Thomas. Using the resources within your reach to get a certain outcome. Do it. I don't want to have to go to them in your stead once you've disappeared as well. You're too good of a friend for me to let that happen. But after all's said and done, do you have a plan for what you'll do if you succeed?"

I stared at her blankly. "I'll have brought Pitezel to justice. Avenged Ruby. What else is there?"

Phebe dropped her fork. "Really? What happens if he's put to death? You can say you've given up on religion all you like, but something tells me that's still going to weigh on your conscience."

"That isn't—"

"If Pitezel were to come in this restaurant right now and attack you, would you be able to defend yourself?"

"Of course."

She laughed and shook her head. "It's one thing to think it, and another thing to do it. My gut says you'd freeze. Too busy worrying about what the right thing to do would be. To succeed at this, you need to stop thinking about right and wrong and just do what needs doing. If you can't do that, your conscience is going to eat you alive."

"It won't come to that," I insisted. "I'm going to catch him. Prove what he's been doing, and turn him over to the authorities."

"What comes next in your daydream?"

I flushed. "I don't appreciate being—"

"I'm not making light of you," Phebe said, her eyebrows raised and earnest. "I'm saying you should know what your dream is. There's no way to reach it if you don't plan it out."

"Oh." Her tone and expression mollified my pride somewhat. "Well, people won't question my abilities anymore, to begin with."

"And?"

"And...the Pinkertons will apologize. And offer me a job."

"And?"

I sighed. "And...I'll go home and confront my father and force him to see the error of his ways. Then I'll come back to Chicago and solve cases with Sherlock Holmes, who will move here when he reads of the wonders of my escapades."

Phebe laughed. "That's more like it. Dream big, I say. The bigger, the better."

I had the next morning free, offering the perfect chance to head downtown. The time for writing letters was over. I needed his input now, not a response next week.

I spent the entire walk there checking the back sides of trousers on the off chance one would magically appear that matched the torn fabric and button in my possession, but, of course, it never happened. Pitezel had to have burned those trousers. Checking was as useless as knocking on wood to ward off evil.

Thomas lived in a brick townhome not far from Chicago's center. A fat butler answered the door, scowling at me as if I smelled unpleasant. "Yes?"

My voice abandoned me, and suddenly I was Zuretta, fresh off the train and petrified. "Is Thomas here?"

The butler's expression darkened. "Mr. Chalmers is away on business."

"When will he return?"

"Mr. Chalmers' affairs are his own." He began to close the door.

I put my hand up, stopping him. "Can I leave him a note?"

"And you are?" he asked me, peering down his nose. It didn't help that there was a step up to get into the house, so the butler was naturally above me, as if he were a judge sitting in court.

"A friend," I said, an edge creeping into my voice. "May I leave a note or not?"

He sighed and held out a hand, as if I had the note pre-written.

"I shall require pen and paper," I said.

You would think I had told him I needed to drill into his teeth. But something in my bearing made him go back inside the house and return minutes later with stationery.

I used the time to consider what to write. This butler would almost certainly be reading it, and I didn't want to be too overt. In the end, I settled on:

Thomas,

I have come upon some developments in the case I first approached you about. I need to meet with you as soon as you can. Lives may well depend upon it. I am at the World's Fair Hotel, more commonly known as the Castle, in Englewood. Send me a letter about where we may meet in person. We should not meet at the Castle.

Sincerely,
Zuretta

It had taken me two minutes to settle on the proper way to conclude the letter. Yours? Gratefully? Respectfully? At last I had scrawled *sincerely* and been done with it.

My trip back to the Castle was filled with doubt, and it didn't get any easier once I arrived. Minnie and Anna's trouble weighed on my mind, and I found myself constantly stopping in the middle of my work, certain I heard a scream. I would pause from time to time to listen to walls and floorboards, until a guest caught me crouched on the floor, my ear to the ground, and I had to pretend I'd been looking for a lost coin underneath a chest of drawers.

I should go to the police. The thought repeated itself in my mind several times an hour. But the rational explanation held me back. Like it or not, Phebe and I were just novice detectives. Could Minnie and Anna have left suddenly? Yes. And if I brought the police and it turned out I'd cried wolf, I would have alerted Pitezel to my intent.

The next few days crawled by. Mr. Holmes was in a daze, shutting himself in his room and refusing to emerge. Pitezel took over in his stead, barking orders and snapping when they weren't carried out quickly enough.

I caught him staring at me from time to time. Did he know I suspected? Was I next on his list? I prayed each morning that Thomas would respond to my request. For as reluctant as I'd been to contact the man in the first place, his answer became increasingly important to me, as if its appearance would solve my troubles at once.

With each day that Thomas failed to appear, I began to consider other options. What if he had given up on me? Dismissed me the same way so many other men had throughout my life? I needed proof that what I was saying was true. The second floor was barred to me, but perhaps I could find something on the third.

It was a stretch, but it gave me something to do. I'd approach it methodically, as if I'd never tried a real search of the floor yet. I'd pretend I was a Pinkerton presented with a tough problem to solve and see if my claims might sway someone else.

For the first hour, my pessimism was confirmed. I used my hand-drawn maps as a guide, marking off areas as I searched them, coming back to the ones that were occupied when I first tried. The guest rooms showed nothing of interest. The storage rooms were just storage rooms. It was almost enough to make me feel like Mr. Holmes's claims that the house had simply been constructed haphazardly were justifiable.

Mrs. Patterson came through the third floor, a whirlwind of activity. "Have you seen it?" she asked.

I could only give her a blank stare. "Seen what?"

"His pocket watch, of course! What else have I been looking for this past half hour, fool girl? What have you been doing?"

"A guest spilled ink on the floor in the corner room. I've been scrubbing it clean, and I almost have it finished, but if I wait much longer, the stain will set."

The lie came to my lips without effort: reason enough to skip the search for the watch, but general enough that I could brush it aside after. I'd been through this floor thirty times on my own searches. I didn't want to waste more time going over it again. Mrs. Patterson listened with half an ear, setting her keys down on the hall table as she searched its drawers and then got on her hands and knees to scan beneath it. "Useless," she called out, almost as an afterthought, as she continued farther down the hall.

Leaving the key ring behind her.

My eyes flicked from the keys to Mrs. Patterson's retreating form. Surely she would remember them. If she came back to find them gone, would she suspect me? But I'd been in her shoes often enough to know what would happen: in her search of the whole building, she'd forget where she'd left her keys as well. I could return them to her later, saying I found them anywhere I pleased, and she'd be none the wiser.

I slipped the keys down the front of my blouse, then hurried off to the corner room where the "ink stain" supposedly lay. (I'd been in the room ten minutes before and knew it was empty.)

Once there, I removed the key ring, not quite believing I had it. Those keys would let me into any room in the Castle. Surely there were some places I hadn't searched yet in all my efforts. Places that had been barred to me.

I opened my map and consulted my notes. Other than the secret rooms on the second floor that I'd yet to find an entrance to, there wasn't much unmarked. But before I put the map away in frustration, my eyes fell upon one place I'd had yet to visit: the small room next to mine. Mrs. Patterson had called it a "storage room," and the door had always been locked.

Not today.

I hurried to my room, having to remind myself not to literally run there. I still arrived flushed and breathless, closing my door behind me and locking it. Now wasn't the time for anyone to surprise me. I fumbled through the keys until I found the match for the unknown room. The lock clicked open, and I twisted the knob.

My heart pounded. What mysteries might I find?

The door revealed a small antechamber with cabinets that ran from the floor to the ceiling along one wall, and a few chests and drawers along the other. A storage room, and a very small one at that.

I tried not to give into despair, rifling through the drawers and cupboards. They contained nothing more exciting than sheets and silverware.

A pit gaped open where my heart should have been. All my efforts came to nothing, even when I thought I'd finally turned the corner. I removed my map yet again and glared at it, as if the fault for my failure were to be placed on it and not on my own shortcomings.

The real clues must be in the secret rooms on the second floor. How might I enter them? Would one of the keys fit a hidden—

I checked the map of the third floor again, then flicked back and forth between them. If my measuring was correct, one of the empty spaces was right beneath my room. There had to be a reason this small closet on the third floor was always locked, mustn't there?

It might conceal a trap door that led to that secret room.

I dropped to all fours, my hands trailing around on the floor, searching for a catch or something out of the ordinary.

The left edge of one of the chests of drawers was pushed out. Mrs. Patterson was a stickler for things being set properly, so that bit of crookedness stood out.

I pushed the drawers to the side, inspecting the wall behind them for a switch or a latch, but it was blank and plain, without any cracks or joints where an entrance might be hidden.

The crooked chest might have been nothing more than the

effect of someone bumping against it in a rush. That was the simplest explanation, after all, and almost always the simplest...

The floorboards underneath the chest stuck up in a strange pattern.

You would get that in a house, of course, as the wood warped over time. But that was typically a board here or there. This was four of them in a row, and the edges didn't line up. It was as if an entire section of the floor was pushed up ever so slightly.

I knelt down, prying at one of the boards with my fingers. It moved a fraction of an inch up.

My heart pounding in earnest now, I scrambled to find a tool I might use to gain more leverage on the board. The base of candlestick from my bedroom was small and thin enough that I could use it to press against the board and get some traction. After five attempts, I lifted the board high enough for my fingers to gain purchase.

The entire section of the floor swung upward, revealing darkness beneath me. For a moment, I pictured the corpses of dead girls rushing up through that chasm to clutch at my clothes and drag me down with them.

But nothing appeared, and there were no noises.

I hurried to get matches, for I already had a candle. Light flared moments later, and I held the candle down into the hole, wincing at first as the flame burned my wrist in my excitement. That would be all I needed, to light myself on fire just before I had a breakthrough.

Below me, I'd hoped to find a ladder leading to the depths of the basement. Instead, the light glinted off a series of glass beakers and tubes. It was a small room, neatly kept with a desk and a chair, a bookcase filled with vials and tomes.

And a skeleton standing in the corner.

I almost dropped the candle when I saw those bleached, white bones, the empty sockets staring up at me, mouth wide in a macabre grin. But I recovered my wits, looked about me, and clambered down the ladder I found along the trapdoor's side.

It was over, and I wanted to shout with joy. I had the piece of real proof I needed to show to the police or the Pinkertons so they would sit up and take notice of the Castle. Give it the investigation it truly deserved. Sledgehammers and pickaxes would provide an entrance to the mysterious basement quickly enough.

I studied the beakers and vials, examining the neatly lettered, blocky handwriting. *PANCREAS, F, 43. LIVER, M, 27. BRAIN, F, 25.* It was almost mechanical in its precision, and I had seen none like that penmanship around the Castle. He was keeping particular care to make sure he could not be traced.

All the glass on the desk was empty and clean, though there were many chemicals and powders on the shelves, along with various objects suspended in liquid. The last jar I came to had floating eyeballs staring back at me. I shuddered. Could it be a simple house of wax? Surely they couldn't all be authentic specimens.

The books were medical texts bound in leather, with the same blocky notations in the margins. There was no trace of dust in the room, and everything was neatly washed and taken care of. It all spoke of a precise mind that thought things through, both before and after.

The skeleton was like one I'd expect to see in a doctor's office, if I'd ever been in a doctor's office that owned a skeleton. The bones were bound together with wire, and the whole thing hung on a metal frame.

There were no bodies, moldering or otherwise, but I had found evidence that *something* strange was happening at the Castle. No one would be able to dismiss my claims, and I pictured myself striding into the offices of the Pinkertons, head high and confident.

But the picture was off. I could see his skeptical face and those disappointed eyes. Would he take one look at what I had and demand a full investigation?

What, exactly, did I have?

There was Mrs. Patterson's vanished notebook that contained evidence of many girls coming and going from the Castle, but I already knew that was a common enough phenomenon here in Chicago. There was the Castle itself, with its strange corridors and unsettling architecture, but that was hardly incriminating of anything other than poor design. Pitezel would have a ready explanation for that.

This laboratory was the strongest bit I had, but even that seemed tenuous as I pictured myself entreating Mr. Pinkerton.

The skeleton wasn't a victim, or else hundreds of doctors across the nation would be guilty of crimes. The same held true for the tissue samples in jars—if they were even authentic.

Pitezel might be guilty of conducting experiments, but that was hardly a hanging offense. I could see him explaining it as a private hobby. The laboratory nothing more than a grown boy's fancy. Men, being men, would be so much more likely to listen to each other than they would to listen to me, a woman.

In my mind, I was being dismissed again already. Once that happened, Pitezel would disappear. The state of this laboratory was proof enough of that. He likely already had a plan in place. All I needed to do was find it. Surely there would be evidence of that somewhere in here.

I did not have hours to go through the notes at my leisure, but I could scan the books more thoroughly. There might be notes or a journal of some sort. Anything physical I could take with me to the Pinkertons.

After going through at least twenty books of varying degrees of scientific focus, I came across a thin leather-bound book with a blank cover. I thumbed through the pages in the flickering candlelight.

JRC—1.15.91—ASPHYXIATION. ACCIDENTAL.

BDH—4.3.91—ETHER. SUBSEQUENTLY DIED OF BLOOD LOSS AFTER THREE DAYS.

DKC—4.7.91—BLUNT TRAUMA TO HEAD. DISSOLVED
IN ACID. TIME TO CONSUMPTION: 3HRS 17 MIN.

Line after line of neatly printed entries, each detailing a grisly death in a few short words. Later in the book, each of those entries were expanded upon.

THE DEATH OF PEARL, HER LITTLE DAUGHTER, WAS
CAUSED BY POISON...I BELIEVED THE CHILD WAS OLD ENOUGH
TO REMEMBER HER MOTHER'S SICKNESS AND DEATH.

Not from a house of wax, after all.

As soon as I realized what I held, I leafed through the entries, desperate to find the one that really mattered. It took a few moments of scanning, but there it was at last:

RP—9.15.92—GAS. TIME TO ASPHYXIATION: 30
MINUTES.
PERHAPS THE SEAL WASN'T AS TIGHT AS INTENDED?
MORE EXPERIMENTATION NECESSARY.

Seeing the words in print was almost physically painful. I gripped the book tighter than I intended, crinkling some of the pages in my hand. It was all I could do not to throw it across the small chamber and begin smashing everything in sight. I closed my eyes, took a deep breath, and tried to calm down. I was too close to my goal to make a rash mistake now.

I glanced above me, convinced I would be found. Surely my luck couldn't hold. To have a detailed log book of all the murders in one spot? Something I could bring with me to the Pinkertons and end this once and for all? What did it matter if the killer had masked his handwriting and didn't mention himself by name? With the proof of the crimes, it would be a small matter to line up alibis for each and see who had the opportunity to commit each.

I scanned through the room, straightening any messes I might have caused. Time to be gone as quickly as I could. I'd leave the Castle at once and take this to Thomas, the Pinkertons, or the police. Anywhere but here would be safer.

Victory!

I hurried back up the ladder, closed the trapdoor, and restored the chest of drawers to their original position, taking care to leave it ever so slightly askew.

Whomever the murderer was, he clearly paid attention to small details. I didn't want to give him cause to think the noose was tightening around his neck. Not until I had it ready for his fall.

Except when I tried to leave the Castle, Mrs. Patterson intercepted me with a laundry list of tasks that needed doing. Mr. Pitezel was down in the pharmacy repairing a door, and did he stare at me longer than necessary?

Perhaps it would be safer to leave at a more opportune moment. The incriminating book stayed on my person, tucked into my top and secured fast against me by my belt.

I deposited Mrs. Patterson's keys underneath a table on the third floor when no one was looking. Someone would find them and return them to her. After that, I busied myself with sweeping and mopping, waiting for the right time to leave.

It seemed everyone was watching me, as if I had a sign hung from my neck announcing my intentions. If the killer knew what I had—how I might reveal him in less than an hour—he would stop at nothing to get in my way. It would be a simple enough matter to follow me from the Castle.

Mr. Holmes had retreated to his rooms, but Mr. Pitezel seemed to be everywhere. After he was done in the pharmacy, I ran into him on the third floor as I was dusting the lamp shades. Then he was outside bickering with a deliveryman over being charged too much. Mrs. Patterson came back to me with more chores at five, and I was kept hopping from room to room straight until nine o'clock.

Even then, Pitezel was still up, standing in the main hallway of the first floor as he worked on fixing a water leak.

Could I have tried to leave and not come back? Certainly. But it felt like too great a risk. If I did anything to make the killer notice me, I risked having him follow me or stopping me somehow. I had to be sure there was nothing to make him suspicious. I'd stayed weeks and weeks in the Castle already. One night couldn't do me in. I had left that letter for Thomas. He might appear on his own tomorrow and save me the trouble of needing to leave at all.

That didn't mean I slept easily. I was up the entire night, one hand on the incriminating journal and the other clenched tight around my knife.

No one tried to enter my room. No one walked past in the hallway.

Tomorrow, it would all be finished.

CHAPTER EIGHTEEN

I suggested that he live with the woman in the Castle for a time,
and later, if his life became unpleasant to him, we would kill
her and divide her wealth. Soon, he suggested it was time to
take his companion's life. This was done by my administering
chloroform while he controlled her violent struggles.

———

M RS. PATTERSON CAME FOR ME at 5:00 a.m., forcing me,
bleary-eyed, out of my room and down to a guest room
where a man had been sick the night before. I'd had the sense to
tuck the journal back into my dress, but when I saw the state of
the room, I knew I'd be there for at least an hour, crouching and
twisting as I tried to clean all the crevices. The journal might well
slip out of my dress, and then where would I be? What if Mrs.
Patterson noticed it? True, she might be as shocked as she should
be, but she might also be in on the crimes. I didn't want to trust
anyone. She stood there, watching me sweat as I tried to get the
stink out of the cracks between the hardwood.

"He made a mess of the bed sheets as well," she said. "Trudy left those in a pile for you down in the washing room."

I stared up at her, my face to dripping from the exertion in the humidity. I felt as if I'd jumped into a lake. A stuffy, warm, rancid lake. "She didn't clean them herself?"

"We don't all have spare time to flirt with the management," Mrs. Patterson said. "Don't forget the towels need folding as well. You're falling behind."

No. Keeping the journal with me would not do. As soon as Mrs. Patterson stalked off to boss someone else around, I dashed back to my room and secreted the journal beneath my mattress, right by the wall, before resuming my task. Two hours later, I was down in one of the storage rooms, folding towels into the neat stacks Mrs. Patterson required. The room was hardly four feet square, with shelves that took up most of what little space there was. Behind me, the light grew dim as someone came to stand in the doorway. No doubt Mrs. Patterson, fresh with more chores I should have been doing hours ago.

I didn't even bother to turn around. "What is it this time?" I asked. "Did a child throw up all over the dinner table? Did someone dump a pile of manure in the hallway?"

Pitezel's voice answered, low and harsh. "You're getting above yourself."

I gasped, whirling and dropping a number of towels to the floor. "Mr. Pitezel! I—I'm sorry. I thought…"

He filled the entire doorframe. "Henry might be sweet on you, but you're still hired to do a job at this establishment, and I'll have no lip from you."

I couldn't have gotten away if I'd tried. Was this how he had dispatched the others? What if there were a secret passage in this closet? I'd inspected it, but there was no way to know. What if this were the way to the basement? Or maybe there was a chute he could push me into. I'd slide down into unimaginable horrors waiting for me below.

Pitezel stepped forward, now no more than a foot away from me. I clutched what towels I had close to my chest, as if they might keep him from coming even closer.

"I knew your sister," he said, his voice a low murmur. "Ruby. I saw the resemblance the moment you showed up here, asking for work. Did she write about me in her letters home, Zuretta?"

I had never used my real name, but why should that be the thing that caused me most unease at that moment? If he were revealing this now, it meant he had made up his mind.

It would take me too long to get to my knife. Precious seconds that would give Pitezel all the time he needed to incapacitate me.

He kept talking. "I saw her writing. Saw her make her little trips to send them off, week in, week out. Even asked her about it. She said it was none of my business. And then she got really comfy with Henry, same as you. Always together."

I swallowed my fear and tried to push around him. "Excuse

me," I said, though my voice came out as little more than a whisper. "Mrs. Patterson wants me to—"

"Where is she now?" Pitezel asked. "What happened to all those happy smiles to Henry? Her hugs in the hallways? She disappeared, the same as the rest. You might disappear too."

My pulse pounded in my ears. I felt faint.

He reached into his suit jacket pocket, and I scrambled to think of what I would do if he pulled out his own knife. The man was twice my size, with strong arms that could overpower me. But before he could show me whatever he was searching for, another person came into view behind him.

"What seems to be going on here?" Thomas asked, and I could have leapt into his arms.

Pitezel froze and glanced over his shoulder. "This is a supply closet. You want the main stairs; they're back down the other way."

"I know that young woman, and I came here to speak with her. Back away from her immediately or face the wrath of the Pinkertons."

I adored seeing the way the blood drained from Pitezel's face when he heard those dreaded words. Didn't he deserve every shred of fear they brought him? Perhaps that was the moment he realized he'd overstretched. That his string of killings or kidnappings was to end now.

But those words might give him the warning he needed. I wanted him caught and imprisoned at the very least. Hanged, if I could manage it. If he ran because of what Thomas had told him...

"It's fine," I said, struggling to keep my voice level. When that didn't quite work, I forced a laugh that sounded slightly better. "Mr. Pitezel was simply talking to me about some tasks I haven't had a chance to finish. Thomas, this is Mr. Pitezel, one of my supervisors here at the hotel. Mr. Pitezel, this is Thomas Chalmers, a man who came to my aid when I first arrived in Chicago."

The two men eyed each other like feral cats arguing over a piece of meat. Not exactly a charming way for your knight in white armor to behave the moment he shows up to rescue you.

"May I have a moment with Thomas?" I asked Pitezel, willing every ounce of feminine wiles I had at my facility into the question. I had no idea if I was doing it in the correct way, but he nodded, turned, and left me alone.

When he was far enough off, I snatched Thomas by the hand and dragged him out of the building, wishing I'd kept that journal with me. When Thomas tried to speak or stop me, I wrenched his wrist and walked faster.

Once we were a block away from the Castle, Thomas grabbed me by the shoulders, forcing me to stop walking. "What. Is. Going. On?"

Perhaps it was the pressure of having been doing this on my own for so long. The thought of having a true ally with the ability to shine the light into this situation it so desperately needed. Or maybe it was because I had thought Pitezel was going to murder me moments before. In either case, my bottom lip began to quiver, and tears welled up in my eyes as I tried to speak.

I clenched my eyes closed, forcing the tears back, and bit down on the inside of my lip hard enough to make it bleed. I took a deep breath, reached up, and removed Thomas's hands from my shoulders, then began to walk at a statelier pace.

"Someone is killing women in the Castle," I told him, and my voice was light and breezy, and there was a smile on my face. No one passing by would suspect what we were discussing. No tales would return to Pitezel's waiting ears.

For the next hour, Thomas and I walked the streets of Englewood. I dumped out every shred of evidence I'd built up during my search. He kept trying to interrupt me, but I forced him to wait, uncertain whether I would lose my train of thought if I derailed it even once. After the first ten minutes, he gave up, too engrossed in the story as it unfolded.

"You're sure it's this Pitezel man?" he asked me once I finished.

"He was about to knife me in that storage room if you hadn't shown up," I said. "I'm as sure as sure gets."

We walked in silence, each of us staring straight ahead. "It isn't possible," Thomas said at last. "You're describing a monster. That might happen in detective novels, but this is real life."

"Jack the Ripper was real enough," I told him.

"The Ripper murdered five women—maybe as many as eleven. Prostitutes off the street. That's the only case we have in modern history. It's because it's so unique that it garnered so much attention."

A group of school children walked by, holding hands as they traipsed through the city streets like a trail of paper dolls.

"If it happened with the Ripper, it could happen in Chicago," I said.

"But the only reason he got away with it was because the murders were isolated. No one knew where he would strike next. You're claiming Pitezel built an entire building for the express purpose of murder, and he's been doing it for months without anyone catching wind. It's impossible."

I shoved him into the entryway of a hardware store. "When I arrived in Chicago and went to the police, they told me how many people go missing. If someone wanted to kill many people at once, Chicago is the perfect place for it. It's happening, and you have to believe me. Come back to the Castle, and I'll show you myself."

His eyebrows shot up, and he glanced behind him, apparently worried someone might try to exit the store and run into us. Or perhaps he was concerned our behavior might be construed as inappropriate. But I was beyond worrying about what strangers thought was right or wrong.

"Fine," he said. "I'll go back to headquarters, and we should be able to have some men out here in a few hours. My uncle won't like it, but—"

"Not a few hours," I cut in. "Now. If we give Pitezel the chance to escape, he'll take it. I'm not even sure he'll be there when we return."

Thomas shook his head. "There's no way I can order detectives to come with me now. I might believe you, but you know my uncle won't without a long explanation from me. So you'll have to choose. I can come right now and inspect whatever you'd like, or we can wait until later and do this right."

I could see his point, and I agonized for a few moments, trying to see my way to the right decision. In the end, simple numbers made up my mind.

"Come now," I said, thinking of the hidden room, the skeleton, and the jars of body parts. The journal. If that didn't convince the Pinkertons to look more closely, I might as well give up now. "I already know where to look, and once you have that proof, you can take him into custody, can't you?"

Thomas sighed but nodded, and we hurried back to the Castle.

CHAPTER NINETEEN

So horrible was this torture that in writing it I have been
tempted to attribute his death to some more humane means;
not with a wish to spare myself, but because I fear that
it will not be believed that one could be so heartless and
depraved.

F OR ALL OF THOMAS'S UNCERTAINTY, he knew how to play the
part of a Pinkerton Detective. He barged into the Castle in
stark contrast to his timid approach before, pounding on doors and
glaring at people left and right.

"Thomas Chalmers, Pinkerton Detective Agency," he repeated
several times. "I'm here to interview Benjamin Pitezel. Where is
he?" All he had to do was follow the stunned fingers as they pointed
the way farther into the building. I trailed along in his wake.

Pitezel was on the third floor, poring over some documents
with Mr. Holmes. They looked up in surprise as Thomas threw the
door open.

"Benjamin Pitezel?" he barked.

It was a joy to see Pitezel's look of sheer astonishment. The way his jaw dropped. How he backpedaled and nervously picked at his suit jacket. "Y-yes?"

"Thomas Chalmers, Pinkerton Detective Agency. I have allegations that you've been leading improper dealings on these premises, and I'm here to inspect those allegations. You will come along with me as I do so. If they prove to be false, you'll have my apologies, and you'll hear no more from me. But, if they are true, I will take you under custody immediately. Do you have any objections?"

I wasn't sure if anything Thomas had rattled off was even remotely legal, but it sounded very authoritative, and the word "Pinkerton" made almost anyone in the United States sit up and pay attention.

Mr. Holmes turned to Pitezel. "Benjamin? What's this all about?"

The man sputtered for a moment, but he leveled off quickly, standing up straight and regaining his balance. "I have no idea. I assure you, however, I am innocent."

Thomas nodded. "Of course you are, sir. But I'd like to inspect the premises nonetheless. You'll accompany me?"

"I will," Pitezel said, and now he glared at me.

"I'm the manager of this building," Mr. Holmes said. "I feel duty bound to come with you as well."

"Excellent," Thomas said. "I'm sure this will be cleared up in no time." He turned to me. "If you'll lead us, ma'am?"

I found myself at the head of a small train of men. I went straight for my room. No sense giving them the time or opportunity to find the book I'd secreted beneath my mattress.

Once we arrived, I pointed to my bed. "Underneath the mattress is all the proof you'll need. A ledger of the crimes."

Thomas stepped forward and picked up the mattress all at once.

Beneath it lay nothing but bare wood.

I gasped and leaned forward, craning my neck to see where the book might have fallen, then taking the sheets off as I scrambled to find it. But no matter how hard I looked, it stayed vanished.

My stomach twisted. *He'd found out.* It must have been the confrontation with Thomas. Pitezel had gotten worried and come to my room. Why hadn't I taken the book with me?

"He must have taken it," I said. "But there's more." Surely an entire room wouldn't be so easily disposed of.

The side room next to mine was as I had left it, the drawers back in place, with no sign of a trap door. I pointed to where it was, however. "Lift that up," I said. "Beneath it, you'll find a ladder to a science lab hidden on the second floor, with no other entrance from that floor."

Thomas shoved the drawers out of the way and ran his hand over the floor. "How does it open?"

I hadn't considered it would be so smoothly shut. "There's a door built into the floorboards," I said. "I'm not sure how it normally opens, but if you had a pry bar, you'd see what I mean soon enough."

This took longer to procure, but Mr. Holmes sent for Mrs. Patterson, who rummaged through the workroom and came back minutes later, pry bar in hand.

Thomas grabbed it from her, jammed it into the end of the floorboard, right where I had pointed, and threw his weight into it. With the amount of pressure he was exerting, any normal door would have popped open easily.

The board stayed firm.

Had I remembered the wrong spot? I cleared my throat and pointed to a different area. "Try there, instead."

One of the floorboards there splintered up, revealing a dusty space beneath it, but nothing resembling a ladder.

I was left speechless for a moment, but I caught my bearings. "He must have sealed it up," I said. "Covered his tracks. But the second floor is a maze, with staircases that lead nowhere. Doors that are nothing more than facades. It…"

Even as I said it, though, I knew what was going to happen, and it did. Pitezel and Mr. Holmes began to speak of complications that happened during the building process. All of them sounded reasonable and straightforward. A series of minor misunderstandings that culminated in major mistakes, though they assured Thomas the mistakes were being rectified.

"I blame myself," Mr. Holmes concluded. "Etta is clearly overtired. We've been working her too hard."

For it to come to that—to not just be disbelieved, but to have people openly question my abilities—was perhaps the worst blow of all.

Thomas's shoulders were no longer quite so square. His chin didn't jut out the same way. "What about the basement?" he asked.

Pitezel's eyebrows raised, and he gave a half smile. "The basement?"

"Underneath the building. I'm led to believe there might be further evidence down there."

Now Pitezel even laughed. "I'm sorry to make light of the situation, but there *is* no basement in this hotel. Another trick of the construction plans. One had been built originally, but the soil in the Chicago area is fickle at best. Later construction efforts decided the foundation couldn't support a basement and three stories above it, so we had to fill it in."

Thomas turned to me, and there I stood, without any explanation at all. I'd put everything I had into this ploy, and now it was falling apart while I watched, helpless.

From there, the men took over. Thomas apologized for his intrusion, and Mr. Holmes waved it off, even as Pitezel glowered and rumbled about lawsuits.

I could tell when someone began to worry more about minimizing damage to reputation than doing the right thing. Thomas had stopped believing me.

He did get Mr. Holmes and Pitezel to commit to not holding it against me, claiming most of it had been a rash misunderstanding on his part. And while it was a valiant gesture, I didn't believe it would do much good. I had shown my hand, and now Pitezel knew what a threat I was.

Would I live out the night?

Thomas had me escort him out of the house. There he paused, staring at me hesitantly. "I believe you believe what you saw," he said at last, his voice low and soothing. "But perhaps you've been working too hard. You've overtaxed yourself. Have you considered going back to Utah? I would still pay for your ticket. You could leave this place. It's a beast of a hotel. How anyone can stay here and feel comfortable is beyond me. I don't blame you for thinking of it as a dungeon of horrors."

"It's Pitezel," I repeated, hating my voice for sounding so weak. "He knows I'm after him now. He might kill me next."

"Then come away. Leave. There's nothing tying you to this place."

Thomas was right. Staying any longer would be a huge risk. Pitezel would know how close I'd come to revealing him. But if I left, I would be allowing Ruby's killer to walk free. And if he walked free, he'd kill again.

I couldn't allow that to happen.

And so I shook my head, feeling my resolve harden. "I'm staying. He can't make me disappear. If he does, and you hear of it, he might as well admit what he's been doing." I stared into Thomas's blue eyes, keeping my voice steady. "I will send you a letter every morning. If I miss a morning, it will be because I'm trapped. Someone might try to say I ran away. That I couldn't face the shame. I am telling you right now: if someone tells that to you, they'll be lying. I'm not leaving here until my sister's killer is in chains or dead."

Thomas winced and sighed. "You're being overdramatic. Can't you admit you've been too focused on why your sister stopped writing you? A reason other than she just wanted to start a new life?"

"You're not listening to me," I started. "I saw her entry, and—"

Thomas cut in, flushing, his arms thrown up. "You're right. I'm not. Because, when I *did* listen to you, I bet my entire family's reputation on you being right. I'm done, Etta. My uncle was right. If you really think you're in trouble, you should leave Chicago."

He turned and walked away without waiting for me to say another word.

I stood there, wondering what in the world I was supposed to do now. All of my efforts had assumed that, when I found something, I'd be able to get help. Was I really supposed to take on the murderer on my own?

"I'm sorry about that," a voice said behind me.

Mr. Holmes stepped up behind me, his brown eyes sad and full of pity.

"Sorry?" I asked.

"For how you were treated," he said. "For ignoring you in front of your friend. I'll admit your story seems far-fetched, but I was watching Benjamin. He's up to something. I believe you're right."

My heart melted in relief, but I hesitated. "Then why didn't you say so?"

"Because Benjamin was too prepared," Mr. Holmes answered, then glanced above him, as if he could see through the floors to wherever the man waited. "He caught wind of your suspicions, and it was clear he was ready for anything. The Pinkertons aren't going to help you. We're going to have to take care of this on our own."

I gasped and took a slight step backward. "What do you mean?"

"You go to him now. Confront him while I listen outside the door. If he tries anything against you, I'll rush in and stop him, but I don't think he will. As you said, anything done against you now will only make him appear guilty. But if you can get him to reveal details of his crimes, I'll testify to what I hear. Now is the perfect time to do it! While he's still glorying in his success at evading capture."

The thought of going into Pitezel's lair and staring him down left me weak in the knees and lightheaded. I shook my head. "It's too dangerous."

"If what you say is right," Mr. Holmes said, "it's far more dangerous to let him go free. He might run away or come up with a way for you to meet an unfortunate accident. We need to strike now, before he has further time to plan."

And when he put it that way, what other choice did I have? I nodded once, though it felt like I was putting a final seal on my fate, and I glanced once more in the direction Thomas had left.

CHAPTER TWENTY

I determined to use this man in my various business dealings, and did so for a time, until I found he had not the ability I had at first thought he possessed, and I therefore decided to kill him. This was done, but as I had not had any dealings with the "stiff" dealer for some time previous to this murder, I decided to bury the body in the basement of the house.

=====

P ITEZEL WAS IN HIS ROOM when we returned to the Castle. Every step I had taken back to the third floor had felt like I was burdened down with a load of iron. My feet dragged. My mind unable to think of anything but the horrid possibilities ahead of me.

He could attack me straight off. Slit my throat before Mr. Holmes had a chance to rescue me. He might snap my neck or shoot me dead. It was one thing to be confident a gun was empty, but putting it to your temple and pulling the trigger still took a certain nerve.

If Mr. Holmes hadn't been there, I don't think I could have gone through with it. But he continued to encourage me and strengthen my resolve. More than anything, it was the thought of trying to go to sleep tonight in my bed that gave me the final push necessary.

Mr. Holmes was right. Pitezel could try to do any number of things to me. He might well be unbalanced at this point. I thought of the time the Harris's bull was startled by a rattlesnake. It had broken out of its pen and run into their barn, and when I'd come to them hours later, it looked as if someone had set off dynamite in the building.

So I climbed the stairs one at a time. Wove my way through the third-floor corridors until I stood outside Pitezel's door, which was outlined with light. From inside came the sound of drawers being pulled open and slammed, papers shuffling around, and footsteps pacing back and forth. The noise of a man unnerved or searching wildly for something.

I stepped up to the door and raised my hand to knock, but froze.

"You can do it," Mr. Holmes whispered to me, and his voice was so reassuring and familiar that I found myself knocking almost without knowing what I was doing. He ducked next to the wall beside the door so as to be unseen.

The door swung open, revealing Pitezel, his shirt untucked and his hair in disarray. He scowled when he saw me. I stood straighter and glared back at him, too foolish to at least refrain from antagonizing the man.

"I want an explanation," I said, and my voice didn't quaver at all.

He grunted. "Seems like you got one back when your friend the detective was here. You were wrong. End of story."

I glanced up and down the hallway, my eyes passing straight over Mr. Holmes, set on not giving away his presence. "Can I come and speak with you in private?" It was only then that I realized how scandalous this would seem. A young woman asking a grown man to visit him in his private bedroom?

The Zuretta who'd shown up to Chicago months ago would have never dreamed of doing this.

After a pause, Pitezel moved to the side, allowing me to pass.

Papers lay scattered all over the floor, clothes strewn across the bed. A far cry from how it had been the last time I'd come there. Pitezel closed the door behind me, and it boomed like a safe slamming shut.

Part of me was braced for an attack right then. The man would rush in to throttle me. But Pitezel simply folded his arms and stood in front of the door, staring me down.

"You've been busy," I said at last.

He didn't respond.

"Thomas's appearance earlier in the day made you worried."

Still no response.

"Hiding the laboratory entrance was a nice touch," I continued, thinking perhaps flattery would open his mouth. "It must have taken some time. I'm surprised you were able to do it without any of the guests hearing."

Pitezel grunted and said, "We packed the walls full of asbestos when we built the rooms. They're soundproof enough. I made sure of that."

He'd threatened me before. Mentioned the possibility of me disappearing, but this was the first time he'd come right out and admitted his knowledge of the inner workings of the Castle. I had to get more out of him. "Why are they soundproof?" I asked, feigning ignorance.

Pitezel chuckled. "So smart when your friends are behind you, and now it's suddenly all gone. Poof!" He made a motion by his head, as if it had exploded. "The girls disappear. But do you know where they go?"

I shook my head, all moisture gone from my mouth.

"Corpses fetch a pretty penny with the right buyer," Pitezel said.

"No one would pay for a murder victim."

He smiled. "They would if they didn't know that's who they were buying. Hard to tell who's who when all the skin and fat and muscle's boiled away. You think that was just a doctor's skeleton in that laboratory? That was Julia Conner. Cute young thing when she was walking around. Her husband worked at the jewelry counter downstairs, until she and Henry took a fancy to each other and the husband stormed off. Left Julia here with her daughter. Little Pearl. Doctors don't pay for small skeletons, though. So only Julia's still around. Lost a lot of weight, though."

The door swung open behind Pitezel: Mr. Holmes entering. Pitezel noticed the movement and let out a yelp of surprise. He tried to slam the door shut, but Mr. Holmes pushed on the other side with such force it threw Pitezel back into the room.

Mr. Holmes squirmed through the opening, and the two men squared off. I watched it unfold, not quite believing what was happening. None of this had been part of the plan, and it had all happened so quickly! Pitezel was wary, his face covered in confusion. He had the advantage on Mr. Holmes by weight and height. I'd seen a few men fight over the years, and I didn't believe Mr. Holmes would be able to walk away victorious. Perhaps Mr. Holmes had worried about Pitezel's dangerous tone and thought he needed to come rescue me before things went too far. Regardless, there was no going back now.

I took out my knife, thankful at last I had a chance to use it and see what I was trying to hit.

"What are you—" Pitezel began, but Mr. Holmes rushed forward, not bothering with punches but going straight into a grapple. The two men spun around the room, crashing into the bed and drawers alike. I jumped out of the way to stay clear of the struggle. Mr. Holmes seemed to be trying to put his arm around Pitezel's neck, and Pitezel was throwing blows whenever he could.

I ducked and weaved around the men in an effort to remain unscathed, all the while looking for an opening to slash out at Pitezel, knowing if he were to defeat Mr. Holmes, I was as good as dead. But the two men were struggling too violently for me to feel any sort of confidence in my aim. For the first while, I managed to guess their path correctly and steer clear of the fray, but Pitezel landed a crushing blow to Mr. Holmes's stomach. He fell forward in pain, and Pitezel began to kick wildly at his head, his eyes wide and his face in a frozen grimace of concentration. He wore his heavy work boots. There was no way Henry would be able to withstand the onslaught, but it gave me the opening I'd been searching for.

I lunged forward, sweeping my knife down in an arc aimed at Pitezel's unprotected side. He casually backhanded me across the face, the blow whipping my head around and making my vision go gray. The knife skittered across the floor.

When I could see again, I found myself lying in the corner in a crumpled heap. Something was jabbing into my side. The men still fought like terrors, with Mr. Holmes giving up on the choke hold and simply punching back at Pitezel.

As I got to my feet, I discovered what had been poking me: the clawed back of Pitezel's hammer. I snatched it up, its handle smooth and cold in my right hand.

When I stood, I stared at the fight, hunting for another opening. Calculating how I might best assist. It was a testament to how soundproof these rooms could be that no one had come to check if the hotel were about to fall down around us.

And then they were locked in a draw, both standing as each struggled against the other. I didn't think. Didn't hesitate. Pitezel stood for everything evil in my life. He had murdered my sister and bragged about it. Killed who knew how many other women. He was the symbol of all the ways men had tried to ruin me.

I brought the hammer back and whipped it forward with every ounce of strength I could muster, bringing it crashing on the back of Pitezel's unprotected head.

The tool crunched into Pitezel's skull with a moist crack, and blood welled around the edges of the wound, streaming down Pitezel's scalp and onto his neck and back.

He gasped in surprise and stiffened, putting a hand to his head.

Mr. Holmes rained punches on the now defenseless man. When he noticed the change in his opponent he stopped for a moment, then scrambled back and patted down his pockets, emerging with a small vial and a handkerchief. Unstoppering the vial, he poured its contents on the handkerchief and then held the soaked cloth over Pitezel's nose and mouth.

Within moments, the man's struggles and spasms had ceased, and he went limp.

Mr. Holmes exhaled in relief, then turned Benjamin around to get a better view of the wound.

"That was quite the blow," he said, sounding surprised. He looked up at me. "You saved my life. Thank you."

I thought myself used to anything the world might throw at me, now. I had been in constant danger and feared for my life. Growing up, I had watched my parents kill animals for food. Death was a common occurrence on a farm. But my eyes would not leave the wound I had created.

"Is he going to…die?"

"It's hard to say." Mr. Holmes inspected Pitezel again. "Much of it depends on how deep you hit him."

He continued, but I couldn't keep track of his words anymore. The room began to spin. Ruby stood in the corner, the same rotting corpse that had been haunting my dreams for weeks. She shook her head. Disappointed in me. "Murderer," she whispered.

Thomas joined her, his face slack with shock. "Murderer."

My head spun even more quickly, and I blacked out.

CHAPTER TWENTY-ONE

I proceeded to burn him alive, saturating his clothing and his face with benzine, and igniting it with a match.

═══════════

I WOKE IN MY BED, SURPRISED to even be waking at all. And for a few blessed moments, I lay there, simply happy to be breathing. But then I remembered the feeling as the hammer crushed down on Pitezel's skull, and my happiness fled.

My entire life I'd been taught how wicked murder was. How hard it would be to ever repent of that sin. If I had taken another's life…hadn't I become as evil as Pitezel himself? I'd wanted to bring him to justice.

Instead I might have ended his life.

I wanted to be sure he'd been trying to kill Mr. Holmes, but I couldn't say that with certainty. They'd been fighting, yes. But men fought all the time without killing each other.

Pitezel hadn't even threatened me. He'd been gloating over his string of murders, true, but he hadn't done anything to show he was about to add me to them, and no amount of scrutinizing my memories came up with anything different.

I had been scared.

But had I killed him? Part of me wanted to rush out and find out this moment, but a larger part worried what the answer would be.

A thought came through, clear and full of hope: the memory of a man who'd been kicked in the head by a horse. The hoof had caved in his skull far worse than the blow my hammer had made, and yet he'd lived for years afterward. He couldn't speak, and he'd had trouble moving, but he had survived.

Mr. Holmes was a doctor. He might have saved Pitezel.

And it was with that shred of light that I got out of bed and got ready for the day, my hands working at my clothes and hair out of rote. As I prepared to go downstairs, I consoled myself with the fact that I'd avenged Ruby. Pitezel would no longer be harming young women, and, perhaps, the price I paid would be worth that.

Where would things go from here? If Pitezel were alive, then I had my testimony and Mr. Holmes to prove what he'd been doing. Hopefully we'd be able to find more evidence of his actions amid the belongings he left behind.

If he were dead, I would likely go to prison. Would there be a trial? The Pinkerton stories always ended with them capturing the evildoer. I'd never paid attention past that.

The house was silent. No guests about. No maids cleaning. My footsteps echoed through the corridors, and the floorboards squeaked and protested my passing. Strange. The halls were loud, but the rooms were silent in this house—like each of us lived our lives. A public face everyone saw, and a private one no could truly understand.

I didn't see a soul until I was on the main floor. Mrs. Patterson was there, her face lined with tears. When she saw me, I was ready for her accusatory looks and any reproach she might give me. Instead, she ran toward me, threw her arms around me, and hugged me tight.

"You poor, sweet girl," she said, her voice quaking with emotion. "It's at times like these we must remind ourselves how precious life is."

There'd been many responses I'd imagined to my actions, but nothing like this. I stood there, too confused to know what else to do.

She ducked her head to my shoulder and sobbed harder. "Think of his wife. His children! He had so much to live for. Why would he throw it all away?"

So perhaps the entire story had come to light. Had Mr. Holmes told the staff what I'd done but explained it by telling them of Pitezel's villainy as well?

I pushed Mrs. Patterson away, wanting to see her eyes. "What happened?" I asked. Better to keep things vague until I understood more.

She raised her eyebrows. "You mean you don't know? It's Mr. Pitezel, my dear. He killed himself last night."

I stumbled backward in shock. "Killed himself?" How could anyone think a man had crushed the back of his own skull in with a hammer?

"Burned himself to the bone, and nearly brought the whole building down with him. Mr. Holmes came across the scene and put out the fire. Too late for that poor, troubled man, I'm afraid."

I rushed back down the hall and through the entire hotel, searching for Henry. What had gone on last night after I had passed out? Pitezel's body had *burned*?

Mr. Holmes was coming back from a walk when I ran into him coming in the door by the barber's. I skidded to a halt, and he glanced from side to side before hurrying toward me, taking my arm, and pulling me back to one of the storage rooms.

"I thought you'd sleep longer," he murmured to me.

"What happened?" I asked. "Pitezel was burned somehow? How did he…"

Mr. Holmes stared at me, his eyes fierce and intense. "You were never in his room last night. That didn't happen. At the very least we can shield you from any scandal. As best I can figure, Pitezel's conscience caught up with him last night after our confrontation. While I was taking you to your room, he must have come to. He doused himself with benzene and set himself alight. I came across him burning and managed to sound the alarm. We put out the fire before it spread. Pitezel might have brought down this entire structure with his guilty heart. I've been to see the police, and they're on their way to inspect the premises. It's vital you stay with that explanation."

The statement left me speechless. It was too much, too fast, and so my upbringing took over. I shook my head. "No," I said. "That's not right. That's not honest."

Mr. Holmes checked around us once again. "What's not honest about it? I carried you to your room after you passed out. Pitezel was bleeding himself out on his floor, and I had no idea what I was to do with him. In between the time it took me to get you situated, he recovered enough to end his life in a horrible manner."

I backed up. "But we don't know why he did. Perhaps he was overcome with pain. No reasonable man would burn himself to death. I played a part in it. I have you as my witness of what he was trying to do before I struck him. Surely the law will be lenient." My words sounded hollow in my ears. I could already picture the judge staring down at me as I tried them in court. If I didn't believe them, who would? And it was so tempting to let the lie stand. Such a relief to think I might not have to admit to the world what I'd done.

Mr. Holmes shook his head. "Far better to never let this go to trial. Benjamin was a horrible man. Think what it will do to his wife and children if that becomes splashed over the newspapers."

"But won't their names be tarnished no matter what?"

"There's a strong difference between suspicion and fact. Let people wonder," Mr. Holmes explained. "Besides, there's the reputation of my hotel at stake as well. I'll be ruined if this is revealed. If you won't do it for yourself, please do it for me."

I'd already thought I'd committed the most heinous sin imaginable. Compared to that, a simple lie seemed innocent enough, especially after I'd told so many others. I wouldn't have done it to save myself. I felt that I should pay for what I had done, but it didn't make sense to make others pay as well. Shouldn't Pitezel be held somewhat accountable?

"I want to see it," I said, the words tumbling from my mouth before I even knew I would speak them.

Mr. Holmes frowned. "See what?"

"The body."

"Why?"

"To know it's over. I want to see it, Mr. Holmes."

He sighed. "Fine, but on one condition."

"That is?"

"You stop calling me Mr. Holmes. The two of us have been through enough together. I think it's safe for you to call me Henry, don't you?"

I flushed, then nodded, my eyes sinking to the floor.

Mr. Holmes—no, *Henry*—escorted me to the third floor. Pitezel's room reeked of smoke and something I couldn't identify. Most of his belongings had caught fire as well. The entire place was blackened and charred, and in the middle of it all lay Pitezel himself.

Henry saw me flinch back and pulled at me, trying to get me to leave the room, but I shook him off.

Of course they hadn't covered the body. The police would want to see the scene exactly as Henry had found it. I forced myself to step into the room, and then I recognized the other smell.

Burnt flesh.

The fire had not been kind to Pitezel. His clothes were completely gone, leaving in their wake nothing but ashes. I had expected that. His body, however, was much different than my imagination had painted. I'd assumed he'd be nothing more than a charred remain, like wood after fire has swept over it. But his flesh wasn't just black; it was mottled red and white, some of it bubbled and blistered where the fire must not have burned as hot. Bones peeked through in areas, and there was far more blood than I'd been ready for.

Stranger still, he appeared smaller than I would have expected. In life, Pitezel had been so imposing. So strong and muscled. But here he was now, and it was as if all that might had evaporated. Did his muscles just burn away?

I could only stomach examining the body for so long before I simply had to turn away. There was the rest of the room, after all. (Anything to avoid looking at the wreckage that had been Pitezel.)

For a moment, I allowed a stray beam of hope to distract me: the fire would have uncovered a hidden compartment or a sealed-up wall, and I'd discover the infamous torn suspender button on Pitezel's trousers, or mementos from all the missing women. Anything that would give physical evidence to what he had done.

For his death had taken away the chance for concrete answers. Who he had killed, and why. Why would a person do that sort of thing to another person? I believed in evil in the world, for I'd seen enough of it in my life. But there was such a difference between beatings and cruelty and outright murder.

And the entire Castle has been built to facilitate those killings. The winding corridors. The confusion. The heavy feeling of oppression and grief that washed over me in some of the rooms and hallways. Evil deeds had occurred within these walls, and I longed to understand why.

But there were no hidden chambers or compartments. No ripped suspender button revealed itself in the wreckage of Pitezel's room, and no matter how much I tried to ignore the body in the middle of the floor, it still crouched there, its lips charred away to give it a permanent smile or grimace, its hands held up to ward off an imagined blow.

"He was alive when he did this?" I asked.

Henry shrugged. "He must have been, though I wouldn't hazard to guess how much he knew of what was happening. You mustn't worry yourself about him. He was a monster, and he deserved his fate. All he did was hurry along what the courts would have done eventually."

This *thing* had murdered Ruby. Why did I feel guilt about its fate? The world was a better place without him in it.

I turned to Henry. "The police won't suspect anything? I can't imagine Thomas will ignore it, which means the Pinkertons might get involved."

He spread his hands wide. "Let them."

"A body found like this in the middle of a hotel? The man I accused yesterday of murdering numerous women? This story will be all over the newspapers by tomorrow."

"I think you overestimate the interest this will attract if we don't give it more material to ignite."

"How so?"

"The Pinkertons were here already. How would it look to the public if it turned out their representative had done nothing to try to apprehend the villain? 'We never sleep' is their motto. But if Pitezel is as evil as we know he is, and the Pinkertons walked away? They did nothing *but* sleep in this case. I doubt they even inform the police what they already know. And the police have better things to do with themselves than scurry off over suicides. If we say nothing, this will go away."

The idea that my life might resume—that I'd be able to exist without Ruby's killer loose, and that I could simply enjoy Chicago without some sort of overarching mission hanging over me—was too appealing.

In the end, I agreed.

I went down to my room and wrote my letter to Thomas, as I'd promised I would. I explained that Pitezel had committed suicide and thanked Thomas for all his help and support and told him his services were no longer required.

The police came, and the police went. I pretended to be as shocked as the rest of the staff, and they paid me no special attention.

The officer even seemed bored, asking me the same questions he asked everyone else. Did I know Pitezel? Did I have any reason to suspect he was suicidal? Had he been acting strangely?

I lied. It made my stomach twist itself into knots, but if the police had done their job in the first place, I wouldn't have been left to investigate on my own. Why punish myself now that they were taking interest?

True to Henry's promise, the police left with little fanfare. The mortician was called. The body was examined and removed, and Mrs. Patterson began directing the efforts to clean and sanitize the room.

I volunteered for the duty, of course, because there might be evidence I needed to hide or clues I might uncover. Though neither of those occurred. By the time it was over, however, I needed to go to someone not connected to any of this. A place where I could recover a shred of normalcy.

I showed up on Phebe's doorstep at ten in the evening. Her hair was tousled and her eyes roaring with irritation when she opened the door, but all of that vanished when she saw me. Wake Phebe up after a long day and face her wrath, but she was a true friend no matter how tired she might have been.

"It wasn't your fault," she told me bluntly after the tea had been poured and I was halfway through my second cup. She'd listened to everything I'd said, all of the events bursting out of me one after another. "Simple self-defense."

"But I lied about it," I said, her words not making the guilt go away.

"People lie about a lot of things. Sometimes it's the best choice. Just be glad you're through with the man. You did it, Etta! He attacked you, and you still managed to come away from it. If I'm being honest, I was half convinced I'd be at your funeral before the summer was out. That or wondering where you'd disappeared to. If the worst that comes from this is a bit of guilt over a lie, that's still a happy ending as far as I'm concerned."

"And the answers?" I asked. "What about those?"

"Easier to get answers when you don't have a bloodthirsty demon lurking around the corner. That Mr. Holmes is on your side now, and he runs the place. Give it some time to die down, and then the two of you can get to the bottom of it all. What you need now is time, though. A good night's rest, and it'll all seem clearer in the morning."

She was kind enough to let me sleep there, but I did nothing but stare at the ceiling for hours. It reminded me of the first few days of my time in the city, searching for my sister and coming back to Phebe's each night to wonder what the future held. Now that I knew, what would I have told myself back then?

If only I could learn to forget the feel of the hammer crushing his skull. The thought of his body, the flames curling up and around his skin. And the sickening remnant of flesh that he'd left behind.

My mind kept churning, flicking back and forth between my memories of Pitezel alive and that of his charred body. Of Phebe's reassurances and my own doubts. Something didn't add up, and I was desperate to figure out why.

CHAPTER TWENTY-TWO

It will be understood that from the first hour of our acquaintance, even before I knew he had a family, I intended to kill him, and all my subsequent care of him and his, as well as my apparent trust in him by placing in his name large amounts of property, were steps taken to gain his confidence and that of his family so when the time was ripe they would the more readily fall into my hands.

———

I WALKED INTO HENRY'S ROOM THE next morning. He sat at his table, poring over the newspaper, perhaps for any sign of articles about what had happened at the Castle.

"It wasn't him," I said.

Henry looked up at me, his forehead wrinkled in confusion. "Excuse me?"

"Pitezel," I said. "That wasn't his body we saw in his room. It had to have been someone else. He's still alive."

Henry laughed off my statement. "Preposterous."

"His remains were too small," I said.

"Fire does strange things to a corpse, I suppose. Isn't a log much smaller once it's burnt?"

I shook my head, insistent. Phebe had been right. Everything had been clearer this morning, even if I hadn't slept well at all. I'd gotten up and come straight back to the Castle, leaving with my friend rooting me on. "What makes more sense: That the villain burned himself after suddenly being overcome with guilt or that he burned some other victim to fake his own death, once he knew the noose was tightening?"

Henry sighed and stood, walking around his desk to place his hands on my shoulders. "You've been thinking about this too much, and I don't blame you. It's been a horrendous week. With what we've been through, even the hardest soul would crack under the pressure."

He pulled me into an embrace, wrapping his arms around me. I fought off the desire to give in and let myself become a sobbing wreck. What if Pitezel were truly alive? The man began to take on an inhuman figure in my mind, able to conquer even the powers of death to inflict his bloody desires on my life.

I tried to push back from Henry, but he held me close, and I relented, accepting the hug in the consoling spirit it was intended. He patted my back. "Pitezel is dead. He can't hurt you now. But what *can* hurt you is dwelling too much on these dark deeds. I understand where you're coming from. Ruby, Minnie, Anna—it's enough to make us want to give up. Could you do something for me, though?"

He pushed me out of the embrace so he could look into my eyes. "Come with me to the exposition?"

"The fair?"

Henry nodded. "It'll help take our minds off our sorrows and give us the strength we need to make it through whatever else might come. Part of me wants to become purely analytical and dive into the endless details that must be taken care of. I need to contact Minnie's family. Need to confront the horrors Pitezel might have left behind. But can't we set that all aside, at least for one day?"

When phrased that way, it made sense. I'd been forcing myself too hard. No wonder I was having nightmares of rotting corpses and ominous threats. Perhaps if I gave myself some time away—some perspective—it wouldn't seem as insurmountable.

Perhaps if I'd done that earlier, I never would have wounded Pitezel at all.

"Fine," I found myself saying, and Henry beamed at me so happily I cast my eyes to the ground, unable to maintain the gaze.

Henry whirled into action, directing Mrs. Patterson to keep the hotel running in his absence, and ignoring the flurry of objections she made. He gathered his jacket and wallet and stopped in to see some of the various shopkeepers and assure them all would be well. Somehow, he even managed to make it sound like he believed that.

For me, every shadow contained a waiting threat. The thought of Pitezel lurching along behind me caused me to stop and cast a backward glance more than once as we walked from the Castle over to the exposition.

Ruby and I had dreamed of visiting this place long ago, and now look at us. My sister murdered, and I a murderer. The exposition had seemed like a fairy tale as we heard about the many wonders it would hold. A lake for boats. Museums bigger than towns. People from all around the world assembled in a fair that would rival even the wonders of Paris from a few years ago. Paris had its tower, and Chicago had its wheel made by Mr. Ferris.

Now I was going there at last. What would it have been like if I'd gone with Ruby back on that fateful night? Would I have been able to save her from Pitezel's clutches, or would my skeleton be grinning next to hers in some doctor's lab?

All of that was in the past, however, and I resolved to do my best to keep it there for today, just as Henry had suggested. I'd had plenty of practice pretending life was fine even while my father was making it anything but each evening.

The crowds thickened as we approached the gates, a sea of people jammed together to get into the exposition. Short, fat, tall, thin, white, brown, and more. Exotic languages and accents. Strange styles of clothing. It was everything I'd felt when I'd first come to Chicago, all over again.

And then we were through the gates and into the open spaces of the fair. I had to stop for a moment to take it in. Enormous white buildings with pillars and manicured lawns. Statues and fountains. Vendors crying their wares around open squares.

There were so many things to see and do. Moving pictures on a thing called a kinetoscope. Strange food, from "shredded wheat" to "Cracker Jack." Ingenious creations. I marveled at a new invention called a "zipper" that somehow managed to bind two pieces of cloth together with metal teeth, and then unbind them just as easily.

Throngs of people had a new type of camera made by a company called Kodak, which was renting the devices. There must have been so many pictures of each building and statue that someone could have made a book out of them.

Not all the inventions were so innocent. Someone had come up with a way to kill a man by strapping him to a chair and shooting electricity through his body. They said it would be more humane than hangings, but it made my skin crawl and brought images of charred flesh to mind. I quickly moved Henry past the display.

Of course, he'd brought Minnie and Anna here so many times, he had the entire place memorized. But he seemed to enjoy seeing my reactions, and it was all new and fresh enough that we were able to escape the terrible events and focus on the moment.

"The buildings are really temporary?" I asked Henry after an hour of wandering the grounds.

He nodded. "They weren't built to be lasting. They'll be gone in less than a decade, I'd wager. What else would people use them for? This fair is just for the people who can make it here now."

We weren't able to get tickets for the Wheel until the evening, but Henry assured me it was a sight better seen at night. "The exposition is spread out before you like a million stars. It's as if you're soaring above it all and lighter than air."

So the day went by in a pleasant haze, as I allowed all the new sights and sounds to wash over me. They were almost always enough to keep my mind distracted, and Henry clearly wanted to ensure I never dwelled on Pitezel. It was flattering to see the lengths he would go to entertain me, acting quite the fool from time to time, just to see me smile or laugh. It was a new experience for me, who had always been content to tuck myself away into the shadow of my sister.

And no amount of antics or cavorting that day could erase my concerns completely. I would find myself examining the suspenders on the trousers of passing men, still idly engaging in the habit before I reminded myself the fiend had been found, if not (perhaps?) eliminated. And when that would happen, I'd search through the crowd, wondering if Pitezel might be out there, following us.

It was preposterous, of course. No one attacked us. There were no signs of Pitezel other than the ones my frantic mind created out of thin air.

As dusk began to fall, Henry rushed me to the Canals of Venice, an area that looked just as it was named. "What's the hurry?" I asked as he pulled me along. It had been a day filled with strolls and meanderings, and my feet had long since begun to protest.

"I want to surprise you," he said, smiling.

At the Canals, we boarded a gondola, and the gondolier pushed us out into the water, Henry sitting facing me, his eyes bright and full of excitement. I half-frowned at him in confusion, then realized how I was enjoying myself, and how inappropriate it was.

The area exploded with bright white light as they switched the electricity on. It was as if someone had turned on the sun in the middle of the night. I gasped and smiled, and Henry was right there in front of me, drinking in my every expression.

"Do you like it?" he asked.

"It's incredible," I said. "I'd seen it from the horizon, but I never imagined…"

There were light bulbs along the rooflines and inside the buildings. Lights on the columns. Lights along the shoreline, as if someone had painted with electricity, and the World's Fair was the perfect canvas. It had wide-open greens with sight lines that let you see many buildings at once. Plazas to gather in with beautiful fountains in the center of each, and now each one's water jets were streaked with light.

"How did you know when it would come on?" I asked.

The smile drained away from his eyes and became more wooden. Forced. "I've been here often enough, and I surprised Minnie…" He clapped his hands and shook his head to clear it. "No gloomy thoughts tonight. Live in the moment and forget about everything else."

We enjoyed the rest of the gondola ride, though the magic

bubble had been pricked. Still, we did our best, and when we were back on land, my mood brightened once again as I realized the time for our ride on the Wheel had arrived at last.

To look at Ferris's Wheel in the day was to be filled with skepticism. According to the brochure, it towered 264 feet into the air: two giant rings of metal holding thirty-six cars in place, each of which could hold sixty people, if you believed it. If it looked tall from far away, it was taller still once it was dark and you were standing next to it, craning your neck and wondering how it would feel to be at the top of the circles.

Henry and I joined the other fifty-eight people who would be making the journey with us, and our car rumbled into position. It, too, was made of metal and wood, and as we filed in, nerves fluttered in my stomach. It only grew worse as the door shut and the car left the station.

The entire vehicle rocked back and forth like a swing! I lurched from side to side, trying to find my balance and convinced we were moments away from crashing to our deaths. I was not the only one to be so afraid. Several others—men among them—exclaimed in fear as we continued to rise, though the sounds turned more to astonishment than terror as we arced ever higher.

Outside, the fair continued to unfold. Bit by bit, as each subsequent car was unloaded and loaded again, we ascended to the top, soaring like a bird. The city spread out before me, and it truly did seem like I was above the stars, with all those twinkling lights below.

It gave me goose bumps, and I put my arms around myself to try and fend them off. Henry, noting my action, removed his jacket and draped it across my shoulders. Ever the gallant host. The car fell silent as we all stared out at the exposition.

Across the car, someone exclaimed, "Fire!" and then the car was full of a different kind of silence. I scrambled backward, pushing against the wall as I thought of being trapped helpless, hundreds of feet above the ground, while I burned to death like the charred body in Pitezel's room. Everyone else looked up as one and spotted what had actually caused the call: not the car itself, but a building across the grounds of the fair.

The whole car shifted as people crammed toward the side with the best view, and I worried for a moment the weight would cause us to topple. Was it designed to handle this? Surely all the other people in all the other cars were doing the same thing this instant, causing the weight of the entire Wheel to move to one side. It could strain the welds holding the two circles together, and an image of us plummeting to the ground once again flashed through my mind.

I held back from the press of the crowd, unwilling to contribute to my potential demise, though Henry pushed forward with the rest of them. Still, I was able to see the basics of what was happening.

Orange flames lashed at the air from atop a tower, and a group of spectators were already around the base of the building, staring up at the unfolding drama. Firefighters rushed in and scaled the outside of the building, pounding in stakes to the wall to use as a crude ladder. They worked their way a hundred feet into the air without anything to prevent their fall.

I stepped farther back to the other end of the car and tried to calm myself. Looking anywhere else felt cheap to me, however. Why should I be enjoying the view while lives were in danger?

Henry was pressed forward with the rest of the group, craning to get every glimpse, his white shirt almost bright in contrast to his dark suit, since I still had his jacket around my shoulders. As he went on tip toes to try to see around a particularly tall man in front of him, I noticed his suspenders at the back attached to the pants with two buttons on each strap, yet the one on the right hung loose, with only one button fastened.

It must have come undone at some—

A chill washed over me, like ice water on a cold winter's morning.

I stepped forward to get a better look. Stray threads sprouted from the spot where the button should have been. It had been torn away, and I knew as soon as I saw them that I had the matching piece of fabric in my dresser back in my room.

Torn from the pants of the man who had attacked me in the middle of the night at the Castle.

Ripped from my sister's killer.

Dr. Henry Holmes.

CHAPTER TWENTY-THREE

As soon as he had ceased to breathe I cut his body into pieces that would pass through the door of the stove, and by the combined use of gas and corncobs, proceeded to burn it, with as little feeling as though it had been some inanimate article.

———————

HOLMES HADN'T NOTICED MY SHOCKED expression. He was too busy focusing on the fire down below. I was proud I didn't panic. I did what any good detective would do: analyze the situation and choose the best response.

I could yell out for help from the others, but they were all strangers, and I was a woman. I'd had plenty of experience to this point about how the words of women held up against the words of a convincing man. Whether in here or on the ground at the fair, Holmes would no doubt explain to anyone I ran to how the fire had made me hysterical, or some other nonsense. And he was persuasive. He'd succeed.

Running was another option. Once we were in the chaos of the exposition, I could lose him in the crowd. He might waste an hour or two looking for me, and in that time, I could rush to Thomas or the police. But how many times had I relied upon men to save me, only to be disappointed?

I'd been burned too often to give it another chance. There had to be another way, but the only tool I had at hand was the fact I now knew him for what he was, and he was unaware of it. I could use that surprise as my chance.

No doubt Holmes thought it highly amusing, to ape around the exposition with the sister of one of his victims, all the while duping her into believing he was her friend. My insides clenched with anger.

Had he planned to kill me later this evening, or was he hoping to see how long he could keep me deluded? Perhaps he'd even propose marriage to me. He'd killed his last two fiancées. (At least!) How could I have thought he was simply unlucky? And what about Pitezel?

The time for worrying about that was past. I would have to focus every effort on showing no changes to him now that I knew the truth. He couldn't find out, or else the consequences would be too dire for me to imagine. To do that, I would need to come up with some explanation. I knew myself too well to think I'd truly be able to fool a man as accomplished at the art as Holmes.

But my time hunting for Ruby had made me quick on my toes. When Holmes glanced back at me, I was quick with a horrified look, using the fire as a justification for the change in my demeanor. He gave a quick grimace of commiseration but returned to his study of the battle against the flames.

The firefighters had reached the upper windows of the building and had pulled up hoses behind them. For a moment, it appeared they'd conquered the disaster. A chorus of cheers erupted from below as water spouts burst through the flames from inside the building.

Moments later, the fire exploded to new heights, and those cheers turned to screams. The firefighters began to pour from the building, shadowed shapes against the brightness of the flames, some of the men fully engulfed as they leapt clear of the chaos, choosing a quick death to the horror they were experiencing.

One man, still unburnt, tied a hose to a girder and used that to slide down to rescuers below. Seconds later, another man tried the same feat, only to have the hose burn through partway. He screamed all the way until he crashed into the earth, and I couldn't help but think once more of the charred, unrecognizable corpse sprawled on the floor of Pitezel's bedroom.

All through this, the Wheel continued its revolution, taking us back to the same place we had started.

As the carnage worsened, I was joined by others in the car, and at some point it became too macabre for most to continue gawking at others' tragedies. The rest of the trip was much more subdued than the ride up had been. Holmes put his arm around me, and I forced myself to lean into him, because wasn't that what I would have done five minutes before?

All the time, I was considering my options. Appealing to strangers was out. I debated trying to kill Holmes for a moment. My recent experience with Pitezel made me realize I was no cold-blooded killer. No, I'd want to trap Holmes. Keep him captive so I could bring Thomas back into the picture.

And the moment I thought of that—trapping Holmes—the plan sprang into my head, fully formed. For hadn't I been dreaming of the vault in his office for months? Perhaps God had sent those dreams to me as a sign. If I could get Holmes in there, all my problems would be solved.

Since I'd arrived in Chicago, the one thing I could depend upon men for was to underestimate me. If I could turn that to my advantage—use it to get Holmes to do what I wanted…

Together we walked off the wheel and back into the crowd. Holmes hoped to head toward the burning building, but I pulled him back. "I can't," I explained. "It's too…"

"You're right," he said. "I'm sorry. I got caught up in the moment. It's late. We should be heading home."

Which was exactly what I wanted. I tried to think of how I would be acting under normal circumstances. I couldn't feign to be bright and cheery, because I'd just seen a terrible tragedy. But if I was too brooding, would Holmes get suspicious? I needed to surprise him if I was to have any hope of bringing him to justice.

And then I realized I'd been mute for at least a hundred yards. I needed something to discuss. Didn't I? "The fire was terrible," I blurted out, then cursed myself as soon as I'd spoken. As if a fire were a matter for casual conversation.

"I'm sorry you had to see that," Holmes said, and he sounded sincere. Did he expect me to swoon into his arms? Turn to him for comfort? He'd been flirting with me all day. I grit my teeth and edged closer to him, allowing my arm to brush against his.

He reached down and took my hand, his grip gentle and light. I pictured my hand trailing along the skin of a rattlesnake, and it was a struggle not to flinch away. Instead, I ducked my head and gave Holmes a half smile. Let him think I was being bashful and shy. But I also gave his hand a slight squeeze. What I hoped seemed like appreciation.

At least it excused me from needing to talk.

I thought through my options if this plan went awry. If his hand clenched around mine like a vise, showing I'd been caught, I'd do everything I could to escape. Holmes was a man, yes, but he wasn't a foreboding figure. If I'd been up against Pitezel, I would have been in trouble, but Holmes seemed like a person I could fight and walk away from victorious. His strength was found in his guile, and I was immune to that now. He wouldn't surprise me.

Part of me *wanted* him to catch on so that I no longer had an excuse to humor him. If he knew I was on to him, then I'd no longer have a chance at tricking him, and I could lash out. I could smash my knee between his legs, and I was quite sure he'd fall to the floor the same as any man. At that point, it was just a matter of kicking the soft spots: stomach, face, neck. True, I'd never tried such an approach against my father, but that was because I'd been cowed.

I wouldn't make that mistake against Holmes. But the walk continued, and we stayed hand in hand. Perhaps all my practice over the last few months had prepared me enough to pass this final test.

"Would it be too forward of me to ask what your plans are for the future?" Holmes asked me.

Watching as you're hung by the neck until dead. "What do you mean?"

"Do you think you'll be able to return to cleaning hotel rooms after all you've seen and done?"

"Oh," I said. "I-I'm not sure if I can stay on at the Castle. The memories…"

"Would…would you be interested in staying on in another role?"

Now I frowned in true confusion. "What do you mean?"

He cleared his throat. "I know it's not the most appropriate… but we're almost in the twentieth century. Don't you believe the time has come for us to put outdated thoughts behind us?"

My frown deepened. "Outdated thoughts?"

"Etta, would it be wrong of me to admit I'd noticed you since the day you arrived at the Castle? That perhaps I even came to feel something for you that first day? At the time I wondered why, shocked I would even consider anyone other than my sweet Minnie." He trailed off once again, and I said nothing.

At last he continued. "Perhaps you reminded me of my earlier love for your sister. And, as I've seen you work, I've come to admire you. You're brave. Fearless. Watching you fight against Pitezel..."

I dropped my hand from his, unable to continue to touch a man who would talk of such things at a time like this. Instead, I folded my arms across my chest, continuing to walk. But then I reconsidered. He must be kept distracted until the time came for the next part of my plan. Would it work?

"I don't know if I'm ready to discuss such things," I said. "It's all been a whirl. Forgive me."

He forced a laugh, sounding every inch the rueful suitor. "No. I should be asking your pardon. It was ill-timed."

We strolled in silence once more, the street mostly empty this far from the exposition and this late in the evening. Englewood was far from downtown, after all. As we proceeded, I began to have second thoughts. Was this really my best choice?

Several possibilities went through my head, some more outlandish than others. I could pretend I was going to kiss him and then smash him over the head with a pipe. Or I could get hold of some ether and use it to knock him out. What if I claimed to be frightened and asked him to accompany me to a police station, where I then accused him in public? Perhaps he had a gun somewhere in the Castle, though I'd never found one. A gun might even the field considerably.

Each of the ideas were dismissed one by one. Pipes and guns

weren't going to magically appear out of thin air, and I had no idea where I might obtain ether. Asking to go to a police station might alarm Holmes too much.

Our footsteps echoed off the street. It was late, and the buildings stood like gravestones on either side of us, tall and intimidating and uncaring. The Castle was getting ever closer, and I wouldn't come up with a better plan. We were alone now. If I tried to scream and run, he'd be on me in an instant.

"In a hurry?" Holmes asked me.

I had quickened my pace and was now practically pulling at Holmes to get him to speed up. "Oh," I said, then laughed nervously, something which didn't require any acting at all. "I'm…I suppose it's just unnerving."

He nodded, the gas lights casting a yellow light on his hat, which left his eyes hooded in shadow. All you could easily see was his mustached mouth and chin. "There's no shame in that. We had our day of fun, and now we must return to deal with the problems we did our best to forget."

The problems he had caused. But I kept my face blank, my eyes downturned, and only nodded. "You're certain Pitezel cannot harm us?" I asked, laying foundation for my plan.

Holmes put his arm around me once again, and it was all I could do not to shove him away or claw at his face. "He's dead, Etta. All your worries are unfounded."

"I don't see how you can be so certain," I said. "It's not as if we all see burned corpses every day. How can you know what fire does to a body? It was so much smaller than—"

He stopped and put his hand under my chin, forcing me to look up. His eyes were nothing more than glints under his hat brim, and I wondered how I'd ever looked to this man for comfort or thought him charming. Could I keep my feelings from showing? The street was deserted, and his hand was inches away from my neck. All he had to do was turn it and squeeze, and I wouldn't be able to make a sound.

I should run. Push him down and flee. Pound on a door and cry for help. Who was I, to try to do something so foolish? This man was a cold-blooded killer, and I was a nobody from Manti, Utah. A girl so idiotic that she lived for weeks with this monster and never saw him for what he was.

Behind him, a vision flickered in and out of existence. The sea of rotting women who had haunted my dreams, all of them in different states of decay. Each of them glaring at Holmes.

I gasped. There was no way to hide it. Holmes's eyes widened, and he glanced behind him. "What was it?" he asked. "What did you see?"

The street was empty. But I had to have some reason for my fright. Something he'd believe. I tucked my head down and pushed myself into his chest.

"I've been having nightmares," I said, my mouth muffled against his shirt. His jacket was still around my shoulders. "For weeks. The ghosts of all Pitezel's victims have been visiting me while I slept, calling for vengeance."

He laughed. "Nightmares of ghosts? Etta! You're on the verge of hysterics. This is all the more reason to get you home and into bed. I've read about cases like yours in medical school. You need sleep and rest."

"But they were there," I said. "On the street. Behind you. And they all looked so angry at me."

"Tomorrow, we'll go to the police," Holmes told me, his voice soothing. "Anything to make you calm down. Okay?"

What I wanted to say was "By tomorrow you'll be in chains, and then I'll be calm at last," but I only nodded. Better to have him think me hysterical. It would make what came next that much easier to believe.

We walked the rest of the way in silence. It was simpler not to speak, and I pretended to be terrified and in need of comfort, forcing myself to tuck my head down and press it to his shoulder. That devil was all too ready to pat my back and tell me all would be well.

At last the Castle loomed into sight. I recognized the shops on either side of us. The bakery that sold those marvelous rolls. The shoemaker's shop where I'd gotten my boot fixed two months ago. One hundred yards to go. Mere seconds until I had to begin. I focused my mind and went through the steps. I'd have to be perfect in the performance, but I thought it was in my reach.

When we were fifty yards away, I straightened. "You're right," I said. "I can't let myself live in fear."

We walked ten more steps, and I raised my eyes to stare at the Castle. At those ugly, ungainly walls. The jutting windows. The haphazard design. And I screamed into the night air as loudly as I could, putting every shred of fear and frustration and anger into my voice as my hand jutted up, pointing at the third floor.

Holmes stopped short, his eyes going to where I was pointing. A gust of wind rushed past us, clutching at my skirts and tearing at my hair. "What is it? What did you see?"

Several windows opened along the street, people putting out their heads to see what had happened.

"It was him!" I said, putting a tremor into my voice. "Pitezel. In the window of your office."

Holmes frowned and checked again. "The light is off. You couldn't have seen anyone, even if they had been there."

"What's going on down there?" a voice called out. "Has someone died?"

"Nothing!" Holmes shouted back. "She saw a rat and took a fright. That's all."

The grumbles on both sides of the street were audible, and windows shut once more, but not before a couple of people complained about "silly women" and "hysterics over nothing."

A rat? As if I'd respond like that to a simple rodent. But I bit my tongue and continued to pretend sob as I pressed myself into

Holmes's shoulder. "It was him," I repeated. "He's alive, and he's going to kill me."

Holmes took me by the shoulders and shook me. "He's dead," he hissed. "Why can't you believe that?"

I raised my head to stare at him. "Are you saying I've gone mad? I know what I saw."

He groaned and pulled me into motion again, hurrying us to the Castle. "We can settle this easily enough."

The building was silent when we entered, our footsteps echoing with every step up the stairs. Holmes moved quickly, his fingers digging into my arm. I held back, focused on keeping the pretense of being convinced we were walking to our doom.

We reached the hall that led to his offices. My heart beat faster, and my throat tightened.

Holmes threw open the door and switched on the gas lights, going through the different chambers one at a time, flinging open closets. "Do you see? No one here. There never *was* anyone here." He was the very picture of a man confident in his knowledge, mostly patient as he described the way things were to a foolish little woman.

I trailed along behind him, trembling as I peered into each of the rooms. When I got to the vault, I gasped (not wanting to screech too loudly and wake the guests—not for what I had planned ahead) and stumbled backward, pointing once again.

Holmes frowned and walked back so he could see into the vault. "What is it?"

"It's Pitezel," I said. "In the vault? Can you not see him?"

He stepped forward, closer to the vault, then glanced back at me. "You need rest, Etta. You're delusional."

"He'll kill us all!" I gasped.

When Holmes turned once more to look in the vault, I rushed up to barrel into his back and propel him into the vault. Once that was accomplished, all I had to do was slam the door closed and turn the lock, capturing the man in a place where he could do no one harm, and giving me the time I needed to get the police and the Pinkertons involved.

That was the plan, at least. It would be glorious. As I reached out to push Holmes forward, a vision of the future flashed through my mind. Mr. Pinkerton apologizing for the way he'd treated me. Offering me a spot in his company, and praise for my tenacity. Thomas looking on, beaming with approval.

But at the last moment, Holmes twisted, turning his body so he dodged my shove. I stumbled forward into the vault instead.

I tried to catch my balance, but I'd put all my faith in that one simple move. There was no going back. I fell to the floor of the vault, the iron cold against my palms and knees. I spun around, but Holmes was already standing there, his form outlined by the light behind him.

"You finally spotted the missing button, didn't you?" His voice was devoid of emotion. "I noticed you'd held on to it for all this time. It was endearing, really. Watching you search every man's trousers when you thought no one was looking. Sometimes I'd wear those pants just to spite you, always turning to keep the missing button out of your view. It was an entertaining enough game, for a time. I admit I didn't think you'd be able to see it this evening in the car, though it was exhilarating knowing you might when I gave you my jacket. I have to thank you, Etta."

"Thank me?" He was talking, which meant I still had time. But to do what?

Holmes nodded. "These past few months have been some of my most enjoyable. It's likely your fault I killed Minnie and Anna when I did. They weren't nearly as captivating as you were."

"What happened to Pitezel?" I asked.

He shrugged. "You'll find out soon enough." Holmes reached into his pants pocket and emerged with a syringe.

I scrambled to my feet as he held the syringe to the light, tapping it to remove any stray bubbles.

"Often I use ether or chloroform," he said, "but they're too unreliable, and I respect you far too much to resort to such cheap tactics. This will be far more suitable. You'll want to struggle, I'm sure, but believe me when I say it will go much better for you if you—"

I tucked my head down and barreled forward. The man wasn't as solid as Pitezel. Perhaps if I had enough speed, I might still push past him. But, once again, Holmes anticipated my move. Instead of trying to grapple with me, he stepped to the side and stuck out his foot. I tripped over it, landing with a thump on the floor.

He was on me in a moment, pushing aside the collar of my dress as he tried to stab me with the syringe. Suddenly I was back in Manti, my father bearing down on me, his belt at the ready. A surge of panic lent extra force to my movement, and I twisted my way free of the man. My left elbow landed a solid blow on his temple, and he groaned in pain and frustration.

I was able to roll to my right and work my way clear of him, scrambling to my feet and racing to the door. If I could just get someone else to hear me. A guest or Mrs. Patterson or anyone at all.

The door was locked, and I pulled and twisted at the knob in frustration. I pounded on the wood and screamed as loud as I could, then whirled around to see Holmes bearing down on me once again, his face cast in shadows, the needle still ready.

I darted toward one of the windows. If I could break it and scream out into the night air, then at least someone might—

Holmes anticipated the move, grabbing my wrist and then jerking me off balance. I fell to my knees, sobbing in terror as he pulled my arm up and back, threatening to pop the entire limb out of its socket.

"This will be much easier for you if you'd just stop fighting."

I thrashed back and forth again, but the pain in my arm was too much. Something pricked me in the back of my neck, and everything went black.

CHAPTER TWENTY-FOUR

I asked her to look about my offices and finally to look within the vault, and, having once passed that fatal door, she never came forth alive. She did not die at once, however, and her anger when she first realized that she was deprived of her liberty, then her offer of the entire forty thousand dollars in exchange for same and finally her prayers are something terrible to remember.

———————

S HADOWS FLICKERED ACROSS THE CEILING.
  I awoke gradually, like a series of veils lifting from my eyes, one at a time. Each almost transparent, but put enough of them in the way, and they were impossible to see through.

My eyes didn't want to focus, and I tried to reach up and wipe them, but my arm wouldn't move. When I attempted to use my other hand, that arm was stuck as well, though my mind was still groggy enough that this didn't make much of an impact on me. Perhaps I'd merely slept in an awkward position?

When I tried to roll over and discovered I couldn't, I knew something was seriously wrong.

I blinked and shook my head to clear it. And that was when everything rushed back. The torn button. The confrontation with Holmes. Getting captured.

I thrashed from side to side, trying to free myself from whatever bonds might be holding me. And in the process, I discovered I was spread-eagled on a table with rope tying each of my limbs in place. The bonds cut into my skin as I struggled, the pain sharp and fierce, clearing my mind further.

Complete panic took over. I screamed and cried, twisting so much that my joints came close to popping. He would get me. Cut me. Torture me. My nightmares flashed through my mind. I was going to die. Why had I ever thought I was up to this investigation?

As I continued to struggle and make no headway, my brain caught up with my instincts. This was doing nothing more than hurting myself. If I was going to get away from Holmes's clutches, I'd need to keep my wits about me. My mind wasn't bound, but it might as well be if I didn't give it the freedom it needed to focus. I had to come up with a plan, and that meant analyzing my situation.

I stopped moving and took a few deep breaths, willing my heart rate to slow and my thoughts to calm.

Concentrate.

The room was long and squat. Large enough that the far reaches were bathed in shadows, and short enough that I guessed a tall man might have to stoop to walk between the exposed rafters. If I arched my head back, I could see a furnace of some sort burning behind me, its fire providing the one source of light in the room. Why it was burning in the middle of the summer was beyond me. Who had stoked it? Did they want it to be so sweltering down here? Basements should be cool in the summer, not like this.

The floor was dirt, piled high in places and packed hard in others with no real pattern to it. Two feet to my right, a severed arm lay on the ground, its stump ragged, as if it had been hacked off by a blunt knife.

I squealed in fright when I realized what I was looking at, scrabbling against my bonds to try and get farther away from the thing, though that did nothing. My breath came in quick gasps, sweat streaming down my forehead. I wanted to explode. This was a scene straight from my nightmares, and yet I knew this was no dream. The details were too precise. The smell of the earth. The coarse texture of the rope against my ankles. The hard pressure of the wooden table beneath my back. The phlegm in my throat.

Why was I trying to be quiet? What was I afraid of?

I screamed again. Loud and long. Screamed until my throat was raw and my lungs ached. But the room seemed to have a way of absorbing all the sound, or my ears grew used to the noise. Certainly no one noticed my calls for help. There were no footsteps from above. No shouts for the police.

And there's only so long a person can be terrified.

Eventually I calmed down again, reminding myself every moment I was down here was another moment I had that I might be able to think of something that could help me when Holmes returned.

Because it was most definitely "down here." I was in the basement of the Castle. Staring at the ceiling, I could even get a feel for the layout of the floor above me. Those beams over there supported the floor of the pharmacy. Behind me would be the jewelry counter, where, even now, a man might be picking out a ring for his beloved. I'd arrived in the very place I'd wanted to find all this time. I'd just found it in the worst possible way.

Knowing where I was and what I might expect, I turned my attention once more toward a systematic study of the room. What else did it contain? Where would Holmes be coming from when he arrived?

There was a ladder on the wall toward my feet, leading to a trap door between the rafters. When Holmes opened the door to come down, whatever soundproofing he'd put in place would be weaker than otherwise. I could scream then, and hope and pray someone might notice.

That was a helpful thought. I needed more of those.

It was hard to think helpful thoughts when so much of me wanted to dwell on other courses of action I might have taken. Why hadn't I gone to the police last night? Why had I shrunk back from accusing Holmes in the middle of the car on the Wheel? I'd told myself no one would listen to a woman over a man, but was that really the cause? Or had I wanted to capture Holmes on my own? To not let someone else get the credit?

Or my knife! I'd spent all these months strapping it to my leg every morning, and then when the time had come for me to use it, I'd shied away. I should have tried to stab Holmes in the back instead of simply shoving him. Maybe it would have gone better for me.

I concentrated, shifting my hips and my legs as much as I could, trying to see if I could feel if the knife had been removed. It was hard to tell, spread-eagled as I was, but I thought at least the strap was still on my thigh. If only there were a way for me to reach it.

My throat was parched from all the screams, and it was hot and stuffy in the basement. The air smelled stale and rotten. Stagnant and full of the reek of mice. I breathed through my mouth more than my nose, though that helped only a little.

I studied every aspect of the room, craning my neck until it cramped from the awkward positions I forced it into, then resting it and craning it again once I could.

My first focus was the arm.

It was a woman's arm. That much was clear by its slender shape and delicate hand. Someone young, and dead for a quite some time, judging by the state of the flesh. My guess would be Anna's or Minnie's, and I only prayed whoever it was taken from had already been dead when it was hacked off.

Other body parts were scattered around, though harder to see and in much worse condition. Dusty bones. A hand in the corner. Rib cage over by the furnace. Something that might have been a skull in the far reaches of the room, bathed in shadow.

Holmes had been busy.

The room had two other tables. Blood caked their surfaces, and, coupled with the trays of knives, pincers, and surgical implements, it didn't take much imagination to think what Holmes might do to his victims. When I thought of the pain and misery this room had seen, I became physically ill, and I had to concentrate on something else—anything else—to take my mind away from the brink of madness again.

Why?

I kept coming back to that simple question. Why would Holmes do such a thing? Why kill so many people? He didn't seem insane, and he was far from sadistic in his everyday life. I'd spent hours around him, and I hadn't seen anything "wrong" with him. Nor had anyone else.

And yet, the lengths he'd gone to with his obsession were horrifying. How he'd lured so many women into relationships with him only to kill them.

A grating sound interrupted my thoughts. Metal on metal, somewhere above me.

"Hello?" I called out. "Help me!"

The grating stopped, and then was followed by a series of

muffled thuds, culminating in an object slamming into the floor twenty feet to my left. It made a crunch as it landed.

I stared at the flesh-colored pile for a moment, my mind unable or unwilling to process what it was. But then I picked out the arms and the feet, and once that happened, I was amazed I hadn't spotted the face right away, though it was in far from pristine condition.

Pitezel looked much worse in death than he'd ever looked in life. His skin was now tinged gray, and he was completely naked. None of his body was burned. (So whose corpse had Holmes used upstairs as a decoy?) He'd landed on his head, and the crushing of his neck and skull had been the sound I'd heard moments before.

You did this to me.

I wanted to turn away from him, but I couldn't. This could be my fate. Perhaps it's what I deserved for being so blind to Holmes.

"I'm sorry for killing you," I said, or tried to. All that came out was a muffled croak.

And Pitezel didn't want to listen to my excuses.

The fires of the furnace began to dim, turning the light from bright yellow to dull orange. My throat became ever more parched, and I ached for a drink of water. The circulation in my limbs was poor, as they were constantly stretched. The ropes dug into my skin, itching and irritating it.

Time was difficult to gauge. I guessed I'd been awake for two hours, judging by the way the fire had died down. It was almost dark now. As time continued to drag, I began to wonder whether

Holmes planned to see me at all. Perhaps he'd leave me tied to this table until thirst and hunger did me in.

Pitezel's body twitched.

It was hard to tell with as dark as it was, and I stared long and hard at it, waiting for another movement.

His one good eye blinked, then again.

I struggled against my bindings, thrashing my arms and legs in a futile effort to get away, and reopening the cuts I'd made in my wrists and ankles previously. But I was still just as caught as before.

Pitezel cocked his head to the side with an audible crack, and he gasped. His arms and legs unfolded. They, too, had been broken in the fall. His right forearm bent in the middle, and, when he stood, his left foot folded to the side as soon as weight was placed on it. The result was that he balanced on one foot and one ankle.

I called for help. No one heard. No one came.

"You did this to me," Pitezel said. He reached up, took hold of his head, and turned it back to face forward. "Always snooping and prying and thinking you knew everything. But you didn't, did you? And now you're worse off than I am."

"I'm sorry," I tried to say again, but once more I couldn't manage more than a croaked vowel or two.

"What's that?" Pitezel asked. "Apologies? Too late for that, poppet." He stepped toward me, his gait unbalanced and lilting. The bones on his left ankle tore through the skin and dug into the dirt beneath it. He struggled to lift that leg high enough to make complete steps, and the jagged bone left a trail in the dirt as it passed.

He came to stand to my left, looming over me as he stared into my eyes. The fire was bloodred at this point, casting its color on everything it touched. "Not that I didn't deserve it," he said with a little shrug. Or an attempted shrug. His shoulders didn't line up, and the movement made his head flop forward once again.

After he had righted it, he continued. "I did know what was going on, after all. Mr. Holmes always enjoyed the fun bits, but when it came to disposing of them after the fun was over, he didn't care much for the follow-through. He'd perk right up once the bones were boiled and the skin had sloughed off. But he didn't have much use for dead meat. Nothing to experiment on. Nothing to scream when you poked it."

Pitezel reached out a finger and prodded my rib cage. I shrieked at the contact and tried to edge away from it.

Another voice spoke from the other side of me. Ruby. "Can't get upset by a little prod," she told me, and appeared in my vision, smiling down at me. Though it was hard to tell if she was smiling on purpose, because her lips were almost completely rotted away now.

Ruby laughed. "Always thought you were so resourceful. You were going to change everything. Avenge me. Avenge us. Didn't work out that well, did it?"

"I tried," I said, my voice trembling. "I didn't see it until it was too—"

"Oh," Ruby said lightly, interrupting me and glancing at Pitezel. "She tried. Well, that makes it all better, doesn't it? As long as you tried so hard, then I guess none of the rest of it matters."

Pitezel chuckled and nodded. "After all, she got away from her daddy for a few months, didn't she? Got to see the big city and the exposition. Got to pretend to be a detective. A grand adventure, I'd say." He placed a hand on my left thigh. It felt like a scorpion perched, ready to strike.

"Very," Ruby added.

"I could still get away," I stammered.

The two of them broke up in laughter. Pitezel's head fell backward, and Ruby's lower jaw popped one of its hinges so that it swung below her face, almost falling off completely.

"You're not getting away," she said. "Not ever again. You're going to join me. Join us."

"*If* I let her waste away like you," Pitezel said. "A juicy morsel like her? Would be a shame not to have a taste before she turned."

"Be my guest," Ruby said. "I don't care about failures."

I frowned in confusion as Pitezel leaned back over me, grabbing onto my hair with one hand and my left shoulder with the other. And then he surged down at my neck all at once, his teeth ripping into my flesh with a wet squelch.

I screamed and struggled, writhing this way and that, wishing I could escape. Panicked at what was happening. That went on for seconds. Minutes, perhaps, until I noticed there was no pain.

I opened my eyes. No corpses stood above me. I checked the floor at my left. Pitezel's body still sat there in the same position it had landed in.

Another nightmare. Nothing more.

Though, when Holmes decided to show up, something told me it would be much worse than anything I'd dreamed.

CHAPTER TWENTY-FIVE

The location of this store was such that it would have been
hazardous to have sent out a large box containing a body,
and I therefore interred her remains in the store basement.

———————

I HAD NO IDEA HOW LONG I was in that basement alone. Long enough for the fire to completely die, and then long enough for my parched throat to be in agony. For my tongue to begin to swell and me to wonder what it felt like to die of thirst.

Long enough for several more hallucinations. More visits from Pitezel, Ruby, and the other victims. They were each more horrid than the first, and it seemed there was nothing my imagination was not prepared to show me in excruciating detail, depicting women I'd never seen before in real life, filling in the blanks to flesh them out.

I began to wish for Holmes's visit, if only for him to bring an end to this existence. Would I go mad before he arrived, or would he ever arrive at all? Was it the lack of water making me see those apparitions? Perhaps they were reality, and the interludes between them were when I slipped into unconsciousness.

It must have been a full day before anything changed, though I saw no hint of light anywhere. No sign the sun had risen, although it became more sweltering and stuffier, as if the fires of hell had been stoked, ready to greet me.

But I had no way of really knowing, and that was its own form of torture.

The heat had begun to subside (perhaps) when the trapdoor at the top of the ladder opened. A dim pool of light appeared on the floor, cast from somewhere high above. The second floor perhaps? Or could it have been the third? Having gone so long in darkness, it felt like a small anchor of stability had returned to me. I knew which way was up and down, and I was grateful. All my plans on shouting for help once the door opened had fled. My throat was too dry for anything more than a parched gasp, though I did try to call out as hard as I could.

My voice wouldn't have gotten the attention of a person across the room, let alone of someone on a different floor.

The light lessened as someone climbed through the door and descended the ladder. I lay there praying Holmes would kill me quickly, but I doubted I would be so lucky.

He had brought a lit candle with him, its flame casting unsteady light into the room. Holmes walked over to stand above me, his face clouded with worry.

"I didn't mean to leave you down here this long unattended," he said. "There were more police by today, asking questions about poor Benjamin, and I had to ensure no one caught wind of my operations. I even had to shove his body down the shaft without proper preparations. Shoddy work, and I might end up paying for it later. The skull was already damaged from your hammer blow, so it might be difficult to find a doctor who'll buy it. Hopefully he kept you good company."

I closed my eyes, tears leaking from the edges.

Holmes fumbled at his belt and took off something metallic, from the sound of it. His belt buckle? Moments later, he was dribbling water into my mouth. I lapped it up eagerly, and it was fresh and cool, and I didn't even consider until afterward that Holmes might have poisoned it.

At some point, I became less focused on drinking and more focused on coming up with a way to turn this situation to my advantage. Holmes seemed genuinely contrite. What sort of a human could do the things he'd done and yet still feel bad for the person he'd endangered?

At last the flow of water trickled to nothing. The canteen had been large, but it was empty. "I can bring more in a few hours," Holmes told me. "I don't plan on sleeping much tonight. You and I should have plenty of time to get this done."

A chill ran down my neck. "What do you mean?" I asked, and I was pleased to hear my voice working better. With the thirst gone, my body was reminding me of all its other woes: The cuts on my wrists and ankles. The way my arms and legs were unnaturally positioned.

"I like to take my time with this," Holmes said. "Especially with someone who proved to be such an excellent competitor."

"What are you talking about?" I didn't want him to leave. To give him more time to cover his tracks and prepare for whatever was coming.

"The resemblance between you and Ruby is clear," he told me. "I was so impressed to see a girl of your age appear. To show the sort of resolve it took to travel here from Utah. Ruby never thought you'd be able to leave your home. Not even for the wedding. She died well, if it's any consolation. No sniveling from your sister. A much better death than some of the other girls I've killed. I sold her skeleton to a medical university, right after I collected the insurance money."

"What?" I pulled against the bonds that held me tight, slowly, so as not to alert Holmes to what I was doing. But they were still as firm as ever.

"It's not all fun," Holmes told me. "When I can, I try and get the girls to take out insurance policies on themselves. That was my mistake with a couple of the richer ones. Families go into mourning, but insurance companies go into action. They send investigators around. Whisper the most alarming things into the wrong ears. It's why I didn't bother with you. Don't take it personally."

Holmes might as well have been discussing the weather, or what we were to eat for supper.

"Why are you doing this?" I asked.

He shrugged. "Talking to you? Because I so rarely get a chance for people to appreciate what I've accomplished."

"Killing people," I said. "Why?"

Holmes thought for a moment, frowning in irritation. "I'd say it was the money, but that would be a lie. Control?" He stood there in silence, staring at a piece of wall to my right as he mulled the question over.

"Feelings," Holmes said at last. "I do it for the power it gives me. It's addictive, and I grow to crave it when I don't have it. It's a game. Picking out a victim. Seeing how much of her trust I can gain. Testing how much I can reveal of my true self without her catching on. If you had tried to call out in the car last night, I would have had to kill you earlier. I was happy you didn't, but even I couldn't tempt fate any further. Not even for the game."

He was dead inside. How had I missed it before? This was a *game* to him? "How many have you killed?" I asked.

"I haven't actually counted in quite some time. Well over a hundred, I'd guess. Probably closer to two?"

The ease with which the number slipped off his tongue, and the sheer size of it, left my head spinning. Hundreds? "There's no way," I blurted out. "You never could have—"

His face clouded over. "No way? I don't think you're in a position to judge what I can and can't do. You came specifically looking for me, and see how you ended up. I've had plenty of practice, and I'm careful. Extremely careful. Part of that means I don't prattle on with my victims. Even the ones I respect."

He turned and used the candle to light several gas fixtures around the basement. Somehow the bright light made things even more grisly, as if what I'd been staring at for hours had been some imagined story, yet here it all was, just like it had been in the dark. The dismembered arm. The bones. The other body parts. The torture instruments.

"What are you going to do with me?" I called out, frightened of the response, but more worried not knowing.

He busied himself assembling an array of pincers, scalpels, knives, and saws. He picked up a heavy scale and lugged it over to the table next to mine, then brought a notebook bursting with stray papers and placed it next to the scale. From there, he began assembling a series of vials and jars and bottles, some of them empty, some of them not. And he put on a long jacket that might have been pure white at some point in its history but had met far too many stains since then—and I could imagine how he came by them.

"You're going to torture me to death?" I asked, and once again, my voice betrayed me, cracking and shaking. My bottom lip quivered, out of my control. My eyes fixed on one of the steel saws: an enormous thing with sharp metal teeth, more like one of Father's farm tools than something a doctor might use on a person.

The thought of it digging through my flesh, cutting into my bone, sent my heart rate spiking even higher.

Holmes smiled to himself and continued his work. He began sharpening the knives, taking them to a leather strop and a whetstone one at a time, examining the edges for nicks.

He had wanted to talk to me for the first while. Had been content answering a few of my questions. But now he wasn't. What had changed? I scrambled to review our conversations. He'd gotten angry when I'd questioned how many people he'd murdered, and he'd ignored me since then. If he kept ignoring my questions, I might as well be dead. I needed him to react. Respond. And to do that, I'd have to try the one thing that had gotten results.

Taking a deep breath, I focused. I closed my eyes and tried to find a center somewhere within me. And did I pray for God's help? With every fiber of my being. Never mind whatever doubts I'd harbored in years or weeks or days past. I'd take any help I could get, and I'd need some of it to be divine if I were going to see another sunrise.

My bottom lip stopped quivering. My hands ceased their shaking. I opened my eyes and turned toward Holmes. "You're not smart enough," I said in a matter-of-fact tone.

He paused his sharpening for a moment. Long enough for me to know it was in response to my statement, though he tried to mask it by resuming his chores as quickly as he could. This was all the encouragement I needed.

"It's clear what you're trying to do. You've been to medical school, and you fancy yourself a doctor, don't you? Though if you were worthy of the title, I hardly think you'd be tinkering around in a poorly constructed basement of a shoddy hotel that isn't even in downtown Chicago. You're a failure, and you hope to make up for your inadequacies by taking it out on unsuspecting girls. You're a coward."

He continued to ignore me, though the blood rose to his face. I tried not to think too closely on what he would do in response when he snapped.

Instead, I forced a smile and hoped it seemed genuine. "I see the blush creep over your face. You know what I'm saying is true. Coward. Spineless and gutless and unable to make it anywhere back east. You slunk out here to make yourself feel like you were good at something. And now that I'm not playing along with it, it makes you angry, doesn't it? You want me quivering with terror, not telling you what a pathetic excuse of a man you are."

He sprang to his feet, rushing over to the table next to me and slamming some of the jars into place.

I laughed at him, encouraged by the increased emotion. "What an inept little toad you are," I said. "The only reason you've been able to get away with it is because no one in this city has cared to follow you. No one's bothered to look, though I wouldn't be surprised if you hadn't killed even a tenth of the number you claimed. Two hundred? More like a dozen, if that. Six, I'd guess. Or less. You can't even—"

"No!" he screamed, lunging at me and slamming a scalpel into the table right in front of my eyes. It stood there, quivering, inches from my face. "You don't get to make those claims," he sputtered, spittle flying from his lips. "I know what I've done, and I know what I'm doing."

"Coward," I repeated, keeping my voice level and controlled. The wilder he became, the less emotion I tried to show.

"No," Holmes repeated.

"Look at you. Tying a seventeen-year-old girl to a table, leaving her to starve for a day, and only then trusting yourself to come down and face her. If that's not the sign of cowardice, I don't know what is."

He picked up the scalpel and sliced at my dress, carving open the skirt in one quick motion. It took a moment before pain registered with me. He had cut into my leg as well. I wanted to scream. Wanted to run and hide. But I forced myself to ignore the pain.

"Is that supposed to make me quake in terror?" I asked. "You can't even muster the courage to kill me with my arms untied, and I'll be damned if I give you the pleasure of hearing me beg for my life like this."

Holmes pounded on the table with his fists. "No!" he shouted at last. "You don't get to ruin it. I was going to make it easy on you. Give you something for the pain. Do it the right way. But I will not stand for this!"

He sliced at the rope with a knife, cutting my arms free, the blade snapping the corded twine with no trouble at all. I gasped as my arms fell back into something like a normal position, my muscles in more agony now they were free.

Holmes cut my feet loose as well. In that brief moment of freedom, I brushed my hand against my leg, feeling for the outline of my knife. With the blood still tingling in my limbs, it took twice to be sure, but then there was no mistaking: it was still strapped to me, waiting.

If only my hands could grip anything. I needed time to recover.

Holmes picked me up and slung me over his shoulder as easily as a man might move a bale of hay. But the ceiling was low, and he had to crouch as he carried me to the far reaches of the room where a vat sat. A squat, long rectangular pool that held a black liquid. He rammed my back into a rafter, and dust rained down from the ceiling. It sizzled where it landed in the vat.

Acid.

When I left Manti, I'd thought I'd have to learn a whole slate of new things to cope with on my search. And I had. But perhaps the biggest asset I'd had all along was the same one that had served me so well against Father all those years: my ability to keep getting up, even when I hurt.

I'd carried my share of animals around the farm. I knew how the weight could shift and make it difficult, and I knew how to roll to transfer my own weight as Holmes stepped away. Put the pressure over to the ball of my right foot and drop my hip and turn...so.

Holmes toppled to the floor, off balance, one arm moving forward to catch him before he fell face-first into the acid bath.

As he did, I pushed away from him, tumbling to the ground myself. I rolled away, trying to put as much space between us as I could. The movement and sheer terror helped me move my legs and arms no matter how much they protested. I staggered up into a crawl, and then a run, desperate for a place to hide. Behind me, Holmes cried out in pain, accompanied by a faint sizzling noise.

I turned to face him, my hand darting up underneath my dress and ripping away the knife, strap and all. Holmes's face twisted in pain, his left hand cradled against his body. "You're going to regret that," he said through clenched teeth.

My knife was still in its sheath, and I shook the blade clear and waved it back and forth in front of me. What did I intend to do with it, though? I had no training on using a knife in a fight. Did Holmes? He surely had more experience with inflicting pain than I did. I wasn't sure I'd be able to beat him in a fair fight, even with one of his hands burned by acid.

There had to be a way to even the field more.

He'd only lit the lamps in the corner of the basement where he'd kept me. The other areas remained bathed in shadows. I backed up, keeping my eyes on him as I retreated farther into the darkness.

Holmes spent a few seconds grabbing a roll of gauze, wrapping it around his injured hand as he watched me retreat. He smiled then, an expression with more than a hint of snarl in it. "I should have known you would have put up more of a fight," he said. "My mistake to underestimate you. It won't happen again."

As I continued to back up, my right foot hit open air, and I had to whirl my arms for a moment to catch my balance. I glanced behind me: I stood at the edge of an open grave. Waiting for my body, perhaps? Or for what pieces of me the monster couldn't sell off? Other graves lay next to it, five or six in all, some of them with higher mounds of dirt than others.

Holmes hadn't rushed me in my distraction, but he'd advanced. "I will enjoy this. I'll have to. It will be harder without Pitezel's help for the next while. Not that he helped me all the time, but it was nice to have someone handle the bodies once they were of no use."

He still knew where I was. If I was going to be able to strike out at him, I'd need to do it from a direction he didn't see coming. I knew from Father how much stronger men could be than me, and I worried about wasting whatever chance I had to beat Holmes.

I turned and ran away as fast as I could, turning left to where the light could reach, back behind the furnace or oven or whatever it was Holmes had built down here. I was sure he would chase me, confident even now he was closing the distance, his hands reaching out, grasping for my hair. Any moment, I'd be jerked back and come face-to-face with him looming over me.

But the hands never came.

Instead, I ran face-first into a brick wall, narrowly avoiding knocking myself out, though I was still left breathless.

He laughed again, his voice muffled by the dirt floor. "It won't do you any good," he said. "You seem to think the darkness bothers me. I've spent hours down here. Days. I'm as comfortable here as I am in my bedroom. More, perhaps. Here, I don't have to hide who I am."

My breath came in gasps. Holmes was a figure outlined in gaslight, a faceless monster stepping toward me. Inescapable. I edged against the wall and kept going to my left. Maybe there were would be a pile of boxes or a chest. A place to hide or set up a trap.

"I built this place," he continued. "Planned out every inch of it, from the mazes on the second floor to the airtight rooms. A house where I could have complete control. I've bricked people into rooms. Suffocated them with gas at night. Burned them in a kiln down here. I've boiled their bodies and sold their corpses to doctors eager for specimens. There are passages between walls. Places for me to peer out and see what the tenants are doing. I've watched you sleep just as I watched your sister before you. Looking forward to when you would finally understand."

Sooner or later I would come to the corner of the building. He knew it. I knew it. Somehow, I'd have to come up with a solution before then. And still he advanced, speaking all the time.

"At first I did it for money. Insurance policies, mainly. But, after a time, I did it to pass the time. It's a sort of entertainment better than anything else I've found. That feeling of desperation you feel rolling off a victim. They'll say anything. Do anything. Just to escape. Just to think they might be free again, even though they know better. Why would I let a witness escape? You don't maneuver your way into building the Castle without being able to make meticulous plans and see them through. You have to hide what one construction crew did while you're persuading another to do something nonsensical."

My arm hit something other than brick. I reached out, fumbling around as I tried to decipher what it was. It took a moment before the rungs became clear: a ladder. Suddenly attacking Holmes seemed far too risky. If I could get out, just for enough time to scream so people could hear me, it would be over. This entire hotel rested on people remaining ignorant of what was really going on.

I began to climb.

It wasn't until I was on the fifth rung that I realized Holmes had gone silent. My body froze of its own will, my ears desperate to hear where he might be.

A hand snaked up from beneath me, wrapped around my ankle, and pulled me off the ladder. I kicked out as I fell, my foot making solid contact with something. He cried out in frustration or pain, and the two of us landed in a heap on the dirt floor. My hand hit first, the ground knocking the knife clear of my grip.

I whirled to face Holmes, slapping and clawing at any piece of exposed skin on him that I could. I gouged at his eyes, ripped at his cheeks, my knees jutting up into his stomach and groin.

He fought back just as fiercely, batting away my attacks and punching me in the ribs before clasping his hands around my throat. It might as well have been a vice, crushing the air out of me. We rolled until he was on top of me, staring down into my eyes, his face outlined by the distant gaslight. His eyes were two empty pools.

I was going to die. He was going to kill me as he'd killed Ruby and countless others. Worse yet, I was going to *fail*. Fail just as I'd failed to stand up to Father. And no one would know, and no one would care.

I might as well have been a gnat for all he cared about my blows to his face. I didn't have the strength to follow through with them, so I gave up that attack and, with my last ounces of energy, felt around my head blindly for something. Anything that might give me an advantage.

And then I brushed against it: the hard, sharp edge of a blade, cutting into the back of my hand. My eyes widened as I realized what it was—as I listened to myself choke and gag to death. As my legs spasmed beneath me and Holmes pressed his full weight on my chest.

I moved my hand and gripped the knife in a quick motion, then brought it up as hard as I could, stabbing Holmes deep in the shoulder.

He cried out, his grip loosening on me. I repeated the blow before he could recover, making two more quick strikes on his unprotected back before smashing the handle into his right temple.

And then I was full of energy and fury, rolling over so that now I was on top of him, operating on pure instinct. I punched him three times in quick succession: his ear, his jaw, his mouth. A bloody tooth sailed out between his lips. His eyes were closed, and he lay there, unconscious.

But I still wasn't satisfied. I raised the blade up, readying to smash it down into his eye and end him once and for all.

Except I paused, staring down at the shape of his lifeless body in the dark. This wasn't the plan. I wanted revenge, yes, but I wanted it in my own way. Not his. I'd like to say I spared him because I knew it was God's will, or because I had a merciful heart, but that would be a lie and only make my sins worse.

Mercy wasn't what stayed my hand. Selfishness was. Killing him would do nothing for me. It would leave too many unanswered questions, and it would deprive me of something I wanted even more.

Recognition.

I wanted people to hear about what he had done and to know I was the one who had stopped him. To have the Pinkerton agents be forced to admit what they'd let fester under their noses for years. I wanted to gloat, and I wanted this waste of human breath to suffer in prison and then be hung for his crimes.

If my heart had been full of mercy, I would have simply put the knife down then. Instead, I slammed the hilt into his shoulders, his arms, his chest. Aiming to do as much damage as I could.

I might not have wanted Holmes to die, but that didn't mean he should avoid suffering. Once I was through with him, it would be a miracle if he walked anytime soon. He wasn't going to woo any ladies anymore, with his jaw being in the condition I left it.

And for a moment (while I was catching my breath and debating whether I was finished punishing the man or not, for using a knife that way is tiring work), I thought I saw Ruby's ghost, standing behind Holmes's body and staring down at the ruin of a man.

She looked up at me and nodded once, her face bathed in shadows. She turned and left. I cast the knife away, got to my feet, and dragged him back to the light, where I bound his hands and legs with the remnants of rope that had held me captive all day. After that, I tottered up the ladder to go find help.

My sister's shade never visited my dreams again.

CHAPTER TWENTY-SIX

The eighteen intervening months I have passed in solitary
confinement, and in a few days am to be led forth to my death.

P INKERTON HEADQUARTERS DIDN'T SEEM NEARLY as imposing as it had months ago when I'd come to it on my first full
day in Chicago. This time, I was dressed in clothes I'd purchased
with money I had earned. It was a week after the incident at the
Castle. Enough time had passed for the news stories to die down
(somewhat), though I had plenty of people recognize me on the
street as I walked downtown.

Bringing the most infamous murderer since Jack the Ripper to
justice had a way of making people sit up and take notice when you
walked past.

I checked in at the front desk, and the secretary there leapt to
his feet, ushering me personally through the building and up the
stairs past the sea of typists and reports being filed. I might have felt
different, but the headquarters hadn't changed.

Jack, Mr. Pinkerton's personal secretary, greeted me without a hint of exasperation this time, getting up swiftly and shaking my hand with a warm smile.

"Welcome back, Miss Palmer. He's expecting you."

In moments, I was in William Pinkerton's office. Same heavy-set man. Same thick mustache and graying hair. Thomas was sitting on a chair in front of his uncle's desk, getting to his feet the moment the door opened, striding toward me with his arms spread wide and a grin on his face.

"Zuretta!" Thomas called out.

Now wasn't the time for that. I was there on business. "Mr. Pinkerton. Mr. Chalmers. You asked me to come by?"

The smile left Thomas's face, and his uncle responded, standing as well. "Thank you for coming. We've heard so much about you this past week. Remarkable work, that. Remarkable."

There'd been a time when the thought of being welcomed and addressed by Mr. William Pinkerton himself would have left me breathless. Back when Ruby and I were reading the accounts of the Agency and imagining scenarios of daring and adventure.

But I'd had my share of daring and adventure now, and speaking to a man, any man, wasn't something I got excited about.

"Thank you," I said simply.

There was an awkward pause. Thomas and his uncle exchanged glances. "Won't you have a seat?" Thomas asked me.

"I'd rather not." I said. "My back still gives me difficulties. I'm more comfortable standing." Which was an understatement to say the least. The doctors said it would be at least another week before I began to feel myself again. Physically, at least.

I still had nightmares at night, though my sister and the other victims had been replaced by charred bodies and the beaten, mangled face of Henry Holmes.

"Yes," Mr. Pinkerton said and cleared his throat. "You have my apologies about that. My personal apologies. You were right, and I was wrong, and I'm not afraid to admit it."

Did that give me a small thrill of victory? More than a small one, actually. But I kept the smile from my face and simply nodded.

When I again did not continue, Mr. Pinkerton pointed to his nephew. "Tommy's told me all about you, of course. Filling in the details the newspapers never get right. And I must say I'm impressed. Undercover for more than a month, all on your own?"

"I had Phebe," I said, not wanting to take all the credit.

"The maid," Mr. Pinkerton asked. "Your roommate?"

I nodded.

"Good of you to try to spread the credit," he said, trailing off for a moment in thought.

"Will you stay for the trial?" Thomas asked.

"I'll be here for it, yes. Though the lawyers have said they imagine it won't happen for at least nine months. They want to get a full picture of what Holmes has done. The extent of his crimes."

Mr. Pinkerton nodded. "Yes. Usual, that. Sometimes it's easier to kill them and not bother with a trial, I've found."

"I wanted everyone to know what he'd done. And I wanted people like you to have the chance to fully investigate him."

Another uncomfortable pause.

"Holmes asked to see you," Mr. Pinkerton said. "Well, not in so many words. The doctors don't think he'll be able to speak comfortably for another month or two. But he's made his request clear."

"I'll not speak to him again," I said. "But I imagine you didn't ask me to come to your office to chat about the whims of a monster. Is there anything else you'd like to say? I have lunch with Phebe in an hour, and it's across town."

Mr. Pinkerton cleared his throat. "We left last time under less than ideal circumstances. You were angry with me, as I recall, because I didn't believe you. And I've apologized for that, though I hope you can see things from my position, now that you've been in Chicago some."

He came around from behind the desk and stood in front of me.

"Miss Palmer, I run a tight ship at my agency. We have the best of the best from across the country. Agents who aren't afraid to get their hands dirty in the name of getting the truth. Doing the job, whatever it may be. As I've read about your nerve and your daring, and as Thomas has told me more about it, one thing keeps coming to mind. We need you, Miss Palmer. People like you. We have a ladies' division, and I believe you'd be a perfect fit for it. I didn't just ask you here so I could apologize. I asked you here to offer you a job. I don't blame you for being upset with us, and I—"

I held up my hand, cutting him off. No need to let the man prattle. He wanted me for the publicity more than anything, I imagined. "I'd love to work for you. I thought you might offer me a position, in light of what's gone on and the fame it might bring your agency. But I'm afraid I have two items I must settle first. Then, once I've handled them, I'd be happy to begin work for your organization."

"Two items?"

"Yes," I said. "The first I can take care of right now." I turned to Thomas and reached into my purse for a small envelope, which I presented to him. "I promised I'd pay you back for the clothing you purchased."

His eyebrows shot up, and he stumbled to find a response, trying to push the envelope away.

"I insist you take it. A promise is a promise, and I saved more than a little money by working at the Castle and living on the premises. My mind will be more at ease knowing the debt is paid."

Mr. Pinkerton roared with laughter, a wide smile breaking out on his face as he watched his nephew's reaction. "There's something I haven't seen before. Tommy speechless in front of a woman! You'd be a tremendous asset to the agency, Miss. A tremendous asset!"

I nodded, accepting the compliment. "Thank you."

"What's the second item?" he asked.

"A stipulation more than an item. You mentioned you want me in your ladies' division. I'd like to be brought on in your standard detective department, instead."

I could have sliced the silence with a bread knife. The two men exchanged glances, and I wondered, for a moment, if I hadn't pushed them too far. Not that it would have made a difference in my decision. I was done putting up with men shoving me off to the side, one way or the other.

But Mr. Pinkerton's laugh returned, deeper than ever. He reached out and took my hand, shaking it firmly. "I'll have Jack draw up a contract, though I imagine negotiating a salary with you will be more than a little difficult, too, eh? What did your father do with you when you were growing up, I'd like to know."

I gave him a tight smile. "More than I deserved. I look forward to paying him back one day soon."

And if Mr. Pinkerton didn't understand my real meaning, what did a little misdirection matter now and then?

AUTHOR'S NOTE

Much of this book is based on actual events. H. H. Holmes, of course, really did live in Chicago while the World's Fair was going on, and he built the Castle in much the same way that's depicted here. (For an excellent account of both Holmes and the Fair, check out Erik Larson's *The Devil in the White City*.) I tried to re-create the Castle as closely as I could, basing the description off depictions in the newspapers from the time period, though there has been some speculation that those depictions themselves were blown out of proportion in order to sell more papers. The actual Castle has long been torn down, and today the spot is taken up by a post office.

In reality, Holmes went on the run soon after the World's Fair closed down. He did end up burning his accomplice, Benjamin Pitezel, alive, and he then went on the road with Pitezel's wife, conning her out of more money (and killing her children as they went, unbeknownst to her). Thanks to herculean efforts by the Pinkertons and Frank Geyer (a city detective for Philadelphia), Holmes was caught, put on trial, and found guilty. He published a "confession" in the newspapers before he was hanged on May 7, 1896. Excerpts from that confession are quoted in this book at the beginning of each chapter.

Other characters from history in the novel include Minnie and Annie Williams, Emeline Cigrand, and Julia and Pearl Conner. In retrospect, Holmes was clearly a monster, possibly killing as many as two hundred people before he was executed. But in his day-to-day life, he was also clearly adept at hiding that murderous streak. He conned a string of women out of their inheritance and life insurance, weaving his way through multiple affairs and engagements.

ACKNOWLEDGMENTS

A heartfelt thank-you to the many people who helped make this possible. Writing is typically a solitary endeavor, so it's wonderful when other people can help you in different ways. Annie Berger, for her spot-on editing and faith in me; Eddie Schneider and all the JABberwocks, for their support; Susan Chang, for her great suggestions and input; Robb Cundick and Tomas Cundick, for their feedback; Isaac Stewart and Audrey Pike, for their map acumen; my family, for their patience; and my writing group (Brian McClellan and Courtney Alameda), for helping me remember I'm not the only writer out there.

ABOUT THE AUTHOR

Bryce Moore is a librarian in western Maine. When he's not up to his nose in library work, he's watching movies, playing board games, and paying ridiculous amounts of money feeding his Magic the Gathering addiction. Visit him online at brycemoore.com.